"You'll never know," Gail choked out.

She turned her face into the curve of his neck. "Even if I could tell you, you couldn't begin to understand."

"Hey," Rand said, holding her tight. "I don't need any details. I couldn't care less about your past."

"You say that now," she began, "but later—"

He grasped her by the shoulders and gently shook her. "Will you listen to me? As God is my witness, Gail, the past means nothing to me. Yours or mine."

"You don't know what you're saying!"

He shook her again. "I know what I'm feeling, dammit!"

"Do you?" she challenged sadly, her heart sinking.

For as soon as Rand discovered who she really was and why she had come to Texas, he would no longer love her.

He would despise her.

Dear Reader,

Silhouette **Special Edition** welcomes you to romance…
and to summer! June is sure to be the start of a great season,
beginning, of course, with THAT SPECIAL WOMAN!
This month, bestselling author Sherryl Woods takes you
on a journey like you've never experienced…and neither
has her heroine, who gets into more trouble than she can
handle—but she *does* have a sexy adventurer by her side in
Riley's Sleeping Beauty.

June also marks the beginning of a wonderful new trilogy,
MAN, WOMAN AND CHILD, from veteran authors
Christine Flynn, Robin Elliott and Pat Warren. It all begins
this month with *A Father's Wish*, Christine Flynn's story of
a man searching for his lost love and child. Reader favorite
Marie Ferrarella is also back with a poignant story in
Brooding Angel. And a mother's determination not only
reunites her with her child but finds her a ready-made family
in Arlene James's *Child of Her Heart*.

In Trisha Alexander's latest, *The Girl Next Door* decides her
best friend, a freewheeling bachelor and sexy confidant, is the
man she's been looking for all her life. Now she just has to
convince him that they're falling in love. And we wrap up the
month of June by welcoming a new author to **Special Edition**.
A Family for Ronnie by Julie Caille is a touching story sure to
warm your hearts.

So don't miss a moment of these wonderful books. It's just
the beginning of a summer filled with love and romance from
Special Edition!

Sincerely,

Tara Gavin
Senior Editor

Please address questions and book requests to:
Silhouette Reader Service
U.S.: 3010 Walden Ave., P.O. Box 1325, Buffalo, NY 14269
Canadian: P.O. Box 609, Fort Erie, Ont. L2A 5X3

ARLENE JAMES
CHILD OF HER HEART

Published by Silhouette Books
America's Publisher of Contemporary Romance

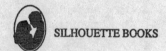 **SILHOUETTE BOOKS**

ISBN 0-373-09964-9

CHILD OF HER HEART

Copyright © 1995 by Arlene James

This edition published by arrangement with Harlequin Enterprises B.V.

® and TM are trademarks of Harlequin Enterprises B.V., used under
license. Trademarks indicated with ® are registered in the United States
Patent and Trademark Office, the Canadian Trade Marks Office and in
other countries.

Printed in U.S.A.

Books by Arlene James

ARLENE JAMES

grew up in Oklahoma and has lived all over the South. In 1976 she married "the most romantic man in the world." The author enjoys traveling with her husband, but writing has always been her chief pastime.

Chapter One

When the phone rang, at first Gail merely looked at it, so accustomed had she become during the past month to utter silence. Then she closed the medical journal she had been reading and reached for the receiver. It jangled again just as her hand covered it. She lifted the receiver and addressed the caller with the same brisk greeting she had been using since leaving medical school.

"Dr. Terry."

"Is this the doc, then?" asked an anxious male voice.

"It is. How may I help you?"

"It's Miss Belle. She fell and..."

Belle? Belle *Grace,* perhaps? The name reverberated through Gail's mind, but she tamped down the flash of excitement that it brought. There could be another. The uncontested societal matriarch of the community might well inspire any number of namesakes. Moreover, duty always took precedence. Gail forced herself to pay attention to the voice at the other end of the line.

"Can't get up," he was saying. "Boss says something could be broke, and the boss would know, I reckon. Anyway, she's hurting real bad. Can you come?"

She was already getting to her feet. "Absolutely. Where is she?"

"The bunkhouse, but don't you worry about that. The boss'll meet you on the way. He's driving a red double-cab dualie with flashing lights."

"Dualie?"

"Dual axle pickup, ma'am. That means it's got two tires on each side in the back."

"I understand. Now, where am I going and how do I get there?"

"You just head south on 67 toward Presidio, ma'am. The boss'll bring you back here. You just put your hazard lights on and pull over once you see that truck. He's done left, so it shouldn't be too far out of town."

"I'm on my way," she said. "As soon as I hang up, I want you to call Alpine for an ambulance."

"We already done that, ma'am, but that ambulance is over sixty miles away, and you're just under thirty. We figured this would be quickest."

"You figured right," she told him briskly, and hung up.

Swiftly she strode into the treatment room, snatched up her ubiquitous black bag, plopped it onto the table, opened it and began selecting items to augment its contents. She chose elastic bandaging and several packages of plaster wrap, as well as a trio of braces and a large quantity of painkillers. She threw in an intravenous setup for good measure and extra saline. With the bag fully loaded, she couldn't close it and didn't even try, just slung the strap of her pocketbook over her shoulder, grabbed a pair of sunglasses and scooped up the medical bag with both arms.

She locked the office door at the front of the house, then let herself out through the apartment at the rear. As she slid behind the wheel of her small, battered, two-door car, she thought wryly that at least there were no appointments to cancel or a waiting room full of patients to disappoint. In the month since she'd replaced old Doc Garlock's shingle with her own, she had barely averaged ten patients a week.

She had been warned, of course. Texas west of the Pecos River was wide open in more ways than one. Doctors were definitely needed. Yet in all those millions of breathtaking acres, only 660,000 people resided, and upward of 620,000 of those lived in El Paso alone. The city boasted a number of fine hospitals and plenty of doctors, but was a couple of hundred miles away from picturesque little Marfa. And while Marfa might need a doctor, that doctor would never be rich. A female doctor might not catch on at all. Gail had heard that warning over and over again, and the prognosticators had not been wrong when they'd predicted that she would not generate enough income to cover her living expenses and make the payments on the exorbitant student loans she'd accumulated during college and medical school. The good citizens of Marfa and the surrounding area would apparently rather drive the thirty or so miles to Alpine and the overworked doctors there. If not for those same doctors, who generously referred patients to her whenever possible, Gail would not have survived the past month.

Nevertheless, she was not ready to give up, nor would she be. Only a single month had passed. It had been a month of settling in, of wondering and waiting, a month of cooling her heels—something she was not used to, coming as she had fresh from a residency at Dallas's busy Parkland Hospital. More than a month of enforced leisure, though, it had been a month of anticipation and worry.

Worry. From the time she had entered her first foster home in California to her graduation from medical school— and then on behalf of various patients—she had lived with worry. But nothing had worried her more than the welfare of her daughter, a daughter she had only briefly seen during the few days following her birth. However, daily life went on, and as always, the immediate concern was getting the bills paid, a feat she was managing, just barely, despite the empty hours spent in the office. Thank God that Doc Garlock had foreseen this difficulty and insisted on carrying her mortgage on the property and equipment for one year without repayment and at minimal interest. He had warned her that it would be years before she could hope to do more than live quite modestly, and he was right, of course. With that mortgage to pay off and the heavy burden of her school loans coming due, she would have her hands full for some time yet. But that didn't matter.

She wasn't there to get rich. She wasn't there, really, to practice medicine, though she had worked long and hard to become a doctor. She was there to find the daughter stolen from her at birth, to uncover some clue to the child's whereabouts after thirteen frustrating, often hopeless, years.

Gail forced her mind away from the subject of her daughter and concentrated on finding her way through the broad, neat streets of Marfa to the narrow highway that ran north and south through town. For a West Coast girl who had negotiated the labyrinth of some of California's most heavily populated areas and then the insanely busy streets of Dallas, small, quiet, logically laid out Marfa was no challenge at all, but she had been warned that the outlying areas could swallow a person whole and leave no clue as to her passing. The broad flat plains and rocky mountain ranges were crisscrossed with dusty, nameless roads and rough tracks that, as often as not, led nowhere and to no one. Moreover, it was all private land, thousands and thousands of acres of it, protected by rightly possessive families whose roots sank deep into the sandy soil. As a newcomer, she hadn't mastered the names or the locations of the surrounding ranches, but in truth only one held any fascination for her. She tried not to think that she might be headed for it now. She tried not to think at all, but the subject wouldn't leave her alone.

In years past, the hectic, sometimes desperate, pace of her work had protected her from thoughts of her only child. During all those months she'd scrimped and saved to gather the funds for private investigators, she'd had the hours of studying and then practice to keep her sane. Time after time she'd gone through the process of amassing the cash, then hiring the investigator and throwing herself into her work to keep her mind occupied until the money ran out and the disappointing news came that no trace of Carel Harte or their daughter had been found. Then finally, two years ago, she'd had her first glimmer of hope. The possibility existed that the man known in California as Carel Harte was in fact one Carel Hartesite of the Hartesite ranching family of far-west Texas. It had taken more of her precious funds and more time to confirm that Carel Harte and Carel Hartesite were likely the same man and then to locate the family ranch near Marfa. After that, Gail had had one goal in mind: to get herself to Marfa and find her daughter. Well, she was established in Marfa, Texas, and racing to the aid of a woman who could well be grandmother to her daughter. Gail said a silent prayer to that effect and turned on her hazard lights as she followed the highway south from town.

Summoning the same determination that had seen her through so much already, Gail focused what had been called "her formidable intellect" on the task at hand. Some eight or nine miles out of town, she spied the flashing lights of the big red truck, and pulled off the road onto the sandy shoulder. The truck drew near and skidded to a stop in the traffic lane. A tall, solidly built cowboy bailed out and crossed the road in long, swift strides. He was wearing a battered gray hat, scuffed tan boots and dusty blue jeans beneath flapping leather chaps. Gail got out of the car. He stopped in his tracks and gave her a quick look down and up again.

"Are *you* the new doc?"

"That's me." She stuck out her right hand. "Gail Terry."

Ignoring her gesture, he took his hat off and rubbed his hand through thick, wavy hair the color of black coffee, exposing an arresting face. Handsome in a rugged, outdoorsy way, with features that were, like the rest of him, large, he had gray-blue eyes set beneath straight, dark

brows, a squarish jaw and a strong chin; lean, shadowed
cheeks and a wide, finely sculpted mouth. But his prominent feature was a long, narrow nose that had been broken
at least once. He stared down that nose at her now, his
skepticism blatant.

"Girl, you don't *look* like a doctor," he said in a low,
tight voice, eyes narrowing.

Gail sighed. Anyone who thought all the battles of sex-
ism had been fought and won was wrong. "See here," she
said sternly, striking a pose with arms folded and one hip
thrown to the side, "I'm getting real tired of this stupid attitude. I'm not just a doctor, cowboy, I'm a *damned fine*
doctor. But I don't have time to argue the merits of my
abilities with you just now. I have an injured patient waiting on me. Now, get in that monster truck and drive!"

He plopped his hat onto his head. "Well, all right," he
said.

Grinning suddenly, he elbowed her aside, reached into her
car, shut off the engine and the hazard lights, then took the
bag from the front seat. Straightening, he tucked the bag
under one arm and lifted the other in invitation, before
turning and heading back toward his truck. She closed her
mouth, squared her shoulders and followed him across the
road.

"Shouldn't I be taking my car?"

"Lady, where this truck is going, that heap couldn't follow."

"Oh."

He hurried her around the front of the truck, opened the
passenger door, tossed the bag in and practically tossed her
in after it. "Slap that belt on," he ordered, running around
the front and sliding through the open door. He put the
transmission in gear, gunned the engine and turned the
wheel hard left.

"My keys!" she said, only then thinking of them.

"Left them in the car."

"What? B-but my purse is in there!"

He slid her an amused glance. "No one's going to bother your things. Folks respect one another's property out here."

"That's a cavalier attitude."

He glowered, his mouth pressed together grimly. "If anything's missing when we get back, I'll replace it. Fair enough?"

It was, actually, but his high-handedness galled her. She changed the subject, determined not to look at the speedometer as the truck barreled down the road. "Tell me about the patient."

He slumped a bit, the slight slackening of muscles betraying his concern. "My mother," he said finally. "She's seventy-three, almost seventy-four, in good health, far as I know. She was hanging some sketches in the bunkhouse."

"Sketches?"

"One of the hands draws. He's real good at it. Mother took some of his best sketches up to Fort Davis and had them framed there. She was hanging them in the bunkhouse dining room as a kind of surprise. She fell. It was just from a stepladder, but she can't seem to get up again, and she's hurting real bad, though she wouldn't admit it for the world and more. That's why I'm pretty sure she broke something."

"Any bleeding?"

"Don't think so. I didn't really wait around to find out. Her leg's sticking out at an unnatural angle. Soon as I saw that, I told the top to call and I started out."

Gail nodded. "The top?"

"That's Bones, the top hand."

"So this Bones is with her?"

He nodded. "Him and the housekeeper, Camelia, who found her. By this time Evert's probably there, too. He's one of the wranglers. He was supposed to head into Alpine with me to meet the train. I've got a bull coming in by rail."

He lifted a hand to the back of his neck. It looked as hard as stone, and something about it triggered a memory for her: Carel cupping their newborn daughter's tiny head in the palm of his hand. Belle. If her investigator was right, and everything seemed to say that he was, Carel's mother's name was Belle Grace. Carel had dark brown hair and pale blue eyes. He had a square chin with a little cleft in it, and a long, patrician nose. He wasn't quite six feet tall, and he was more slender than this man, less muscular. His hands were large, with squarish palms and long, blunt fingers, but whereas this man's were hard, Carel's had merely been firm, the hands of a scholar. Still, there was enough resemblance to make her wonder, make her hope. She cleared her throat.

"You haven't told me your name."

He looked surprised. "Oh, hey, I'm sorry. I just figured you knew. Randal Hartesite. Call me 'Rand.'"

Hartesite. The surname slammed into her consciousness like a fist to her belly. At last. Hartesite. Unless this was all some wild-goose chase, Carel Harte was indeed Carel Hartesite, which meant that this man was some relation of his. At last. She took a deep breath and clamped her teeth down, her tongue imprisoned firmly behind them. It would not do to blurt out Carel's name. It would not do to warn him that she was on his trail, finally. Though in truth, Dr. Gail Terry bore little resemblance beyond the physical to Abigail Walken, the impressionable, lonely nineteen-year-old who had succumbed so easily to the suave graduate student's overtures. She had so needed to be loved, a girl all alone in the world, forever among strangers, wanting so much to make something of herself and a little overwhelmed by her first semester of college. She had been absurdly flattered when Carel had singled her out for his attention and stupidly easy to convince first to share his bed and then, when she'd known she was pregnant, his apartment.

She closed her eyes, remembering the sheer terror of that autumn and then the wonder of it. A baby. Her very own little someone to hold and love. It hadn't seemed to matter when Carel had explained that he couldn't marry her until the spring, when his graduate studies would be finished and he would no longer have to depend upon the goodwill of his

family for financial support. She hadn't cared that she had
to miss the second semester of her first year of college, that
she had to drop out of sight for a while. She hadn't been
ashamed, but she had understood Carel's position. His
family were old-fashioned, he had said. They did not understand him, did not agree with his ambitions. They were
country folk, he had said, living out in the sticks despite the
money left them by his late father. They viewed higher education with a jaundiced eye, labeling it the next thing to
corruption. A pregnant girlfriend would only confirm their
suspicions of the kind of life he led. What did it matter, he
had asked, as long as they loved each other, as long as they
were committed in their hearts?

Gail had told only one other person of her pregnancy, her
college roommate, Faye. She hadn't been prepared for the
vehemence with which Faye had condemned Carel. She had
always thought Faye liked him. But Faye was a moody girl,
easily moved to tears for no apparent reason and not as
talkative as Gail would have liked. Faye's reaction had
awakened in Gail a protectiveness toward her lover. She had
been careful to tell no one else of her condition and had
merely disappeared after that first semester. They'd rented
a little apartment on the other side of town, Carel and she,
and they'd lived as husband and wife for those last months.
Then, in mid-July when the baby had come, they'd been so
happy. She had been so happy. Until the day she'd been
dismissed from the hospital.

She'd signed the obligatory papers without bothering to
read them in her excitement, then she'd dressed and waited
for Carel. She'd waited and waited, and her breasts had
grown heavy with milk. When she'd rung the nurse and
asked her to bring the baby, an odd silence had followed.
Moments later, the stout, middle-aged nurse had stood in
her room and wrung her hands. Didn't she know? Mr. Harte
had come for the baby hours ago. Hadn't that been the arrangement? They had all understood that Mr. Harte would
take the baby so she, Gail—or Abby, as she'd been known

then—could get on with her life, get a college education. She'd signed the papers, after all.

She hadn't believed it—couldn't believe it. She'd run from the hospital in terror and caught a bus to the apartment, but the man who had been waiting there for her was not Carel Harte. He was a lawyer by the name of Esters, and he had patiently, firmly, explained in no-nonsense terms that she could never hope to regain custody of her daughter. Carel and his family would see to that. But she was not to worry. The child would have everything, including a stable home with people who loved her. Mr. Harte had left a check for her "troubles." She had torn the check into shreds and thrown it in Esters's face without even noting the amount. He had shaken his head and sighed. Foolish young girls, trying to use an untimely pregnancy to force marriage on a young man of good family and solid stature.

Numb, broken, more alone than ever, she'd holed up in that apartment for weeks, and finally had pulled herself together and gone out into the daylight. It was then that she'd decided that Carel wouldn't get away with stealing her daughter. Whatever she had to do, however long it took, she would find him and she would fight him. She had tracked him as far as Texas, but this one state as big as five had apparently swallowed him and their daughter. Nevertheless, it was to Texas that she'd headed for her residency, and her doggedness had finally paid off. God willing, she was almost there. Almost. God willing, she was on her way to the Hartesite ranch and, eventually, the daughter she had held in her heart for thirteen long years.

Several more miles down the road, Rand Hartesite sent her a warning look and said, "Hold on." With that, he steered the barreling truck across the empty oncoming traffic lane and onto the sand. The truck threw up a dust cloud that seemed to envelope them.

"I trust you know what you're doing," Gail said anxiously.

His grin stretched wide. "Yes, ma'am. It's called a short-cut."

"I guessed as much, and you're right," she told him as the truck bumped and bucked and flew over a small ravine. "That old car of mine would never have made it, not at these speeds."

"No, ma'am." He slowed a bit and downshifted just as the truck started to climb a short, but steep, embankment. The truck tires churned and slid and bumped up over the edge onto a narrow paved road. He jammed the transmission into a higher gear and they were flying again. After a moment, he took the top of the wheel with his left hand and hiked his right elbow up over the back of the seat, turning a long, measuring gaze on her. "You don't look like a doctor, you know."

Gail sighed and flipped her long, golden ponytail with one hand. "I know." She'd tried cutting her hair short, but that had only made her appear younger. She was fairly tall for a female, five-eight or so, and slender of build except for her chest, which she tried to minimize with loose tops and lab coats. She favored casual clothes—jeans and slacks, athletic shoes, T-shirts and softly tailored blouses—eschewed jewelry as a general rule and kept her thick blond hair cut bluntly. The only makeup she habitually wore was mascara and a touch of brow pencil. She knew that she ought to try a more sophisticated look, and she had made one or two stabs at it, with mixed results, but her busy schedule and tight budget simply hadn't left much space for experimentation, and somewhere along the way she'd made the decision that people were just going to have to accept Gail Terry as she was.

"How old are you, anyway?"

Her mouth dropped open. "And I thought cowboys were supposed to be gentlemen!"

He chuckled. "I didn't figure you for a vain one."

"I'm not. I'll be thirty-two in January."

"That's a good age," he said, rubbing his chin with hi free hand. "Remember it well."

"Is that an invitation to ask your age?" she quipped, little surprised at herself.

"Hell, no. I was going to tell you anyway."

"You were?"

"Why not?" She had no answer for that. "I turned forty one early this month," he said.

"A September birthday," she murmured, but she wa calculating in her head. Carel would have been thirty-six i June. That made Rand nearly five years older than him They could be cousins or brothers.

Now that they were no longer churning up dust, Gai deemed it safer to look around than dwell on a possibl connection between this cowboy and the man who had sto len her child. Hartesite seemed to notice her shift in atten tion. "It's a straight shot from here on out to the house," he told her, and that made sense, considering that the lan lay in plains between the rocky, tumbledown mountai ranges that he pointed out through the windshield an named. They were mostly Spanish-sounding names, whicl again did not surprise her, for they were technically tearin across the massive Chihuahua Desert, though the terrain di not fit her idea of a desert. For one thing, there was to much vegetation, nearly all of it low and scrubby, but gree nonetheless. For another, the climate was surprisingly mild.

As September waned, the days were gloriously golde with comfortable temperatures. Evenings could get down right chilly in the wee hours, but she had found that a goo blanket was all that was needed to sleep soundly. She wa told that she could expect winter temperatures to drop onl rarely and briefly below freezing and that the height o summer brought a blessedly short period of ninety-plu weather. Only the lack of rainfall accounted for the area' desert classification. With averages running about fiv inches a year, moisture was in such short supply that morn ings dawned without even a drop of dew. Gail sensed it, too n her sinuses, eyes, the lining of her mouth and, less obviously, her skin, hair and fingernails. But in these modern times the arid air was relatively simple to combat. One merely drank a lot of bottled water, used moisturizer, hair conditioner and sunscreen regularly and religiously wore sunglasses. Everything else pretty much took care of itself n this wide, regal land.

"You like it out here," Rand declared after a few minutes.

Gail smiled. "Yes, I think I do," she admitted, again a little surprised at herself.

"All right," he said softly, giving her an approving nod. "All right."

Gail had the feeling that she'd just passed some momentous personal test, and she found that she was pleased somehow, pleased and a little proud.

The remainder of the drive passed in an oddly comfortable silence. Almost before she knew it the truck slowed, before swerving into the expansive yard of a sprawling, pristine adobe ranch house with miles of porch beneath its ed shingled roof. The place was enclosed within a low adobe fence, broken at intervals with archways of wrought iron. She caught a glimpse of a number of outbuildings of varying size and purpose as the truck slid smoothly around the main house and tore on toward a long, low building some hundred yards or so beyond. Other than that, Gail had no time for observation as the truck ground to a halt and they spilled out of it into the settling dust. Rand had her medical bag tucked up under his arm again and was holding the screen door open before she even reached the low porch. As she approached, an older man appeared in the doorway.

"'Bout time!" he barked.

Gail judged him to be somewhere in his fifties, mature enough, certainly, to handle an emergency. He had his thumbs hooked into empty belt loops, but his lean, leathery face was twisted with concern.

"This here is Bones," Rand said with a jerk of his head.

The name fit all too well. He was little more than bones wired together with sinew and leathery hide beneath his dusty, faded jeans and thin cotton shirt.

"Bones, this is Dr. Terry."

He took one look and did exactly what Gail expected him to do. He gaped. *"Her?"*

She pushed aside her irritation and headed for the door. "I'm it, mister, Dr. Gail Terry."

The cowboy lifted his battered and sweat-stained straw hat, pushed a scarred hand through his sparse silver-and-blond hair and came to an inevitable decision. "Well, come on then and have a look, but I predict she ain't going to like it," he said looking at Rand.

Rand shook his head. "How is she?"

"Bad" was the terse reply, but it said enough. He backed up and allowed Gail to step through the door into what appeared to be a dining room, with a long plank table hedged by benches in its center. The floor consisted of bare boards, but they were swept free of sand and bleached of stains. She followed the long, thin cowboy through another door in the end wall to a second room of like size. The emphasis there was on relaxation, though. There were no fewer than six recliners placed in a semicircle around a large television. A comfortable couch sat against one wall. Rustic side tables had been strategically situated, some of them holding ash trays, some of them spittoons. The whole place was scrupulously clean, and lying next to the sofa in front of a door that led into what looked to be a narrow hallway was a tall, rawboned woman whose once-red hair was now mostly yellowish white. Kneeling next to her was a plump Mexican woman with strands of gray sweeping through her long black hair. It was the fallen woman, however, on whom Gail focused.

She had a prominent nose, but Gail found that it did not sit nearly so well on her face as her son's did on his. She might be the grande dame of Marfa society, but she had never been a pretty woman, despite the neatness of her per

on and the strong will emanating from her pale-blue eyes.
he was wearing dark jeans this day, a crisp red-and-white
hecked blouse tucked in and held in place by a narrow, sil-
er-tipped belt, and Western-style boots that laced up.
omeone had placed a pillow under her head, and she glared
p at Gail from it, more from pain and embarrassment than
nything else, Gail guessed.

"I heard you were a female," she said sharply. "Kind of
oung, aren't you?"

"I guess that depends on your perspective," Gail an-
wered evenly. "I'm thirty-one." She went down on her
nees beside Belle Grace Hartesite and reached for her wrist,
oting the awkward angle of the right leg. Rand placed her
ag on the floor next to her, and she nodded her thanks.

The pulse was fast and thready. Her skin had an ashy cast
o it, and the pupils of her eyes were contracted into tight
inpoints of black. Intuition told her that only a formida-
le will was keeping the woman conscious. She pulled a
tethoscope from her kit and listened to a rapid heartbeat.
I'm going to give you something for pain," she said, rum-
aging in her bag for syringes and medications, "and
omething to minimize swelling, then I'll have a look at that
g. Now, tell me how this happened."

"I was standing on that stepladder there, driving a nail in
e wall above the door to hang a picture frame on. I kind
f shifted my weight, and the ladder slipped forward. I
wisted and fell hard on my right hip. My foot caught be-
ween the rungs of the ladder."

"Uh-huh. And where and how does it hurt?"

The older woman's lips thinned, but she did not, as Gail
ad feared, refuse to answer.

"Well, my behind hurts, frankly, and all the way down
y leg and into my back. It's a bad, constant ache and if I
ove at all, I get a sharp, stabbing pain that sets my teeth
nd near takes the top of my head off."

"Does your head hurt now?"

"In the front, but I didn't hit it, if that's what you'r wondering."

"Probably stress, then," Gail said, "nothing to worr about. That makes this a little easier." She glanced over he shoulder, syringes ready. "If you gentlemen will excus us..."

Rand shuffled his feet. "I-I don't know..."

She shrugged. "Let's leave it to Mrs. Hartesite, shall we? She looked at Belle Hartesite, explaining, "These have to g in the hip, ma'am."

Belle grimaced and looked at her son. "Go on now," sh said brusquely. "No one's taking my pants down in front c you and that scarecrow."

Rand muttered something, turned and left the room Bones on his heels.

"I haven't dropped my drawers to a man since M Hartesite died, and I don't intend to start," Belle said firml "Guess there's something to be said for female docs aft all."

Gail disciplined a grin. "Could be." She nodded at th Mexican woman, who began loosening Belle's belt an jeans. She liked this feisty old girl, and something told he that the feeling was mutual. That made two Hartesites fc whom she'd formed a tentative respect and general likin and that was two more than she'd expected.

Chapter Two

He was leaning against the end of the table, the heels of his hands braced on its edge, dark head bowed. Gail stepped into the room and assumed her best doctor-to-patient mien. He came instantly to his feet.

"How is she?"

"A little easier, I think. I can't do much more for her just now. Fully sedating her is just too dangerous."

"How bad is she hurt?"

"I can't be sure without X rays, but I'd say her hip is broken."

He looked away, speaking softly under his breath. She did not have the feeling that he was praying. After a moment, he took a deep breath and engaged her again.

"I guess this means a stay in the hospital."

"That's a safe bet, yes."

"I'd better have Camelia get some things together for her." He turned to Bones, who was straddling the bench next to the table and holding a steaming cup of coffee in his

hand. "You'd better get to the radio and put in a call to th
boys. I want Patch to go with Evert to pick up the bull
Can't have twenty thousand dollars standing around on
side rail all day."

The words fell out before she could stop them. "Twent
thousand—"

Hartesite lifted an eyebrow. "Good breeding stock's ex
pensive."

"No kidding!"

He didn't move so much as a hair, but laughter twinkle
in eyes gone almost gray. "All right, Bones, I guess that'
about it. Oh, wait. Since Mother can't do it, somebod
else'll have to pick up the kids from school, and the doc'
gonna need somebody to deliver her car to the house. Tak
care of that, too, will you? I'll get her home when we'r
done."

Bones was on his feet already. He set the coffee on the ta
ble, stepped over the bench and left them, disappearing int
what Gail took to be the kitchen. A moment later, she hear
his boots clumping past the wall to her left and guessed tha
the hallway ran the length of the house. She smiled wanly a
Rand. "I'll stay with Mrs. Hartesite until the ambulanc
comes."

"I'll join you."

She entered the living room ahead of him and stood ove
her patient on the floor. Belle Grace Hartesite looke
peaceful enough. Her eyes were closed, and her breathin
was even. Rand walked around to Camelia, bent and whis
pered in her ear. Nodding, she rose heavily to her feet an
hurried out the door through which they had entered. Ran
looked down at his mother, his brow furrowed.

"Should she be sleeping?" he whispered to Gail, leanin
forward.

Belle's eyes snapped open. "I hurt too damned bad t
sleep," she snapped.

Her words slurred just enough to let Gail know that she was slightly intoxicated from the palliative injection she had received.

Rand went down on one knee beside her, chuckling. "Well, you're not hurt too bad to cuss, if that's a good sign."

"I never cuss," she insisted. "Much." And her mouth twitched with a smile, despite the pain that dulled her pale eyes.

He tenderly brushed her short hair from her forehead. "It won't be long now."

Nodding, she took a deep breath, then suddenly expelled it, her eyes popping open again. "Oh, Rand, what about the children?"

"It's all taken care of. One of the boys will pick them up from the school."

"Not Punch," she said sourly. "Man drives like a loco cow."

Rand chuckled. "No, not Punch. He's heading out with Evert after the bull."

"Lord, we're going in all directions today, aren't we? And it's all my fault."

"Don't I know it," Rand said, a gentle note of mockery in his tone. He glanced up at Gail from beneath the crag of his brow. "What some folks won't do to get out of pulling their own weight around here." Gail hid a smile as Belle's hand came up and popped him on his cheek.

"Smart aleck."

"Ow." He glowered fiercely, then ruined it by catching her hand and holding it lovingly against his face.

"It's just that they depend on me," she said softly. He nodded wordlessly, and she shifted her sluggish gaze to Gail. "You have any children, Dr. Terry?"

Gail swallowed, let her gaze fall to her feet and relied on the truth in masquerade. "I did," she replied softly. "I hope to again."

"Oh, my dear," Belle said, her voice thinning, "to lose a child is just the worst pain."

Rand folded her hand in his and lowered it to her side. "Don't, Mother," he implored gently.

But she gave her head the merest shake. "I can't help it, Rand. Our children aren't just our future. They're the embodiment of all our hopes and dreams. It makes no matter how old they are or how far away, as long as they live, hope lives. But when a child dies, a vital part of a parent dies, as well."

Gail stepped back slightly, feeling as though she were intruding on a very private moment, and yet such words deserved acknowledgment. "That sounds like the voice of experience, ma'am."

Belle Grace Hartesite sighed deeply and gripped her son's hand so tightly that it shook. "It was a car crash," she said, "nearly eleven years ago now, that took my younger boy."

"I am sorry, ma'am," Gail murmured.

Belle seemed not to have even heard her. "I still miss him," she said mournfully. "He was a difficult child and a selfish man, but he was still my son. He was still my Carel."

Carel! Gail reeled mentally and physically, stopping herself from stumbling backward only by sheer force of will. "I'm so sorry, Mrs. Hartesite . . ." Her voice trailed off.

"Eleven years," Belle whispered.

"Carel was my younger brother," Rand explained.

Gail glanced at him and merely nodded.

Carel. Dead. Eleven years. She closed her eyes against the swirl of emotions that threatened to swamp her. She could have claimed her little girl eleven long years ago. Eleven years! Oh, God, where was her daughter now? What had happened to her little girl? Where, oh, where was her baby?

Somehow several minutes passed without her even knowing it, and then a commotion at the doorway jerked her out of her fog. The unshaven cowboy who was standing there doffed his battered hat, shuffled the dusty boots into which his pant legs were crammed and shifted a tobacco plug from one cheek to the other before nodding in Rand's direction. "Am'blance comin' cross the yard now, Boss."

"Okay, Evert. Wave 'em on back here, then you and Patch get on after that bull."

"Yes, sir. Hope you're on the mend real quick, Miss Belle."

"Thank you, Evert. Help me up, Son."

"Not yet, ma'am," Gail said quickly. "You're not to move on your own. You'll only make matters worse and hurt yourself. Just leave the transportation to the professionals, please. That's what they're here for."

Belle grumbled, but she subsided all the same, her face drawn in pain. Rand got to his feet, softly reassuring her as he did so, but he shot a curious look at Gail, which she knew meant trouble. Immediately she sought escape.

"I-I need to speak to the EMT."

"I'll go with you. You lie still, Mother. Won't be long now."

So much for escape. Gail moved stiffly into the other room, desperately searching for the composure that the news of Carel's death had shattered. The ambulance was backing up to the door, and she rushed forward to prop open the screen. "I'm Dr. Terry," she said to the young man who came to meet her. "The patient is a seventy-three-year-old woman who's taken a hard fall and likely broken her right hip. You'll have to be very careful with her. I don't see any signs of shock, but she's in great pain."

The young man listened to her instructions with admirable attention, then began unloading the necessary equipment. Gail stood to one side, arms folded. But if she hoped to avoid Rand Hartesite, her hopes were in vain.

"Are you all right?" he asked, coming to stand beside her.

She had no choice but to bluff her way through. "What? Oh, yes, of course. Why do you ask?"

"I don't know. You seemed...upset in there a little while ago."

She shrugged, her gaze carefully averted. "I'm a doctor, Mr. Hartesite, but I'm human. I take no joy in other people's pain, physical or emotional."

"Must be hard," he murmured, "being around sick people all the time."

Gail almost breathed a sigh of relief. The conversation was moving onto safe ground. "Actually, most of the time it's very rewarding. There's something so ultimately satisfying about helping people heal. There are the losses, of course, and those are devastating, but on balance the victories far outweigh the failures."

"Sounds like dedication to me."

She smiled to herself. "I suppose so. But frankly, in the beginning, I just wanted to be someone."

"Don't we all?" he asked quietly.

"Maybe. I can't speak for anyone else."

"Can't you? That's odd. I could have sworn that you identified very strongly with what my mother had to say in there."

Gail felt the erratic tempo of her heart and willed it to normalcy. "I didn't say I had no empathy."

"No, you didn't. You did say, however, that you'd lost a child."

She closed her eyes. Why was this so hard? It wasn't even a lie, and yet she felt as if he could see right through her. She drew a steadying breath. "Yes."

"I'm sorry," he said softly. "I know what my kids mean to me."

"Thanks, but I'd rather not talk about it."

"Oh, sure. I just... Well, I'd like to know... Does that mean you're married?" he asked softly.

Married? Her gaze flew to his and snagged there. Was that *interest* she saw? Hope? "No! I mean, a-actually, I'm divorced."

"Ah." He smiled, his gaze warming to a soft, hazy blue. "I'm not married, either, anymore."

"Oh." She bit her lip, wondering where this was leading and where that deep sense of relief was coming from. He was Carel's brother, she reminded herself. *Carel is dead,* said a small voice in her ear. She didn't have to be told that Rand Hartesite could likely help her find her daughter, but she wasn't craven enough to believe that that possibility was behind what she was feeling. Suddenly she was frightened, because an attraction to Rand Hartesite was above all things dangerous, and in more ways than one.

The rattling of the gurney across the dining room floor provided distraction and told them that the attendants had made the transfer. Rand hurried to his mother's side.

"Everything okay?"

She nodded, but kept her eyes and mouth firmly closed. The signs of strain were abundant: the paleness of her skin, the shallow rapidity of her breath, the drawn line of her mouth and the tight crinkles at the corners of her eyes. Gail stepped close and laid a comforting hand upon her patient's arm, but it was to Rand that she spoke. "I'll be with her," she told him. "We'll take good care of her. The worst is over now."

Nodding, he stepped back, his fingertips pushing lightly into the tops of his pockets. The attendants swiftly loaded the gurney into the van and took up their respective positions. Gail moved to join them, but Rand called her back, the tone of his voice more arresting than the single word he said.

"Doc."

She turned, missing at first the outstretched hand that he offered. He didn't say anything further, didn't offer explanation, but he didn't have to. She knew well enough that this was an apology for his failure to shake her hand before. She couldn't stop the smile that tugged at her mouth or the warmth that flowed through her when his hand closed around hers. For a long moment they stood there, palm to palm, and then wordlessly she turned and climbed into the back of the ambulance, her spirits magically restored.

* * *

The IV bag swayed as the ambulance turned into the drive and rolled to a stop in the single port of the small hospital in Alpine. Gail had used the time on the road to set up the intravenous kit, along with a heart monitor and a blood-pressure cuff, knowing that each would be needed to ensure the patient's comfort and safety in the hours to come. Belle had hardly batted an eyelash when the shunt was inserted, and Gail was pleased to see that the older woman's vital signs were strong and her veins healthy and freeflowing.

She was not surprised when the back of the van opened to reveal the tall, slender, very gentlemanly middle-aged doctor who had welcomed her into the local professional community with such open arms little more than a month earlier.

"Dr. Terry," he said, "good to see you again. How is she?"

"I'll live," croaked a voice from the gurney.

He chuckled. "I've no doubt of it, Belle," he said warmly. "It would take a lot more than a fall to undo you. Also, you're in very good hands here. This young lady came highly recommended, from Parkland Hospital in Dallas, no less."

"Did she, now?" said Rand, walking up.

The doctor turned to shake Rand's hand and clap his arm. "Indeed. We're very lucky to get her. Why, she's got more emergency-medicine experience than the rest of us around here combined. I thought you'd want to know that, Randal."

"You're right. Thanks."

"Don't you worry, now."

"Why would I? As you said, Mother's in good hands."

He turned a look of confidence on Gail then. It pleased her inordinately, so much so that she felt her color rising. She climbed down from the van and waved everyone back, feeling safe behind the shield of professional authority. The attendants unloaded the gurney and wheeled Belle into the hospital. Gail followed swiftly behind, with the other doctor and Rand bringing up the rear. They stopped inside the emergency bay long enough for Gail to issue orders and make the appropriate notations on the chart started by the attendants in the ambulance. She gave a last word of reassurance to Belle before explaining the procedures that were about to take place and the reasons for them. Finally, when the patient was wheeled away to X ray, she could no longer put off facing Rand again.

The other doctor had made a swift departure. Like everyone else, he had his own duties to attend to. For a moment at least, it was just Rand Hartesite and she.

"I really can't tell you anything else right now, except that her vital signs are stable and strong," she said.

"That's good."

"I want you to know that we'll take great care not to cause her additional pain, but some discomfort is inevitable because of the severity of the injury."

"I understand."

"Fine. Well, I'll see you later, then."

He reached out a hand as if to delay her, but she ignored it in her haste to get away from him. Rand Hartesite was not a man to be ignored, however. He stopped her cold with his next words.

"It's the ponytail, you know."

She swung around. "I beg your pardon?"

He pushed his hat back. "The ponytail," he repeated.

Her hand went automatically to her hair.

"Not that it isn't attractive. It just makes you look about nineteen."

She almost laughed. "Really?"

"I didn't want you to think it was...I don't know... prejudice, I guess, or plain old rudeness."

"What are you talking about?"

"First impressions, mainly, but it goes beyond that, too." He shifted his weight, one leg flexed and extended, his expression thoughtful. "It's this place. You've gotta be tough to make it out here. We just don't have all the things most of the world takes for granted, like an ambulance every square mile or fire stations around every corner. Heck, we hardly even have the corners! What I'm trying to say is that we have to depend on each other out here. We count on our neighbors, whether they're next door or in the next county. We have to know that they're willing and able to meet every emergency, that they're not going to fold when we need them most. And a doctor... Well, it just doesn't get any more vital than that. Folks need to know you're going to stick. They need to know what's in front of that ponytail. You give them a chance to do that, and they'll come around, I promise."

What he was saying made a proud kind of sense, but it was more than just sensible advice. He was telling her that he had no more doubts about her ability, and that was welcome, indeed. She felt, somehow, that she had finally arrived and received the welcome she had needed. She didn't know what to say, except "Thank you for telling me this."

"No thanks needed," he said. "It's what's due. That place you came from, that hospital..."

"Parkland. It's a public hospital."

"I've heard of it. They say it's like a battle zone."

"Sometimes."

"I guess you've about seen it all, then, haven't you?"

"You could say that."

"Probably treated everything from gunshot wounds to drug addiction."

"And a great deal more," she confirmed.

He bowed his head. "A lot of accident victims, I imagine, kids and adults alike."

She didn't say anything to that because it wasn't necessary.

He looked up suddenly, and that gray-blue gaze was now all sparkle and snap. "It ought to show, something like that," he said. "Folks just don't expect a beautiful young woman like you to have that kind of experience."

Beautiful? she thought, and before she'd recovered from the impact of that, a new thought hit her. He was flirting with her! And she liked it. Oh, my, yes. So much that she was likely to be fluttering her eyelashes and giggling nonsense any minute now if she didn't get ahold of herself. She fell right back on that "formidable intellect," coming up with the perfect comment. "Uh, um, I'm older than I look, you know."

He laughed. "Yeah, I know. Thirty-one. Just about right, I'd say."

For the second time within minutes, she felt color burn her cheeks. The urge to flee was so great that she actually began edging away. "R-right. Uh, I'd better...check on your mother."

He smiled warmly at her, and she knew that he knew exactly what effect his flirtation had had on her.

"Okay," he said, "but I'll be waiting."

She couldn't get out of there fast enough. She whirled away, the tail of her lab coat flying, but the excitement he stirred in her was not so easy to escape. The sincerity and the flattery of his words kept it bubbling for a very long time. It was still fresh, in fact, some ninety minutes later when she walked into the treatment room where Belle Grace Hartesite rested.

"Mrs. Hartesite, can you hear me, ma'am?"

Pale eyelids, faintly lined with blue, slowly lifted. The eyes they revealed, though, were relatively strong and bright now.

"I can hear you, Dr. Terry. Go on."

"As we feared, ma'am, the hip *is* broken."

Belle nodded. "Not surprised," she said tiredly.

"I imagine you've been through something like this before, haven't you, ma'am?"

The pale-blue gaze smartly impaled her.

"Whatever do you mean, young woman?"

Gail was neither fooled nor intimidated by the suddenly imperious tone. "I mean that you've broken this hip before, long ago, and it didn't heal properly."

The older woman sighed. "I wasn't certain. We didn't have any way to be certain back then."

Gail laid a hand on her shoulder to tell her that she understood, then she gently pressed her for more information. "How did it happen?"

"I was thrown from a horse. My husband was with me. We both realized that it was bad."

"Did you see a doctor?"

"Old sawbones came all the way from Fort Stockton." She waved a hand weakly. "It was days later. I could hardly stand. Couldn't walk at all. He told me there was nothing to do but stay in bed eight to nine weeks."

"And did you do that, Mrs. Hartesite?"

The pale-blue gaze slid away. "Rand was just two years old," she said. "It was spring, roundup time, and every hand was needed. I found that I could walk without too much pain after the first couple of weeks..."

"And so you did not follow doctor's orders," Gail said, finishing the thought for her. "I imagine it's pained you quite a lot since then."

Belle shrugged negligently. "Sometimes, riding mostly or walking too much."

"I imagine subsequent pregnancies were no picnic, either."

Belle's eyes dampened suspiciously as she shifted her gaze away. "That's why I only had the two. I just couldn't bear another after Carel."

Carel. Gail didn't want to talk about him. She didn't want to *think* about him. She changed the subject to more pertinent matters. "I want to be honest with you, ma'am. The bone didn't knit correctly, and the resulting scar tissue could prove a problem for us now. I wish I could tell you that for certain, but I'm afraid we'll just have to wait and see."

"Wait and see?" Belle echoed warily.

Gail smiled, but her voice was firm when she answered. "That's right. Now, here's what's going to happen. You're going to stay in this hospital for a while. You're *not* going to move without express permission. You're going to let the staff look after you and administer your medications. You're going to take therapy for your lungs to prevent any possibility of pneumonia developing while you're relaxing in bed. And in a couple of weeks, we'll do another X ray. If everything's moving along as it should, you can go home then, but if you get up on that leg before I tell you that you can, you'll wind up right back here, and there's no guarantee you'll *ever* be able to walk again. Now, I hope I've made you understand the severity of this injury."

Belle nodded mutely.

"All right. We'll be moving you to a private room shortly. I suggest you settle in for a good long rest. I'll see you in the morning, bright and early." She patted the slender shoulder beneath her hand and started to move away, but the patient had one more question.

"What happens if I do everything you say and the bone still doesn't knit properly?"

Gail considered her reply carefully. "That's a bridge we can't cross until we come to it, of course, but I'd say surgery was the most likely course of treatment, followed by intense physical therapy. But I have to warn you. Surgery's always risky, especially for someone your age, and it comes with no guarantees."

Belle swallowed noticeably. "I understand."

"Good. Try not to worry. Think of this as a vacation."

Belle snorted. "A vacation where you can't do anything that you want to."

Gail shook her head. "All right, think of it as cruel and unusual punishment, then. Just realize that you can and you must endure it."

"Do the crime—do the time," Belle quipped.

Gail laughed outright. "At least you haven't lost your sense of humor. I'll send your son in once you're settled."

"Thank you. Thank you very much."

One more pat for encouragement, and Gail knew that she'd done all that she could for the moment.

Rand shook his head. He was still upset. He just couldn't believe what Gail Terry had told him as he drove her back to the ranch and her car. Correction. He could believe it all too well. It was signature Belle Grace Hartesite.

He rapped his fist against the steering wheel and gave his tongue free rein. "She never said a word, dammit! Not a word! The woman's as stubborn as a mule!"

Gail merely cocked her head. "I assure you that she was experiencing pain, whether she said anything or not."

He threw up his hand. "Stubborn? She makes a mule look like a pushover! God only knows how many times she's sat on a horse hurting all the while, but would she complain? Hell, no! She's got to prove she's as tough as any man." He remembered the many times he'd called on her for help and how proud he'd been of her performance. He grimaced, feeling guilty as all get out. "Lord knows she's worked like a man most of her life," he admitted. "She can rope and ride as well as any I've ever known, Daddy included, God rest him, and now you tell me it was all in pain! Makes me feel small somehow."

"You couldn't have known," she told him. "She didn't want you to know. I don't think she even thought about it. She just did what she thought she had to."

"Hell, I couldn't do it!"

"And shouldn't," she insisted. "It was the times, I guess. She was a young mother, a wife working next to her husband. No hospital, no doctor to keep an eye on her."

"She and Daddy built that ranch up from nothing," he told her. "They started with eleven hundred acres and wound up with thirty thousand."

"Thirty *thousand!*"

"It's fifty now," he said, not above bragging a little to impress her.

She lifted both brows, her delicate features lined by the soft glow of the dash lights. "Sounds like you've carried on a well-established family tradition."

"Couldn't do anything else," he said. "Daddy worked himself into an early grave building up something his sons could be proud of, and you already know what lengths Mother went to. God, what a woman!" He couldn't quite quell the pride in his voice—or the frustration.

Gail smiled and smoothed the tendrils of her hair back off her forehead. She looked tired and bedraggled, but utterly female, and he was liking her more every minute. What did she think of him? he wondered. Was he just some uncouth cowboy to her? He searched for something to say that might convince her otherwise. He couldn't think of a thing, so he settled for what came to mind.

"I guess you've been around some," he said, stretching his arm out along the back of the seat and checking the rearview mirror.

She nodded. "Some."

"Where you from anyway?"

She looked away, presenting him her profile. She might have been a cameo, a beautiful face carved in ivory.

"California, originally."

"Yeah? I've been there. My brother used to go to college out there. I visited him once." She turned her head away, and he feared he was boring her, but somehow he couldn't let it alone. "Pretty place. Kind of crowded for my taste."

She smiled at that. "Yes, I imagine it is."

"You miss it?"

She shook her head. "No."

Not exactly forthcoming, he mused, but maybe he could draw her out if he tried hard enough. "That where your family is?"

She shrugged. "I have no idea."

He was shocked. "No idea where your family is?" Why, family was everything, at least to his way of thinking. He watched her draw a deep breath, puzzled by the sudden stiffness in her posture. "I mean, it's none of my business but..." He bit off anything further, afraid he'd offend her which was exactly the opposite of what he wanted to do Obviously she didn't want to talk about it.

After a moment, she twisted a little in her seat and turned her face to him. He allowed himself a long, thorough look She was a tall, slender woman, with curves in all the right places, and her face was awfully pretty, a perfect oval, with high cheekbones and a delicately pointed chin. Her eye were shaped like huge teardrops, set beneath gently arching brows separated by the bridge of a dainty nose. They wer hazel in color, with tiny green and gold flecks that re minded him of the shiny chips of bright glass behind the len of a kaleidoscope. But it was her mouth that made him wan to stare. It was plump and rosy and compellingly kissable putting him in mind of strawberries and long drinks o sweet, cool sangria. Heavens! He looked away before he ra the vehicle off the road, and concentrated on the twin beam of the headlights piercing the gathering darkness of night He didn't expect her to say anything after the clumsy com ments he'd made, so he was surprised when she began.

"I never knew my father," she said bluntly, "and m mother took off with...some other man when I was abou nine. It wasn't the first time, but it was the last, 'cause sh never came back."

Oh, Lord, he thought, *no wonder she didn't want to talk about herself.* He tried to think of something encouraging to say and came up with "Well, somebody must've don right by you. Just look at you now."

She stared at him for a moment. "I think it was more like everybody doing everything all wrong, me included."

He couldn't just let that pass. "What do you mean?"

She turned her head to watch out the windshield. "I wa raised in the welfare system, one foster home after another until I just stopped counting."

He didn't know what to say to that, but she didn't seem to expect any comment.

"I wasn't exactly an enthusiastic participant," she went on, "and the harder they tried to make me one, the less enthusiastic I became. I just couldn't see being grateful for the situation I was in, and I guess I was afraid to trust the people who could have helped me most."

"Not surprising," he muttered.

She squared her shoulders, chin high, and he knew that she was refusing pity. He admired her for that, admired her greatly.

"At least they helped me get into college," she said. "My caseworker was a big believer in education, and she helped me fill out the applications and get the available grants and loans to start. One thing about California, there are some pretty forward-thinking people out there, and they were pushing women toward the sciences." She shrugged. "That's where the grants were, so that's where I went, and I guess I finally got lucky, because I stumbled into something I love."

"Trying to be somebody," he said softly.

She shot him a look, but then she seemed to remember having said that earlier, and she softened enough to smile. "Trying to be somebody."

"I'd say you've done right well," he told her gently.

She tilted her head. "I'm not sitting on fifty thousand acres. In fact, I'm hardly even paying the bills at the moment."

"Business is a little slow, I gather."

"A snail with blisters moves faster," she quipped.

He made a firm decision. "It'll get better," he promised. "Just give it some time."

She fixed him with a direct look. "I'm not planning on going anywhere."

He was glad to hear it, real glad, and he meant to see that she didn't start thinking of leaving anytime soon. He meant, in fact, to see that she got *every* kind of encouragement to stay, every kind of encouragement, especially his own very personal kind of encouragement, so personal that his palms were beginning to sweat just thinking of it.

He wasn't quite sure how he was going to go about it. He
just knew that she excited him, more so than any other
woman he'd met. She was a spunky sort, and he sensed that
ribbons of steel ran through her. He liked that. He liked,
too, how she looked—a girl's face on a woman's body and
with all that gold hair, plus that sensual mouth that made
him want...

He shifted his weight, uncomfortable with the pulsing in
his groin, knowing he had to be patient, but this time, he
hoped, it would not be for nothing.

Chapter Three

Neither her excitement nor her nervousness would be diminished. She wished fervently that he had not called first. The novelty of having an actual appointment to record in her book was pleasant, but knowing that she was going to meet *him* again was nerve-racking. She shouldn't be attracted to Carel's brother. Nothing good could come of it, even if he did like her, and she couldn't quite accept that he did, despite his flirtation. Then why had he called? Did his daughters really need physicals so far into the school year— or was he suspicious? Gail caught her breath at the very thought. Had Rand Hartesite somehow figured out who she was?

But that was impossible. Even Carel would not have realized her identity unless they were to meet face-to-face, a possibility she had accepted from the beginning but need not worry about any longer. Dr. Gail Terry, new physician in town, hosted no obvious connection to college freshman Abigail Walken, except the physical, and since Carel could no longer identify her, she had no worries there. Furthermore, she had been married and divorced during a single year previous to her appointment to residency in Dallas, so that foolish girl who had allowed herself to be manipulated by Carel Hartesite would not be very easy to trace. She could be uncovered, of course, but not without some prolonged digging. And Rand Hartesite, unlike his late brother, had no reason to dig. Besides, if he had the least notion who she was, he would not be bringing his daughters in for routine physicals. And she would not feel as if she had swallowed a live eel whole because of it. Pushing aside thoughts of *him,* she tried to concentrate on her goal. She had to find her daughter.

She still could not quite accept the fact of Carel's death eleven long years ago. Eleven years! To think that she might have claimed her daughter without opposition eleven years ago made her both angry and regretful for all she had lost during that time. She could not be sorry that Carel was not there to unmask her and oppose her before she was ready, but she could not rejoice in his death, either, especially now that she knew his family. He had said that he didn't fit in with them, and she could see from the contact she had already had with Belle Grace and Rand Hartesite that he had been truthful in that respect at least. She almost wished that Carel were here so she could vent her frustration on him— and because it seemed somehow more supportable to contemplate confronting him than worming information out of his brother. Maybe she ought simply to identify herself and demand to know where her daughter was. Surely Rand would understand. He had daughters of his own, after all, two of them, as it turned out. Yet she couldn't quite make herself do it, not until she was certain that he would help her. Maybe if he liked her enough... But no, she couldn't think like that. She didn't want to use him that way. Maybe when he got to know her better, though, he'd want to help her. Otherwise she'd just have to wait until someone let something slip about her and Carel's child. She was not very

good at waiting, even after thirteen years. It would be so
much easier if she were busy, really busy, instead of sitting
cross-legged on the floor sorting through the magazines in
the waiting room, weeding out the oldest and most ragged.

She continued sorting the magazines, purposefully
avoiding the clock on the wall and the watch on her wrist.
When she had finished going through them, she discarded
the rejects and organized the remainder by subject in the
wall rack, then proceeded to do the same with the numer-
ous pamphlets scattered about on side tables. This task was
nearing completion, too, when the door opened to the soft
tones of chimes. They were here. In the instant before Gail
turned around, a strange calm, not unlike the kind that
prevailed in the midst of a medical emergency, came over
her. She felt her face arranging itself in the serene, confident lines so necessary in her profession and faced them with
cool, deceptive aplomb.

They were standing just inside the door, Rand at the back,
the two girls side by side before him. They were pretty girls,
similar and yet different. One was taller and plumper, with
more prominent breasts than her shorter, slightly built sister. Her hair was the color of milk chocolate and blunt cut
to just below her chin. She wore it parted in the middle and
tousled slightly around her face, calling attention to her
large eyes of greenish hazel. She would be very pretty one
day soon, and she knew it.

Her sister, too, was going to be a beauty, but of a different sort. Her slender build made her look taller than she
might have otherwise, and saved her from seeming baby-
ish. Her long, almost black hair overpowered her slender
face and weighed down the curl that showed in her wavy
bangs. In Gail's opinion, she would benefit greatly from a
good haircut when she was ready for it. Her eyes were not
as vivid as her sister's and were more blue than green, without even a hint of the yellow that flared in the other girl's.
Her mouth was definitely her best feature. Full and lush, it

seemed to hint at a passionate nature she did not yet know she possessed.

They appeared close in age. She judged the plump one to be the elder of the two, though neither one could be much past fourteen. She wondered if they knew her daughter, and if so, what they thought of their cousin. She would be of a similar age and, Gail hoped, just as pretty. They were bound to know her.

Mindful of that fact, Gail put on her best bedside manner and her warmest smile. She wanted to sweep them into a private room where she could question them, but she resisted the impulse and forced herself to speak first to their father, since he was the only one she actually knew.

"Hello, Rand. Nice to see you again. Have you visited your mother today?"

He nodded and grinned. "She's already agitating to get out of that place, but I'm sure you know that."

"You did warn me."

"It's only going to get worse. She's a strong-willed woman," he said, "and she hates to show weakness of any sort. Plus she's used to getting her way."

Gail laughed. "Maybe she'll *will* that bone to knit properly. Then we won't have to worry about letting her have her way." She turned her attention to the girls, feeling she'd masked her eagerness sufficiently. "Well, ladies, I'm Dr. Terry." She smiled at the bigger girl. "And you are?"

"Mary Grace. You can just call me 'Mary' if you want to."

"Fine. Thank you." She turned to the other girl. "And what's your name?"

"I'm Carel Belle," said the slighter girl, her voice little more than a whisper. "Pleased to meet you, ma'am."

Carel Belle. The shock of that name shimmied through her. With great effort, Gail reinforced her smile. "I'm very pleased to meet you, too, both of you." She tried to suppress thought of the significance of Carel Belle's name. Was she named after her uncle...or possibly her father? She would be about the right age, and it would be understandable if Rand had adopted her as his own. Yes, it was possible. Her heart was pounding so hard that she was afraid someone would see. She retreated, as usual, into professionalism. "Well, who wants to go first?"

"Can't we go together?" asked Mary Grace. "We usually go together."

"No problem."

Gail stepped back and lifted her arm to indicate the way.

Mary Grace quickly went up on her tiptoes and smacked a kiss on Rand's cheek. "Be back in a little while, Uncle Rand."

Uncle Rand! The impact of the endearment hit Gail between the eyes and reverberated down all the way to her toes. Uncle? He was her uncle? Then this must be... Dear God, could *Mary Grace* be her daughter? Then what about Carel Belle? Gail stood frozen to the spot, uncertain what to think, say or do. Suddenly disappointment swamped her, not with either girl, never with these girls, but with herself. She realized that she had expected to somehow *know* her own child. She had been counting on a flood of maternal instinct to reveal her child to her, but these girls were strangers—both of them were strangers. Shouldn't she have known which one was hers? Or were neither hers?

Tears welled up. She turned her head, clearing her throat as she blinked them away.

Rand was hugging Mary tightly. "I'll be fine, sugar. Don't you worry 'bout me." He released her and slipped his arms around Carel Belle, accepting her kiss on his other cheek. "Go on now. Don't keep Dr. Terry waiting." He grinned at Gail over the tops of their heads. "She's a busy lady."

"I wish," she muttered, then added brightly, "this way, ladies."

The professional calm deserted her as she led them around the partition and down the short hall to the examining room, their athletic shoes squeaking on her freshly waxed tile floor. On the way, Gail snatched her clipboard and the new-patient forms from the reception desk. Her ink pen— any ink pen—proved impossible to find with only a cursory look, so she grabbed up a pencil and hurried on, writing "Carel Belle" on the top of one form and "Mary Grace" on the top of the other before putting the girls one at a time on the scale.

Mary Grace was a good twenty pounds heavier and two and a half inches taller than her sister, which might indicate that she was the elder of the two. Important information. Gail's hands shook as she made her notations. One part of her functioned as normal, while another alternately exulted and quaked at the idea of possibly being in her daughter's presence. It was the normally functioning part that allowed Gail to see the similarities between Mary Grace's strong character and her grandmother's, but Gail knew that her topsy-turvy emotions made her observations suspect. Despite a great desire for some sign of commonality, Gail could see only the most superficial resemblance to herself in the girl, only her height and the color of her eyes. On the other hand, Carel Belle seemed to favor her a bit around the mouth, and there was her slender build. But it was hopeless to go at it this way!

She began asking routine questions, making sure that she had the spellings of their names correct, then moving rapidly to such perfunctory matters as addresses, phone numbers and the like. The shock came when, after stopping to clear her throat first, she asked Mary Grace for her birthdate. Mary Grace gave her a date one month and six days after that on which she, Gail, had given birth. One month and six days. Disappointment choked her. She broke the lead in her pencil when she tried to write the numbers on the paper. Hanging on to her composure by only a thread, she excused herself quickly and stood in the hall trying to master her emotions, when the implications of this knowledge hit her.

It had to be Carel Belle. But that didn't explain how Rand had come to be Mary's uncle. Mary Grace had to be Carel's child, too. It was the only explanation. Belle had told Gail herself that she'd had only the two boys. That could only mean that Carel had impregnated some other female, as well, a month and six days after her! The son of a—

How on earth would their father have explained two daughters with birthdates less than five weeks apart? Maybe he'd lied. Given all the other lies, she doubted he'd have so much as paused before handing out a false birthdate for one or both of his daughters. A chill passed through her, a premonition, perhaps of the shock still to come.

Grabbing another pencil, Gail let herself back into the room and put on her smile. She made a little small talk, hardly registering her own words let alone those of the girls, checked the appropriate boxes and filled in the appropriate lines until only one question remained. She hadn't learned a thing to further enlighten her, but she expected the next answer to at least confirm her suspicions.

"Carel Belle," she said in as disinterested a tone as possible, "I need to get your birthdate, too."

She waited for the date, pencil poised over the paper, but Carel Belle merely traded a look with Mary Grace and giggled, her hand coming up to cover her mouth.

Mary Grace rolled her eyes, a wide grin on her face. "Didn't anyone tell you?" she asked.

Gail felt the ground shifting beneath her feet. "Tell me what?"

They looked at each other again. Then Mary Grace came out with it. "We're twins, silly!"

Twins? Twins! Twins. The word seemed to echo inside her head. Twins. Twins. And neither of them hers. Neither of them . . . Gail closed her eyes, stifling the urge to scream. Twins. Oh, God.

"Dr. Terry?"

She heard Mary Grace as if from a great distance, and with a supreme effort of will, Gail pulled herself back to the moment. "Yes. Oh, I-I'm sorry. I was thinking... when..." She shook her head. "N-never mind that now. Let's get your vitals."

Performing routine tasks helped calm her and take her mind off the awful thought that she hadn't found her daughter after all. Or had she? Carel had been all too capable of lies. Without anyone else there to refute him, passing these girls off as twins would have been ridiculously simple. But what of birth certificates and the sort? If she could get her hands on those... She tried to push the thought away, aware that she was not at her most logical and reasonable just then.

The whole experience was quickly becoming a nightmare. She wanted to weep and demand answers, but could only go through the motions of performing routine physicals, despite the fact that her hands shook and her mind constantly wandered. Finally she had done everything that was reasonable. She offered to sign physical forms permitting them to participate in school sports, but there were those traded looks again, and Mary Grace said, "Uh, we had that done at the beginning of the school year."

Hadn't she suspected as much? "Then why—" Gail began, but Carel Belle cut her off with the answer before she could even ask the question.

"He wanted to help you," she said.

"You know how it is," Mary added. "People kind of watch us around here."

"And if Rand Hartesite does something, supports someone, others will, too?" Gail asked.

Mary Grace shrugged. It was a gesture so like Rand's that there was something poignant about it. "It's just that the Hartesite spread is the biggest ranch around here."

Gail folded her arms, feeling oddly warmed—and a bit wary. "I see." It was nice to know that someone around there had her best interests at heart, but she couldn't expect that to continue, not once he knew who she really was and what she wanted. The notion increased her disappointment. Gail swallowed it down and forced a crooked smile. "Well, I guess you don't need me to tell you that you're healthy, lovely girls, but that is my diagnosis."

Mary Grace's smile was quick and a little smug. "Thanks."

Carel Belle said, "Everyone thinks Mary Grace is pretty." There was just a hint of envy in her soft tone.

"We're both pretty," Mary Grace stated flatly. "You just don't act like it is all."

Gail raised an eyebrow, but said only, "Mary Grace is correct, of course. You're each very lovely in your own way."

"You just have to act like you know it for people to notice," Mary Grace said offhandedly.

Gail bent her head, knowing she should bite her tongue, but unable to let that comment pass. "It's true that self-confidence is attractive to others, but arrogance is not, and there's a fine line between the two."

Mary Grace gazed at her through narrowed eyes, but said nothing. Carel Belle looked away.

Gail squared her shoulders. "Well, I guess we're through. I'm going to get those signatures from your—Rand now."

The girls nodded and began whispering. Gail let herself out of the room and took a deep breath before making her way to the reception desk. Rand got up and came to the counter, setting aside a sports magazine he had been perusing.

"Everything okay?"

She gave him a smile. "You know very well that those girls are in perfect health."

He shrugged. "Yeah, well, never hurts to keep an eye out for trouble."

"Two physicals in a single school year?" she said. "Is that your idea of keeping an eye out?"

His face went carefully blank. "I just wanted to get them set up with you here in this office."

"You just wanted to give me your stamp of approval for the whole town to see."

He glanced down at his booted toes and back up again, a sheepish smile growing on his face. "Okay, Doc," he said. "You caught me." His smile grew into a teasing grin. "I hope you're properly grateful."

Gail had to laugh. "You are an operator, Rand Harte-site, but yes, I am grateful. Now, if you don't mind, I have a little business to conduct."

He nodded. "Go ahead. What do you want to know?"

"Um, I hope you won't think me presumptuous, but I had assumed that they were your daughters."

He frowned. "Same as. Technically, I'm their uncle, but they're mine all the same. I've raised them since they were little bitty. Their mother died right after they were born, and their father—my brother—was killed in an accident when they were two, but you know about that."

"Yes," Gail said softly. "Did he, er, have any other children?"

"No. Why?"

She managed a careless shrug despite the almost painful pounding of her heart. "I just like to keep very complete files on my younger patients... for, ah, in case of emergencies."

He seemed to accept that without hesitation.

"Okay. So is that it? I mean, I'm all in favor of being prepared for emergencies."

She licked her lips and plunged on. "Well, now that you mention it, the name and background of their mother would be helpful."

He didn't even hesitate. "I'm afraid I don't know much about her. She was from Canada."

"Canada!" Gail echoed in surprise.

"Yeah, that's where they were born."

"Canada?" Gail put a hand to her head. "I-I thought... that is, I could have sworn... someone told me they were born in California."

He shook his head. "No, Carel was living in California when they were born, but the girls were born in Canada. Apparently it was a difficult pregnancy and their mother went back home to live with family until they were born. I don't think it was a very good arrangement. Her parents were elderly and apparently in poor health. Carel never said so, but we were under the impression that at least one of them died just before the girls were born, and then, afterward, she took her own life—their mother, I mean. Actually, I think there may have been problems with the marriage. Carel blamed it on postpartum blues. Whatever. Anyway, that's why he came home with them."

Gail swallowed, reeling with confusion. Canada. Suicide. Postpartum blues. Thoughts were flying through her head. She latched onto one. "D-did you know her? Had you ever met her?"

"Nope, just knew her name was all. We tried to notify her family after Carel's accident, but we couldn't find any of them."

Gail nodded absently. "Well, could you give me her name then, just for the record?"

"Abby Walken," he said. "Abigail, actually."

Gail gripped the edge of the counter and felt her head spin. *She* was Abigail Walken! She sat down hard on her chair just as the girls came out of the examination room, talking and laughing. Rand glanced from her to the girls and back again.

"You okay?" he asked, leaning across the counter to put his hand on her shoulder.

She shook off the shock, forcing a smile. "But I . . . That is, I-I guess I shouldn't have skipped lunch. My b-blood sugar tends to drop."

His brow was furrowed with concern. "We can fix that," he said. "Why don't you let us take you for a bite to eat?"

"Oh, no, I couldn't!" She gulped, then forcefully brightened her smile. "I-I'm trying to build a practice here, you know. It wouldn't look too good for the new doc to close up shop early, now would it?''

Rand chuckled. "No, I guess not. This doctoring business is serious stuff." He lifted off his hat and pushed his hand through his hair. "We could send you something back.''

She shook her head, too shocked even to note his solicitous treatment. "It'll be f-faster and easier if I just...slip in the back for a quick bite.''

He shrugged, replaced his hat and began wiggling his wallet from his back pocket. "Well, all right," he was saying, "if that's your final word on the matter. I guess you'd better figure up the charges then and—''

"Not this time," she said flatly, waving him away. "I mean it. No charge.''

He lifted an eyebrow, seemed on the verge of arguing, then gave an exasperated sigh and slid his wallet back into place. "This time," he said.

Gail just nodded. "Thank you for trying to help me.''

"My pleasure. Listen, there's something else you could do to help yourself, you know.''

She blinked at him, trying to concentrate, when what she really wanted was to be alone to think. "Oh? And what would that be?''

"Football," he said.

His reply was so unexpected that she laughed. "I beg your pardon?''

"Football," he repeated. "It's the lifeblood of every little town in Texas, the big ones, too, for that matter.''

"I hope you aren't suggesting I suit up!''

"Nah, just turn out.''

She shook her head, muttering, "You'll have to explain that.''

He grinned. "Tomorrow's Friday. There's a game every Friday night during the season. Tomorrow night's game just happens to be a home game. The whole town will be there.

Now, if you happen to attend the game with me, naturally I'll have to introduce you to everybody I know."

He was flirting again! She couldn't help smiling. "Ah, and you'll undoubtedly know every single person in the stands."

He contrived to look affronted. "Don't forget those on the field." He grinned. "Everybody who's anybody around here knows his players and referees well enough to abuse them by name."

She rolled her eyes, but couldn't quell a chuckle. "I see. Seems I have a lot to learn about living in a small Texas town."

"Then you'll let me take you to the game?" he asked smoothly.

A date. She could hardly believe it. Carel Hartesite's brother was asking her out on a date. She was tempted, very tempted, but she knew that it wouldn't be wise to go out on a real date with him. Yet there was so much more she needed to know. Would it be unforgivable of her to accept for that reason? She was so confused that she couldn't think, but instinct told her that this man was dangerous to her in a way that none other had ever been. She fell back on tried-and-true ambivalence, rejection without teeth. "Maybe I'll see you there."

She saw the disappointment that clouded those smoky-blue eyes and impulsively decided that she would go. It wouldn't be a date if she went on her own, and if she happened to see him there... Well, it couldn't hurt her really. Could it? "Um, what time does the game start?"

His grin flashed across his face. "Eight, I think, but you'd better get there early. Parking lot's always crowded."

"I'll remember that."

"We have to go early anyway," Mary Grace said from behind her.

Gail didn't miss the petulant tone of her voice. Neither did Rand. He shot her a scolding look.

Gail rushed to defuse the situation. "Well, it's settled then. This works out best for everyone."

Rand seemed disgruntled, but he merely nodded and pushed his hat down more firmly on his head. "I'll be seeing you, then."

She nodded and pivoted to smile wanly at the girls. *I'm not dead!* she wanted to scream. She swallowed those words and managed a soft goodbye.

"Bye," Mary Grace said shortly, stalking away.

Carel Belle remained to smile shyly. "Nice to have met you," she said softly, and slipped out after her sister.

Rand gave her one last look, touched the brim of his hat and followed the girls out.

Gail let out a long pent-up breath and closed her eyes. Twins born in *Canada* to a supposedly deceased mother named Abigail Walken. Every word a lie, every lie reeking of Carel's unmistakable cachet. What had he done? What on God's earth had he done? And how could she ever unravel it all to the truth that would finally give her back her daughter?

Rand tossed his hat into the seat and slid behind the wheel of the truck. He was still frowning. That hadn't gone at all as he would have liked. He was long out of practice, of course, but he could have done a better job of asking her out if he'd just taken a little more time—and kept Mary Grace out of it. He should have talked this thing over with the girls *before,* he thought belatedly. Well, better late than never. He was determined to prevent at least one mistake from repeating itself.

He started up the truck, but didn't yet engage the transmission. Instead, he slid his arm along the back of the seat and twisted, looking at his girls. Mary Grace had taken her usual place in the front seat and Carel Belle was again sitting quietly in the center of the back. That, too, was a situation he'd been meaning to address. It wasn't fair for Mary Grace always to take the most favored spot. That, however was not the issue at the moment. He shook his head to clear it of extraneous thought and targeted Mary Grace—only to find himself being drilled with those snapping gold-and-green eyes of hers. Gail had gold-and-green eyes. Nice eyes. But not the ones burning holes in him just now. He firmed mentally.

"What?" he demanded.

"You don't really like her, do you?" Mary Graced asked.

He hung one arm over the steering wheel. "I do."

"I think she's nice," Carel Belle said from the back seat.

Mary Grace snorted. "I think she's *weird.*"

"I think you should keep your opinions to yourself," Rand said calmly. "Nobody asked you."

Mary Grace folded her arms and frowned. Rand started the truck and backed out of the dirt lot onto the street, his gaze sliding over his niece. She was the most precious thing in the world to him—one of the most precious—but sometimes he didn't know how to handle her. He thought of his mother and wondered if he ought to leave it to her, then instantly rejected the notion. Belle had enough to deal with just now. She hated to be sick, hated to be idle. *He* hated this petulant silence. He steeled himself and broke it.

"Why shouldn't I like her?" he asked. "She's a perfectly nice woman, smart—a doctor, for pity's sake."

"And pretty!" Mary Grace said sharply.

"And pretty," he conceded. "Something wrong with that?"

She stared out the window, her bottom lip jutting forward in a pout. He shook his head and glanced in the rearview mirror at Carel Belle. She had her nose buried in a textbook, but he wasn't fooled into believing she wasn't aware of every nuance of the conversation. She looked up then and flashed him a conspiratorial wink. He grinned, feeling better. So different, his girls, like opposite sides of the same coin.

Mary Grace couldn't stay silent for long. He waited. She spoke as he turned the truck south, heading out of town.

"You've always said you have too many women on your hands already."

"Come on now, Mary Grace. You know a joke when you hear one." He sent her a sharp look, putting her in her place with a glance. They both knew he didn't have to explain this to her. She was well aware of the attraction that worked between men and women, too aware. She lifted her chin.

"Is it because of Grandma, because she's getting old?"

Rand snorted. "That woman won't be *old* at a hundred. But that's not the point." He tried to think through what he had to say. "It isn't because of any of *you,*" he began finally. "This is about me." *I'm lonely,* he thought, surprised that it was so. He became aware of a tightness in the back of his neck and rubbed it absently. "Look, I'm allowed to like anybody I choose. Adulthood has certain privileges, you know."

"But why her?" Mary Grace asked.

He lifted a brow. "Why not?"

Carel Belle made an impatient sound. "You see any other pretty, smart, single women around lately?" she asked Mary Grace.

Mary twisted around to stick her tongue out at her sister. She hated to be bested in any way, and she glared at Rand as if it were his fault. "I don't like her," she stated boldly.

"But you'll be polite," he said in a tone that left no room for argument.

Her glare got downright nasty, but she stuck her chin in her chest and hunkered down, saying nothing. Rand rubbed his hand over his face and stared at the road stretching out before them. Just what he needed, with everything else that was going on. Well, she'd just have to get over it. Gail Terry compelled him as no other woman ever had, and he meant to further the acquaintance one way or another, no matter who objected. Now all he had to do was make the lovely doctor understand—and hope the feeling was returned. He guessed he'd have some idea about that on Friday night. *If* she showed up.

Chapter Four

Gail heard the sounds of cheering applause and a deep, monotone voice above it all calling out the names of players. She pulled her cardigan closer about her and wished she had worn her coat, but the coat, she knew, would have been too heavy, since it was calf length and made of thick wool tweed lined with quilted sateen. She had bought it at the height of a windy Dallas winter and had worn it seldomly since. She hardly thought she'd have real need of it in Marfa, Texas, but she could see that she was going to have to buy a jacket of some sort or confine her outings to the daytime.

Shuffling her feet to keep her blood flowing, she waited in line behind two teenage cowboys, three giggling little girls and an elderly couple, who were patiently picking coins out of each other's hands in an effort to find exact change to pay their way into the stadium. One of the the little girls poked one of the cowboys in the behind with the edge of the barrette she'd taken from her soft red hair. He swatted at her and yelled, "Stop it, twerp, or I'll tell Mom!"

She stuck out her tongue and withdrew into the safe company of her giggling companions, crowing, "Big butt!"

Gail bowed her head to hide her grin. Kids, it seemed, were just kids, even in remote little Marfa. The elderly couple finally covered the cost of entrance, which was minimal, and passed through the gate. The cowboys started digging their wallets out of their pockets, no mean feat considering how painfully tight and stiff their jeans were. The first one was accepting his change, when one of the little girls turned to Gail, looked her up and down and bluntly asked, "Who are you?"

Gail stuck her hand out. "I'm Dr. Terry. How do you do?"

The child put her hand in Gail's and said, "Fine. Are you really a doctor?"

Gail pumped that little hand most solemnly. "Yes, I am a doctor. I've taken over old Doc Garlock's place."

"Hmm," said the child, her head cocked, her hand remaining in Gail's. "Is it hard?"

"To be a doctor?"

The little head bobbed.

Gail considered. "Yes, I suppose it is, but you could do it if you wanted to and you didn't mind going to school for a very long time."

Delicate eyebrows rose in thought. The tiny hand slipped from Gail's, and a small mouth twisted to one side, then broke into a wide smile just before her friends called and she turned and ran to join them. Gail chuckled, wondering if she'd planted a seed in that fertile little brain.

"One, please," she said to the man collecting entrance fees, but as she dug into the pocket of her jeans, she was trying to picture Mary Grace and Carel Belle at the age of that little girl. What would it have been like to plant such a seed in her own daughter's mind? She felt, for a moment, as if a hand were squeezing her heart, but then she pushed the mental picture away, accepted her change and walked through the gate into the milling group on the walkway. Heads turned and nodded, quick smiles flashed in silent greeting, and Gail knew that if she just maintained eye contact a heartbeat longer, someone would stick out a hand and speak. The knowledge warmed her inside if not out, and she was careful to return every nod and smile, but she shied away from conversation for one reason and one reason only, no matter how much she wanted to deny it. And that reason suddenly appeared at her side.

"Hey, you made it."

"Um-hmm." She seemed to have forgotten just how tall he was. She was used to standing shoulder to shoulder with a man, but with Rand she stood shoulder to biceps, and well-developed biceps at that. She looked up at his smiling mouth and noted with a small shock of interest a tiny scar on his chin. That small flaw seemed merely to draw attention to the male perfection of his handsome face. She quickly glanced away, flipping one side of her hair, worn down for the evening, over an ear nipped by chill.

"Well, look at that," he said, grinning. "No ponytail."

She rolled her eyes, drawing her sweater tighter about her. "I think you like to give me a hard time."

Gray-blue eyes sparkled. "Could be. You cold?"

"A little."

"If you have a jacket in the car, I'll be glad to get it for you."

She smiled at his thoughtfulness, but shook her head. "I didn't come in my car, and even if I had, you couldn't get my jacket for me because I don't own one."

"You didn't come in your car?" he asked, clearly shocked. "How'd you get here?"

"I walked, of course."

He actually laughed. "Bet the sidewalks weren't crowded."

She felt herself smiling again. "No, as a matter of fact, they weren't."

"We'll have to get you a jacket," he said, sliding his down-filled vest off and draping it over her shoulders.

"You'll freeze," she protested.

"Nah, I'll be fine. We'll huddle. Besides, we're sitting low in the stands," he said, telling not asking. He cupped her elbow in his hand, guiding her through the thinning crowd.

She thought about digging in her heels, as she surely would have with any other man, but she had no real desire to do so. *Because he's my connection to my daughter,* she told herself. But it wasn't only that, and she knew it.

"I've got some seats saved," he explained as they were stalled by some spectators standing at the edge of the walk. "The stands usually fill up pretty fast."

They wound their way through the congestion, breaking out at the end side by side. They experienced a moment of physical dissonance as Rand adjusted his stride to hers, but once he adopted the correct rhythm, his hand came up and hovered at the small of her back. Gail found herself feeling alarmingly like a date despite her caution. They walked as far as the middle of the stands, then stepped up to the third row. A couple on the fourth removed a coffee Thermos, a tote bag and a billed cap from the coveted seats. Rand made the introductions.

"Gail, I'd like you to meet the Purdys, Denny and Beth. This is Gail Terry, new doctor in town."

Denny doffed his hat. "Miss Terry."

His wife slid an elbow into his ribs. "*Dr.* Terry."

He apologized with a grimace and a nod. "Beg pardon, ma'am—uh, Doc."

Beth slung that elbow again, but Gail defused the accompanying scold by insisting that they call her "Gail." They shook hands, then Gail and Rand took their seats in front of the Purdys. Gail looked around her for the girls as Rand informed her that the Purdys had a boy, Ronnie, on the team.

"He's just a sophomore," Beth said proudly, "but he's starting this year."

"He's starting as long as he keeps his grades up," Denny said darkly. "We've got that 'No Pass No Play' rule, and it sure makes havoc with these small school teams."

"We'll see how bad he wants to play come report-card time," Beth commented, a note of worry in her voice.

"Aw, he'll do fine," Rand said. "At least until football season's over."

Gail wondered what the girls' grades were like, but could think of no polite, acceptable way to ask. Suddenly a drumroll began. Then a whistle blew shrilly, and the crowd howled as the home team kicked off. Gail pretended to watch the action on the field while scanning faces for the girls. It wasn't until the home team recovered a fumbled ball and the uniformed cheerleaders tumbled onto the edge of the field, whooping and hollering, that she spotted them.

"Cheerleaders!" She spoke aloud, surprised that she hadn't thought of it earlier. But were they old enough for high school cheerleading?

Rand chuckled into her ear, the brim of his hat grazing the top of her head. "Skipped a year," he said softly, pride swelling every syllable into a distinct drawl. "Top students, both of them."

Gail grinned. She couldn't help it. She had decided in the empty dark of a long night that one—or both...was it possible?—of those girls was definitely hers. It had to be, unless Carel had another daughter somewhere that his own family didn't know about. The idea didn't make sense, though. Why take her daughter from her, then hide the child away, while producing two others for his family? And why name her as the mother of those two? No, at least *one* of them was hers. It was the only thing that made sense. But which one? And if both were not hers, who was the other mother? She shook her head, trying to clear it of useless speculation, and concentrated on the moment.

Rand winked at her and she couldn't help but share his pride. The Purdys' boy might struggle with his grades, but the Hartesite girls just naturally waltzed right onto the honor roll every six weeks with enviable regularity. She felt a swelling in her chest and a mistiness about the eyes as she watched Mary Grace and Carel Belle go through their paces with confident precision. She imagined that one of them would be elected homecoming queen eventually, and maybe even student-body president, and achieve all the other things she herself had envied prettier, more popular girls for. But then she reminded herself that she had her medical degree and her private practice, poor as it was, and soon she would have her daughter to hold and love and encourage and praise, maybe even two. Was it possible?

It occurred to her that largely because of the man sitting next to her, those two dark-haired girls cavorting on the sidelines had advantages she had sorely missed. They had a stable home, loving support, financial largesse, an uncle to guide them, a grandmother to nurture them, and each other. She wondered, not for the first time, if it would be terribly selfish of her to separate them. But maybe she wouldn't have to. They *could* both be hers. It wasn't impossible. She'd worked it all out in her mind. An unscrupulous attending physician and his (or her) personal team of handpicked delivery-room staff *could* conceal a second baby from a young, frightened, exhausted mother. It would have been tricky, and it wasn't likely. She couldn't understand why he'd allow her to see one baby and not both, but his motives in all of this were so twisted and baffling she couldn't totally dismiss the possibility. There were two of them, after all, and they were similar enough to be twins. Blood samples and a series of simple tests—not readily available locally, but attainable—could tell her if they were actual twins and if both or either of them were hers. But such tests required signed permission forms and certain other ethical safeguards. Circumventing them could well cost her her license to practice.

Getting blood samples would be so easy to do, though. All she needed was a reason to take the blood. Rand would never have to know that she'd requested the tests, at least not until she was ready to reveal the results—at which point she could be charged with a breach of ethics. These things were usually done by court order, but she doubted that she could get one. For one thing, there was that nonsense about her having given birth in Canada, not to mention the fact that she was supposed to be dead! She suspected that she could find records indicating that she had given birth in California to at least one child, and that Carel Harte was the same man as Carel Hartesite, but she really didn't know whether or not that would be enough to get both girls tested. Besides, she wasn't ready to reveal herself just yet. If only she could decide what to do!

This was turning out to be so much more complicated than she had expected that she was finding herself constantly torn as to her next step, so much so that she was wondering if she ought to do anything at all for a while other than just get to know those two beautiful girls and let them get to know her. That meant, of course, getting to know their uncle, too. But should she allow herself to do that? It could be a very bad idea, considering how attractive he was. Her preference was to try to get to know him without letting him get too close, but was that possible? She didn't fully realize until later how determined Rand Hartesite was to take that decision out of her hands.

He made it quite plain early in the fourth quarter of the game that he was driving her home, period. The local team was hanging on to a relatively safe ten-point lead, when Rand pronounced it all but a done deal and simply got up, his arm at her elbow, pulling her up with him. He asked the Purdys to congratulate their Ronnie on a game well played and to see to it that his nieces knew he would be back for them after he'd escorted Gail home. Gail put on a slightly strained smile, took a last look at *his* girls and permitted herself to be steered down the steps and ultimately out onto the parking lot. Rand kept his hand on her arm and set a steady pace that allowed nothing more than smiles and nods and an occasional word to those they encountered along the way. Once they stepped into the shadows, leaving behind the glare of stadium lights, he released his hold, only to slide his arm lightly about her waist. She felt electrified, anxious, and oddly reluctant to do anything other than let him have his way—a dangerous situation, indeed.

They had passed several rows of vehicles before she found her voice to insist that he shouldn't put himself out like this, but he just laughed and kept walking, his arm sliding up to her shoulders. "No, really," she said, alarmed by the flash of pleasure that accompanied his move. "I walk for the exercise."

"I've got nothing against exercise," he said, an amused curl to his lips, "but not in these boots."

"You don't have to go with me," she argued with a touch of frustration.

"But I do," he said, looking down pointedly, "unless you mean to keep my vest."

"Don't be silly. I don't need it at all. I'll warm up in no time. Why, I'm warming up already," she affirmed brightly, but then she realized that they'd reached his truck and he was opening the door for her.

"Humor me," he said.

His gaze was so warm that she gulped and climbed up onto the bench seat just to escape it.

He strode around and got in on the other side, reaching for the keys in the ignition. He urged the truck forward, gravel crunching beneath all six tires, and turned it out into the traffic lane. At the end of the street, he looked first left and then right, casually stretching his arm out along the edge of the seat so that his hand lay at her nape. She felt as if her blood were slugging thickly through her veins, as if every sense were homed in on that hand at the back of her neck.

They reached her place within minutes. Rand pulled right on around to the private back entrance and, to her dismay, killed the lights and the engine. She smiled, thanked him, shrugged off his vest and reached for the door handle in the same split second, but he wasn't about to let her get away that fast.

"Hold on there," he said, sliding toward her and clamping his hand down on her shoulder.

"Oh, I don't want to hold you up," she babbled. "You really ought to get back for the girls. They'll think they've been abandoned, and you wouldn't want them to think that, now would you?"

He ignored her as if she hadn't even spoken. With deliberate movements, he lifted off his hat with his left hand and tucked it behind the steering wheel, then turned his full attention on her, leaning toward her slightly and fixing his gaze to hers. She gulped, very much fearing what might come next but feeling utterly unable to deflect it.

"Sure glad you came tonight," he drawled, dropping his eyes to her mouth.

"It was fun," she said, adding lamely, "I really ought to go in."

"In a moment," he said. "I want a word with you."

"Oh?"

He nodded, his gaze sweeping her face and coming right back to her mouth before lifting to her eyes again. "My mother turns seventy-four soon. We usually throw a big shindig to celebrate, but I'm worried that she won't be up to it this year, and that's going to be a big disappointment."

"I-I see what you mean."

He nodded and ran a fingertip down the side of her neck. She caught her breath and willed herself not to tremble. He dropped his hand—to her knee. Gail debated with herself whether to ignore it and decided that she didn't dare. She covered his hand with hers and held it in place. The corners of his mouth turned up in a little smile.

"I wondered," he said softly, "if maybe she could attend in a wheelchair."

Wheelchair? Oh. Gail shook herself slightly. "That depends on how well she's healing."

He turned his hand over and neatly threaded his fingers with hers. "When will you know?"

She forced herself to look up. "We'll, uh, take another X ray in a week or so. That will give us an idea."

He squeezed her hand, smiling directly into her eyes. "Okay," he said, "guess we'll wait until then. That'd give me time to get things together."

"Good, uh, fine. That is, I, um, hope it works out."

"So do I," he said. "It'd be nice to have a new face in the crowd this year, especially such a pretty face."

A sweet warmth flushed through her, but she fought it. "Oh, I'm not sure your mother would want to see her doctor at her birthday party. She...probably is sick of my face already."

"I'm not," he said softly. "Don't think I'm likely to be."

The pleasure of that shimmered through her. She was painfully aware of his jeaned thigh next to hers, of the callused pads of his fingers and palm, of that smoky-blue gaze that kept moving from her eyes to her mouth, of the arm draped loosely about her shoulders. She wanted to relax into that arm and feel it fold her against him. Oh, this was dangerous, so very, delightfully, dangerous. She steeled herself and determinedly began to discourage him.

"Rand, I honestly don't think..." She nearly swallowed the word as he gently shook his hand free of hers and ran his fingers lightly up her arm. So intense was the sensation that she looked down to be certain that her sleeves had not fallen away. She gulped, aware that her heart was suddenly pounding in slow, hard beats that seemed to vibrate against the walls of her chest. Desperately she tried to reclaim her train of thought. "I...I really don't think I can..."

"That's all right," he said huskily. "I'm out of practice, but I still remember how."

She blinked, as if that might clear her mind. "How?"

"To kiss."

She opened her mouth to protest, but she couldn't have spoken if her life had depended on it. There seemed nothing else to do but close her eyes, and then his mouth settled gently, briefly, over her own.

For a moment there was absolutely nothing, and she reflected, in some tiny part of her mind, that there had been no shock, no lightning rush of sensation. She knew an instant of disappointment, and then his arms were around her and he was pulling her to him as his mouth came down on hers again.

She knew suddenly that this was what she had expected his kiss to be. Fire sizzled her nerve endings and prickled her skin, then roared through every pore as his hungry exploration forced her head back. In her mind, the truck lifted up, spun and dropped through space. She clamped one hand behind his head and the other over the ridge of his shoulder, just hanging on and riding his kiss out. She'd never felt anything like it in her life, not with Carel, not with her ex-husband, not with anyone.

He did a thorough job of it, swirling his tongue into the cavern of her mouth and inhaling her flavor, gorging himself without apology or hesitation. When they were both winded, he ended it, not before, and even then he didn't loosen his embrace. Instead, he held her tight as he blew out a deep breath. "Whew!"

Her own breath seemed unrecoverable. Her heart was hammering so fast that it seemed to have stolen every molecule of oxygen in her body.

"I think you melted the soles of my boots!" he whispered, nuzzling his way to her ear. When he nipped the sensitive skin behind it, she inhaled suddenly and sharply. He chuckled, puffing hot air into her ear and sending violent shivers through her. "I forgot how erotic a bite could be," he said, sinking his teeth into her neck and gently sucking.

What that did to her body was so intense that she jerked, then melted, then jerked again. "I-I think I've r-reached my limit!" she gasped, pushing him away a few inches.

He laughed, a husky, rumbling sound that vibrated down to the pit of her belly.

"I haven't," he said, and kissed her again with that bone-melting heat.

She was utterly helpless. The possibility of resistance didn't even occur, despite what she'd said. He didn't let her go until she was trembling, her bones mush, her blood boiling in her veins, her mind abandoning thought and reason for the thrall of sensation. He had moved entirely onto her side of the seat, and their legs had somehow tangled. Her arms were clasped tightly about his shoulders. She was shocked and appalled at herself, while he was pleased, very, very pleased. She discovered, much to her mortification, that she did not have the heart to ruin his pleasure.

"Lady," he said breathlessly, "you pack a hell of a wallop!"

She laughed, not with mirth but with irony, for she knew that *he* was the one with the sensual punch. She was still reeling, in body and mind, from the effects, so much so that she had to check to be sure that her mouth was not hanging open!

"I'd better go," he said regretfully. "The girls will be waiting."

But he didn't move so much as an inch. Indeed, his arms seemed to tighten about her. It seemed that she must send him on his way, and she was astonished at the difficulty of making herself do so. Nevertheless she disengaged herself, pulling her arms back to herself and breaking eye contact. "T-thank you," she began, embarrassed by the tremor in her voice. "Uh, for the ride home, I mean."

"My pleasure," he said, grinning.

She sat, stupidly frozen, until he reached across her and opened the door. She slid out, wondering if her legs were going to hold her, and found that they would. The chill air seemed to restore her equilibrium somewhat. She took a deep lungful of it and turned, intending to send him off with a smile and a wave through the opened door, but he had stepped out, too, and she merely came up against him. His arms moved around her. He stood with her that way for a heartbeat, and then his hands came up and gathered handfuls of her hair at the back of her head.

"I like your hair," he said softly, silkily. "I like your mouth. I like the sound of your voice. I'm beginning to think I like everything about you."

"No," she said urgently, "don't."

He tilted her head back so that the moon lit her face. He was smiling. "And why not?"

Because I'm going to turn your life upside down, she thought, but she couldn't say those words. She said, "You hardly know me."

"I intend to remedy that."

She knew she ought not to allow that, but she found herself rationalizing that getting to know him would bring her inevitably closer to his nieces and her daughter. She let him kiss her again. He did so gently this time, and as the first time had been in a way hello, this was goodbye. Afterward, he turned her and slid his arm about her shoulders, folding it about her neck to keep her close to his side. She had little choice but to slip her arm about his waist.

They walked to her door. She had left the outside light burning, having replaced the original white bulb with a yellow one brought from Dallas. He reached up and tapped the glass casing with a fingertip. "You don't really need that, you know."

"I don't?"

"Nope. We don't have many flying bugs out here. Too dry, I guess. You ought to keep an eye out for tarantulas, though. They were as thick as cream in the butter churn last summer. Never saw so many."

"I'll remember that," she said with a twitchy smile.

He grinned broadly and stepped closer, his hands cupping her shoulder blades. "There's a movie showing in Alpine tomorrow night. What do you say—"

"Rand, I can't," she said before he could convince her otherwise. "I-I'm busy."

"Oh?"

She licked her lips, thinking quickly. "I, um, have to do my laundry. I don't have a washer or dryer, so...so I have to use the hospital's. B-but I have to do it on a weekend evening after the laundry workers leave."

"Ah. Well, you could use ours out at the ranch, if you want."

"Oh! Oh, no, I couldn't. I-I have mountains to do! It'll take several machines." That much was true.

He seemed to accept that, nodding his comprehension. "Too bad," he said with a sigh. "We'll do that movie another time."

Relief put a smile on her face. "Thank you for understanding."

"I'll see you."

She nodded. He cupped her chin in his big, sure hand, tilting her face to the light again, his thumb running lightly over her lips, but he did not kiss her, just smiled and left her. She told herself that she was glad, yet the truth was that she was relieved, for if he had pressed her... She didn't even want to think about it, but she knew, her heart sinking, that this wasn't going to be easy. Why did he have to be Carel's brother? Why should he be the one hurt when she finally claimed her child?

They were standing at the curb, the stadium lights blazing in the black sky behind them. Mary Grace had her back to him. She was shouting something to two boys who were walking swiftly away and looking over their shoulders. Rand had the distinct impression that they had been waiting with the girls until he had turned the corner. He wondered if he ought to say anything about it. The girls were too young to date, but he knew they weren't too young to attract the boys. Sometime soon he was going to have to make peace with the idea that some man, sometime, would be doing with one of his girls what he had been doing tonight with Gail—and wanting to do what he was wanting to do. Lordy, he still couldn't sit comfortably.

Maybe he'd been without a woman too long. God knows it had been an age since he'd had the heart for it. Finding a woman out here was hard enough, but devoting the time necessary for getting to know her was a difficult thing in itself. It usually meant driving long distances at late hours. Then, after all that effort, to find that they didn't suit was discouraging beyond words. He had limited himself to the occasional and purely physical relationship after Lynette. Not that he had found their marriage particularly satisfying. Still, he had waited a long time to begin looking for another woman. He supposed that was only understandable, considering how barren the marriage had been in every way and, most of all, how it had ended. He had been disappointed in his search, so much so that he guessed he'd just given up. And now this. He hardly knew what to think.

He'd never felt with anyone else anything like what he'd felt with Gail tonight. But again, it had been a long time. He was surprised to find that he didn't intend for it to be much longer. He wanted in that woman's bed, and he wouldn't be surprised if he found that he wanted to stay there. He wondered if that might be love, but he honestly didn't know. At the moment he didn't really care. Whatever it was, it felt good, damned good.

The girls clambered into the truck, Mary Grace taking the front seat, as was her habit, and Carel Belle failing to challenge her for it, as was hers. He rather wished she would. He worried sometimes that Mary Grace overshadowed Carel Belle too much, and he feared that he would not know if it bothered Carel. She was such a quiet little thing. They were absolute opposites in that way.

As if to prove the point, Mary Grace shot him a cutting look and remarked snidely, "You've got lipstick on your face."

He lifted his hand to his mouth automatically, and in doing so, knew he'd given himself away. He decided that it might be time to give that Mettlesome Mattie a dose of the shocking stuff she liked to give everyone else. He dropped his hand to the steering wheel, started the truck on its way and said, "Gail doesn't wear lipstick, but if she did, I guess I'd be wearing it, too. I might even make a habit of it."

Her mouth dropped open, and he thought that perhaps her face even paled. *Served her right,* he told himself, but he was aware of a niggling concern at the back of his mind. He countered it with a change of subject.

"What was the final score?"

"Twenty-four to fourteen."

"Oh, we scored again."

"You left *that* early?"

Her tone was so scathing that he turned his head to look at her. "It was the fourth quarter."

She folded her arms huffily, sliding a look over her shoulder. "Then you didn't see Carel Belle chosen Game's Best, did you?"

Game's Best Cheerleader! It was the honor given to the girl who displayed the most team spirit during the game. How hard his shy baby must have pushed herself to earn such recognition! His heart dropped to his stomach. He hadn't even watched the cheers tonight. He'd hardly been able to concentrate on the game! He glanced into the rear-view mirror. She was sitting with her head bowed, as she so often did. He felt like the lowest varmint on the face of the earth. "Carel, honey, I'm so sorry! I can't believe I missed that. I hope someone got a picture. Did they?"

"Mrs. Johnson did. I think our sponsor did, too."

"I'll be sure to ask for one. My goodness, Game's Best! I'm so proud of you, but then I always am. Won't Grandmother be pleased! She'll be sorry she wasn't there, too."

"She doesn't like football anyhow," Mary Grace interjected.

"But she'd have been pleased to see her granddaughter chosen Game's Best," Rand said absently, wondering how he could make it up to Carel Belle.

"When's she coming home?" Mary Grace asked.

"If we're lucky, she'll be home in time for her birthday party, but that doesn't mean she'll be up to running you around. She's going to be down for a good long time, and you're just going to have to learn to live with it."

Carel Belle shifted forward in her seat and laid a hand on his shoulder. "Are we going to see her in the hospital tomorrow?"

He patted her hand. "Sure thing, baby. I know she's missing you."

"I miss her, too."

"We both do," Mary Grace declared. "Camelia drives way too slow, and she gets awful nervous about it."

"Well, don't you be giving her a hard time," Rand said. "She's not used to running up and down the road after you two girls."

"I know that!" Mary Grace snapped. "That's what I just said."

"Whoa!" Rand whipped the truck over to the side of the road and brought it to a stop. His foot firmly on the brake, he turned in his seat to glare at her. "You want to tell me just what in blue blazes is going on in that head of yours?"

She folded her arms beneath breasts growing more prominent every day and scorched him with a narrow-eyed look. "I don't like her."

"Who?" As if he didn't know.

"Dr. Terry!"

"Why ever not?"

The girl shrugged, chin tucked down mulishly.

"It doesn't matter whether or not you like her, Mary Grace," he said sternly. "What matters is that *I* like her."

"I don't see why," she muttered.

"You don't have to. You just have to behave yourself."

She glowered, but then she softened a bit. "I'm sorry. It's just...she's not good enough for you."

He had to smile despite himself. "Who would you suggest then? Queen Elizabeth?"

Mary Grace made an ugly face. He patted her shoulder. "Just give her a chance, Mary."

She nodded reluctantly, and Rand let his concerns recede. She'd come around, he told himself. The question was, would Gail Terry?

Chapter Five

The famine was over. Whether it was Rand's bringing the girls in for their unneeded physicals or her appearance at his side at the football game on Friday night, Marfa seemed at last to have discovered Dr. Terry and found itself in need of her services. She took appointments for the rest of the week all Monday long, as well as five walk-ins during that one day. Nearly everyone was amazingly healthy, but then the environment was very nearly free of pollution and stress. Most of the complaints she treated in the early part of the week were easily solved: rashes, scrapes, sprains, heartburn. The one common problem was diet.

This was cattle country, after all, and beef was the staple of every dinner table for miles and miles around. On the other hand, people were used to a good deal more exercise than their big-city cousins, and while that did not quite remedy the attendant problems, it did mitigate them. Actually, she was surprised to find fewer cases of high blood pressure and clogged arteries than she had expected. The dry climate also helped keep down arthritis and ameliorate those cases that did exist. But it was not all good news.

On Thursday afternoon, she examined the sore throat of a forty-seven-year-old mother of five who had smoked two packs of cigarettes a day for thirty-one years. The lesions and lumps were almost definitely cancer, and Gail suspected that it would be found in her lungs, as well. She made arrangements to send the woman to El Paso for definitive tests and treatment, but she did it with a heavy heart, knowing that the prognosis was not good.

That mother's case was not the first potentially devastating one she'd seen. Moreover, like all doctors, she had lost patients, and she had learned to deal with such losses, as all doctors must. But that didn't mean she was used to them. The death of a child always affected her especially deeply. Late at night, almost always unexpectedly, such losses sometimes swamped her and depression settled in. However, she had real successes to balance those sad moments with, sweet faces to recall, faces beaming with health and promise. Yet she found herself unreasonably affected by the ordeal to come for that mother of five, so much so that repeatedly during the afternoon she found herself blinking back tears.

It was as if a dam had been opened within her. She just couldn't seem to get that woman and her family off her mind, and after a while, she didn't even want to. By the time she was sitting alone at the dinner table over a large green salad and a grilled chicken breast, her appetite had completely vanished and her eyes were filling once again. She reminded herself that she was moving ever closer to reclaiming her daughter. Business was improving. Belle Grace seemed to be healing, despite her surly attitude. All in all, things were looking up. And yet those tears hovered disturbingly near the surface, spilling over again and again.

Naturally, one sad thought led to another, and suddenly a number of images were flashing through her mind. She saw that tiny bundle of pink that had been placed in her arms for the first time, the screwed-up face and thin cap of almost colorless hair plastered to a seemingly too large head. She saw that little mouth rooting at her breast and the puffy cheek that flattened in the process. She saw incredibly small hands and pudgy little feet. She saw Carel as she had that last time, smiling, nervous, pledging eternal love and planning betrayal. She saw the smug, supercilious face of his attorney as he coldly explained that she did not deserve her own daughter. Mixed with all the old memories were flashes of Mary Grace and Carel Belle and images of Belle Grace stoically enduring her pain, the pain of loss as well as the pain of injury. Most unsettling of all, however, was the picture burned into her mind's eye of Rand Hartesite's arms folding her close as his mouth covered hers.

Suddenly she was feeling more alone than ever before in her life, completely adrift in an ocean of pain and loss. Overwhelmed, she pushed her dinner away, laid her head down on the table and sobbed, for that poor mother and her family, but also for herself and all the losses she had suffered. She was still sniffing when the phone rang. She almost hoped it was some emergency, something to focus on other than her own battered emotions. It was Rand.

"Hello. Got a few minutes?"

She laughed aloud, absurdly pleased to hear his voice despite the tears wetting her cheeks. "Not as many as I had this time last week," she said. "Which isn't saying much. I'm used to an extremely high level of activity, continuous shifts of thirty-six hours or more, but I'll get the hang of this slower pace sooner or later. I may actually learn to put my feet up!"

"Business still slow?"

She laughed again. "Hardly. It's almost more than I can handle by myself. I'll be looking for office help before long. It's just that I'm used to business being overwhelming."

"Do I hear a yearning for Dallas in your voice?"

She was surprised at her quick answer to that. "No! Not at all."

"Well, I hear a yearning for something."

My daughter, she thought, but remembered sensation flashed over her, so real she could almost feel his arms around her and his tongue sliding into her mouth. She sat down abruptly in the chair she had just abandoned, the phone cord stretched from the kitchen wall to the table.

"Gail?"

Her heart was pounding so hard that she felt certain he could hear it.

"Gail, are you there?"

"Y-yes, I . . ." She looked around wildly, her eyes falling on her untouched dinner. She made a swallowing sound. "I-I was eating dinner. Sorry, that was rude of me."

He sounded vastly relieved. "No problem, I'll call back later."

"No! I-I mean, it's all right. I was just finishing up." She closed her eyes to block out her untouched meal, as if that made the lie all right. She had discovered that she did not like lying, not to this man.

"Okay. I just wanted to touch base with you about Mother. Everything going okay?"

"As far as I can tell. We'll know more in a few days," she promised.

"Guess I'm just anxious," he said. "No fun planning a party the birthday girl can't attend."

"I understand."

"Speaking of which," he said smoothly, "I'm counting on you being here, too. You will, won't you?"

She shouldn't. She even told herself that she wouldn't. All she had to do was make an excuse, any excuse. She took a deep breath, then another. She opened her eyes, feeling flustered and aggravated. She said, "Certainly. I'm looking forward to it."

He expelled a relieved sigh. "I'm going to get you for that," he promised huskily.

"For what?" she asked, pleasure rippling through her.

"For scaring me like that. I thought you were going to beg off!"

She cupped the receiver in her palm, smiling despite the warning bells clanging deep in her mind. "If Miss Belle is going to be there, I'd better be there, too."

"Well, then she just has to be here," he said flatly.

"We'll see. Now then, you'd better tell me what I'm in for, just in case."

"Aw, it's just your average backyard barbecue," he said, "for about two hundred."

"Two hundred guests?"

"Yep. Did I mention dancing? We'll be dancing, too. So wear your jeans and your dancing shoes. And a jacket."

"I don't have a jacket," she reminded him.

"Don't worry, I can keep you warm."

She caught her breath, feeling quite warm already. *I'm sure you can. That's the problem,* she told him silently. Aloud she said, "I'm sure I can find something."

"Oh, I wanted to tell you, just in case you were thinking of it, don't bring a present. Mother hates it when people bring presents. She doesn't even like them from family."

She *had* thought of it, but now she wouldn't. "How about a card?" she asked.

"Ummm, not a mushy one. It might make her cry, and she hates that."

Gail lifted her eyebrows. "Boy, she really doesn't like to unbend, does she?"

He surprised her by laughing. "You got that right. Overt displays of emotion make Mother uncomfortable, always have. She was better about it when Dad was alive. I think she loved him so wholeheartedly that she just couldn't resist his overtures of affection, and Dad was a pretty affectionate sort."

"Like his son," she thought, not realizing she'd said the word aloud.

"I certainly find myself feeling affectionate around you," Rand said softly.

Gail straightened and felt the chill in her face that indicated the blood was leaving it. *Stupid, stupid, stupid.* She was careful not to say *that* aloud, but it was stupid of her to remind him of that kiss, those kisses. She searched her mind for a way to turn him off that subject. "Uh, you-your mother, she must have been...demonstrative when you were small."

"I guess." The lack of enthusiasm in his voice told her clearly that he would have preferred to pursue the former topic, but he humored her, saying, "She was more demonstrative with my brother than with me, though, because he was the baby, I suppose, but then I was a lot closer to Dad than Carel was, so it sort of evened out in a way."

"You don't sound as if you resent her affection for your brother," she ventured cautiously.

"I don't" was the flat answer. "Mother transferred a lot of her unconditional love for my father to me after his death, because I was the one to step into his shoes here at the ranch, I suppose. And," he continued, "Carel might have been her favorite, but he was also her deepest disappointment."

"I see." This information certainly tallied with everything else Gail knew about Carel Hartesite. But she could understand that a mother would love her child regardless of his character. "She must have grieved for him terribly when he died."

"Absolutely. We both did. But I guess we also saw his death as a sort of inevitable justice."

"Now, that's a curious thing to say."

He said nothing more for several heartbeats, but then he sighed. "I'm afraid there was something missing in my brother, something that did not allow him to see and consider the pain of others. It was as though he were helpless before his own selfishness."

Another brief silence followed, and then Rand laughed, but the sound was uneasy, as if he feared he'd said too much and wanted to change the subject.

"Well, this has been an interesting conversation," he said a little too lightly. "But enough about me. I want to talk about you."

A sense of dread enveloped her, yet it had to come. If ever she was to get close to her daughter, she had to be prepared to allow the Hartesites to get to know her, but it was so dangerous, so terrifyingly dangerous. What would he do if he knew who she really was? Would he send her daughter beyond her reach forever? She shuddered at the thought, then summoned her courage. "What do you want to know?"

"Why aren't you married?"

It was a reasonable-enough question, she supposed, but it surprised her. More surprising still was her relief at not having to lie to him. "I was. It didn't work out."

"Why not?" His voice carried more than a hint of command, and he didn't apologize for it.

She renegotiated her position on the chair, uncomfortable with the force behind his question, and tried to decide what to tell him. In the end, it was the truth again. "We were friends. I thought that would be enough. It wasn't."

"Ah, never been in love, then," he said with a satisfaction that he didn't try to hide.

Warning and excitement sizzled through her. He was more interested in her than she realized, and that, too, was dangerous—exciting, but dangerous. She would have to tread carefully here, she knew, but she decided that she must be as honest with him as it was possible for her to be. She wasn't certain why it was necessary, since she knew beyond any doubt that there was no hope for a personal relationship. As soon as he found out who she was and why she'd come, he would despise her. And yet... She shook her head at herself.

"I thought I was in love once," she told him slowly. "I guess you could say that he broke my heart."

"And then some, I'd say," he assessed.

Too close, she thought, mentally scurrying for distance. "It was a long time ago, before medical school even, and believe me, neither med students nor doctors have time to be brokenhearted."

"But you've never forgotten him," he noted none too gently.

"I suppose the hardest lessons are the easiest to remember," she returned lightly.

"Granted," he murmured.

She wondered what he was thinking, if he would ask for a name. He didn't. Of course he wouldn't, never dreaming that he might know the man.

"What about you?" she asked. "I take it you've been married."

"Once," he said.

When he didn't go on, she pressed him as he had her. "What happened?"

"She left." He said it flatly, discouraging further inquiry.

"Oh, I'm sorry," she said quietly, wondering if he had loved his ex-wife very much.

"No need to be," he said. "It was a long time ago, and there was no love lost."

"It must have been rough, though," she said softly.

"Lots of things are rough," he said, "but I don't imagine anything's tougher than losing a child."

"No," she whispered, "nothing, but if you don't mind, I'd rather talk about something else."

"Of course."

She closed her eyes in relief, but knew it was only a reprieve. Still, reprieves sometimes became pardons, didn't they? They made small talk for a few minutes. Rand told her, pride ringing in every syllable, that Carel Belle had been chosen Game's Best Cheerleader the week before. Gail was delighted, surprised that it wasn't Mary Grace, but delighted. She would have to remember to congratulate quiet Carel Belle.

Her chicken was cold by the time she got off the phone with Rand, but her appetite had returned for some reason. She zapped the chicken breast in the microwave and gobbled it down before it could dry out. The salad had remained crisp, and she munched it more leisurely. Perhaps she should have begged off the party, but it was too late for that, and she was in no frame of mind to worry about it. Quite the contrary. She was actually looking forward to it now. She shouldn't be; she knew that. But she couldn't help it, and she didn't want to help it. She wanted to be close to her daughter again. It seemed impossible that both girls would be hers, but she wanted to get to know them. She wanted to get to know Rand Hartesite.

Gail shook her head. Still the fool. All she could ever have with Rand Hartesite was a little time, just a little time, before he began to hate her. She would be far smarter to concentrate her emotional energies on her daughter. Much smarter.

"I have been very good," Belle insisted, as if she could command the report to turn out as she wished.

Rand chuckled fondly. "If you call snapping at the nurses and complaining of boredom every five minutes being good, then I'm going to have to buy you a dictionary."

"Make it a heavy one," she grumbled, "so it'll put a dent in that hard head of yours when I throw it at you!"

"Then we'd both be in here and the ranch would go to ruin," he retorted.

She opened her mouth to hand him a blistering comeback, but the door swung open just then and Gail Terry swept into the room. She was smiling, both hands hidden in the spacious pockets of her lab coat. "Well?" Belle demanded querulously.

Gail bobbed a short, smiling curtsy and whipped folded yellow and pink papers from her pocket. "Your dismissal, madam."

Belle snatched the papers, glanced at them and threw th
covers back.

"Hold on!" Gail clamped a hand down over the olde
woman's shoulder and gently pushed her back down onto
the bed. "I thought you understood," she said, ignoring
Belle's glower, "You're not to put any weight on that leg fo
three more weeks at least."

Belle rolled her eyes. "For goodness' sake, I'm not a
baby! I can get around without putting weight on that leg.'

"You are not to 'get around' at all," Gail pronounced
sternly. She switched her attention to Rand, apparently in
the hope that he would at least listen. He sent her a smile o
encouragement, which seemed only to make her uncom
fortable. "The bone does appear to be mending," she told
him cautiously, "but that does not mean she can get up. An
reinjury of the area will set us back significantly—and per
haps permanently."

"I understand," he said, keeping his tone solemn and
firm. "I'll see to it that she behaves herself if I have to tie he
down."

A snort from Belle told them both what she thought o
that, but Rand ignored her and Gail seemed content to fol
low suit. She nodded at him, apparently satisfied, thougl
her gaze did not quite meet his any longer. "A nurse will be
in shortly with explicit instructions for her care. After that
you can go. You have obtained the wheelchair?"

"Yep, it's already in the truck."

"The nurse will have prescriptions you'll need to fill."

"I'll do it on the way home."

"Fine. I'll check in on her in a day or two. Meanwhile, i
there's any problem, any problem whatsoever, don't hesi
tate to call."

"You can count on it."

"That's it then. Miss Belle, you take care of yourself and
do as you're told—unless you like that bed, because that'
where you'll be if you don't."

Belle huffed. "I think you're making too much of this. But I'll do everything you say," she added quickly.

Gail patted her shoulder. "I know it's difficult for an active woman to stay down, but you absolutely must."

The older woman had the good grace to look abashed. "I'll be good," she vowed. "Just let me do it at home!"

Gail smiled understandingly. "I'll go and let you get on your way."

Almost before he realized what was happening, the door was closing behind her. He shot his mother a quelling look, demanding that she stay right where she was, and went after the doctor. She was halfway down the hall before he caught up with her. He knew darned well that she'd heard him coming, too, but she didn't turn until he touched her arm, and then she whirled around almost defensively. "You have a question?"

He backed up a step, puzzled by her coldness, and put his hands to his waist. "Yeah, I have a question."

She leaned against the wall, arms folded. He noticed that the gesture pulled the fabric of her blouse and lab coat tight across her surprisingly full breasts, and his mouth went dry. Damn. Thoughts of this woman were already driving him nuts. He forced his gaze away from that portion of her anatomy before she could notice what was happening in certain quarters of his.

"I'm listening," she said in a colorless voice, "but please make it quick. I have other patients."

He lifted his brows at that. "Business picking up that much?"

She grimaced and turned her face away before saying gently, "I haven't thanked you properly for that, have I?"

"No thanks due."

She shot him an unreadable look. "I really have to go."

"Okay, okay. In the interest of brevity then, just say yes."

"Yes?"

He grinned. "Good. I'll pick you up about six on Saturday evening." He wheeled around and started back toward his mother's room, wondering just how far he'd get. Not very, as it turned out.

"Hold on there, cowboy!" She hooked a finger in his back belt loop and tugged him to a stop.

He slanted a look over his shoulder. "Not in as much of a hurry as you thought?"

Her eyes narrowed dangerously, moving him to chuckle. She grabbed his shoulder and turned him around. "Explain yourself."

He shrugged, knowing that he was infuriating her. "It's simple. I want to take you to dinner and I *don't* intend to take no for an answer. I was just trying to save you some time, that's all."

She gaped at him, than abruptly clamped her jaw shut on a sputtering sound that either meant she was choking or trying to subdue her temper. He resisted the urge to grin, but just barely.

After a moment, she swallowed down whatever it was that she was trying to subdue and took a deep breath. "I cannot go out to dinner with you on Saturday."

He rocked back on his heels. "Okay. How about I take you to the game on Friday? It's out of town, so we'll have to leave about four, and we won't be getting home much before two in the morning. But I don't mind."

"I keep office hours on Saturday morning," she said. "I couldn't possibly—"

"Saturday night it is, then," he interrupted smoothly.

She made an exasperated sound, her eyes going very wide. "I told you, I can't go out with you on Saturday night!"

"Fine. We'll make it—"

"Or Friday!" she snapped.

He sighed. "I told you, I'm not going to take that for an answer, so you might as well—"

"Oh, for pity's sake!" She threw up her hands. "I already have an engagement!"

He felt himself go cold from the neck down, as if someone had poured ice water through him. "An engagement? As in a *date?*"

She was seeing someone else! Why hadn't he realized that a single woman—especially a good-looking, professional, single woman—would be in great demand around there? He felt an instant flush of anger. He heard her speaking, but somehow he couldn't hear the words. There was only one thing he wanted to know just then—the name of the man who had beaten him to the draw, the identity of the competition. It made no difference that he shouldn't, that he had no right whatsoever; he simply had to ask. But not here.

He flashed a look up and down the hall and then at the door they'd stopped by. There was no name card in the plate screwed to the wall. Hoping the staff was as efficient as they seemed, he grabbed her hand, spun and put his shoulder to the door. It gave easily beneath his weight. He pulled her inside, thankful that the unlit room felt deserted, as indeed it was. One glance showed him the empty bed and the bare table and tray. She was sputtering in outrage, but he was too angry to care.

"Who is it?" he demanded, resisting the urge to shake her by settling his hands at his waist once more.

"Who is *who?*" she cried, thrusting her fisted hands down straight at her sides.

"Who are you seeing Saturday night?" The words roared around the small, darkened room, sounding sharp and bullying even to his own ears, but he simply couldn't think about it just then. He had to know.

"Of all the high-handed, presumptuous—"

"Answer me, damn it!"

She folded her arms stubbornly, but to his surprise, she gave him the name of a local physician.

His eyeballs nearly popped out of his head. He'd never have believed it of her! "He's a married man!" he shouted.

She rolled her eyes. "I know that!" she declared. "He and his wife have invited me to their home for dinner, idiot!"

He and his wife. To their home. Idiot. Relief washed through him, a soothing balm to the jealous beast that had roared to life inside him only moments before. *Holy cow,* he thought sheepishly. He'd never ever made such a fool of himself with a woman. What was it about her? He shook his head. "I thought you were seeing someone else," he admitted bluntly.

"Else?" she retorted. "I wasn't aware that I was seeing *you.*"

"Idiot" was a kind term for him, he realized. Thoroughly distracted, he reached for his hat, but his hat was sitting at the foot of his mother's bed. He rubbed his hand through his hair, feeling more the fool every moment. "I'm trying to fix that now, in case you haven't noticed."

To his vast delight, he watched a smile wiggle across her mouth.

"I noticed," she said. "It's just that..."

Her gaze slid away, alerting him that all was not as it seemed, despite the determination that lifted her chin and brought her eyes to his once more.

"I already have plans this weekend."

"Okay," he said reasonably. "What about next weekend?"

He watched her eyes widen and her delicate brows rise.

"I thought your mother's birthday party was next weekend."

Oh! Could he embarrass himself any more? he wondered, striving for a self-possession he definitely didn't feel. "Well, I... just wanted to make sure we were still on for that."

Her grin told him that he hadn't pulled it off, and suddenly he didn't even want to. He sighed and melted, stepping forward and reaching out for her. He pulled her to him and put his forehead to hers. "It's not just that I'm out of practice," he said apologetically. "You do something to me no woman's ever done."

"Rand—"

He jerked his head up. "Don't tell me you don't feel it, too. I won't believe it. I can't."

She just looked up at him, a great sadness in her green-and-gold eyes. "Don't you think you're going a bit too fast?" she asked gently.

He shook his head, but then he closed his eyes and laid his head back. He spread his hands over her shoulder blades, feeling the softness of her body through the layers of her clothing. He wanted that softness against him, needed it so badly. He wasn't used to feeling this kind of need, this kind of desperation. He took a deep breath and dropped his hands. "You...you're right. I'm being silly. It's just that it's been so long since I've met anyone who interested me even slightly."

"I'm flattered," she said, hugging herself, "but you don't really know me, Rand."

"Then let me get to know you," he responded smoothly. "That's all I'm really asking for."

Her gaze flickered over him uncertainly. "I'm just not so sure that's wise."

"Why not?"

She shook her head, saying nothing. He pressed his fingertips beneath her chin, turning her face up to his. "What are you so afraid of?" he whispered, but she neither answered nor looked at him. He turned his hand and let it slide down her throat, noting with satisfaction the way her breath caught and her eyelids fluttered down. "I'd tear my heart out before I'd hurt you," he promised, and saw her mouth turn up in the saddest smile.

"Why couldn't I have met you first?"

First? He smiled. "Before your ex-husband, you mean?"

"Before anyone!"

He slid his arms around her and pulled her close, tucking her head beneath his chin. "He really did a job on you, didn't he, that college boy?"

She turned her face into the curve of his neck. "You'll never know what he did to me," she said quietly. "Even if I could tell you, you couldn't begin to understand."

"Hey," he said, holding her tight, "I don't need any of the details until *you* feel the need to give them to me. Personally, I couldn't care less about the past, except for how it affects the present."

"You say that now," she began, "but later—"

He grasped her by the shoulders and pushed her away, shaking her gently. "Will you listen to me? I don't care! Whatever it is, I just don't care, and if you'll give me a chance I'll prove it. As God is my witness, Gail, the past means nothing to me, yours or mine."

"You don't know what you're saying."

He shook her again, but not so gently this time. "I know what I'm feeling, dammit!"

"Do you?" she challenged.

He didn't know what else to say to her, so he let action speak for him. In one smooth movement, he pulled her to him and found her mouth with his. She stiffened, but a moment later she made a small, exasperated sound and went all soft and pliable in his arms. Suddenly rockets were going off all around them, and he knew that she had to feel them, too. But just in case, he locked one arm around her waist and sent the other downward, splaying his hand across her bottom, pressing her to him. He didn't want there to be any mistake about how she affected him, and to emphasize it further, he began to rhythmically thrust his tongue into her mouth, letting her know in no uncertain terms what he wanted to do with her. He felt immensely gratified when she wrapped her arms about his neck and buried her hands in his hair, holding his head at the proper angle while she twisted her mouth beneath his. It was madness to be doing this in an empty hospital room with his mother likely raising hell down the hall and demanding to know where he was, but he let the kiss go on and on, until he started thinking about that unmade bed in the room and whether he could get her into it. Too fast, she'd said. If she realized what he was thinking now...

Groaning, he forced himself to break away, confident he'd at least made his point, even if he got his face slapped in the process. But she wasn't in a face-slapping mood. He saw it the moment he looked down into her eyes and recognized the dreaminess that clouded them. He laughed. He couldn't help it. He wanted so badly to know that she was feeling some part of what he felt. Some part? All of it, he'd say.

She blinked—and frowned. Quickly he schooled his expression into a semblance of contrition. "My, um..." He dropped his voice into a silky whisper. "My mother's probably wondering what happened to me. Besides, I'd better go before I get us both in trouble."

She opened her mouth and snapped it shut again right fast, a nod her only answer. He moved around her in a wide circle, not trusting himself to touch her again.

"Anyhow, I'll see you at the party. Right?"

She cleared her throat. "Right." It came out all husky anyway.

It was all he could do not to whoop in delight. "I'll, um, call you."

Another nod.

Satisfied, he spun and pulled open the door, strolling through it with what he knew was a Texas-sized grin on his face. But he didn't care. He hadn't gotten the date he'd wanted, but he'd gotten a reaction that told him all he had to do was bide his time. He could do that. For a while. Long enough, he'd wager, if that kiss was anything to go by. Oh, yeah, he could do that whistling, and to prove it, he reeled off a jaunty little tune as he strolled down the hall. He didn't know he'd left behind a woman in tears.

Chapter Six

It was ridiculous, and she knew it. She didn't know him well enough to feel this way. It wasn't as if she'd lost anything, after all. He wasn't even a friend, really, and yet... She couldn't help feeling that what could have been between them would have been better than anything else she could possibly have with any other man. That warranted a little mourning, didn't it? The truth was, though, that she had passed a *little* mourning days ago. She hadn't even enjoyed dinner with her colleague and his well-meaning wife because she couldn't keep from thinking how much more pleasant it might have been if she'd only had the nerve to invite Rand to escort her. The fact that it would have been a mistake seemed to have no bearing on her feelings in the matter. Why did he have to be Carel Hartesite's brother? She had even put off calling her private investigator to help her determine which of the Hartesite girls might be hers because she hated to think that ultimately she'd be hurting Rand when she claimed her daughter.

Given all that, she ought to have welcomed a Tuesday as busy as this one, but she was facing three waiting patients already, when she heard the sounds of a disturbance in her waiting room. She had been teetering on the razor's edge of impatience all day as it was, and that sudden commotion was just the last straw. She grimaced at the older gentleman around whose arm she had just secured a blood-pressure cuff, then marched to the examination room door, yanked it open and stalked out into the hall. She ran smack into Rand Hartesite's chest.

"This man's bleeding to death!" he yelled. Only then did she notice the two other cowboys at his side, the middle one sagging from arms draped around the shoulders of the others.

She pushed by them and flung open the door of the treatment room. They hauled him inside without question and lifted him up onto the padded table.

She was already busy putting together a suture tray. "What happened?"

"Damned bull gored him. There's another one, too, but at least he's not bleeding like a stuck hog."

"Bring him on in and put him in the other room. Mr. Cole won't mind when you explain."

Rand jerked his head at the man standing next to the injured cowboy. "See to it, Evert."

Evert mumbled something in reply and strode from the room. Gail began pulling on a pair of rubber gloves. A glance over her shoulder told her what else was needed. "Looks like the femoral artery's opened. Get those pants off him."

The injured cowboy struggled up onto his elbows. Even though he was pale and substantially weakened, it was clear that he was appalled.

"I ain't shedding my pants in front of no woman!"

Gail rolled her eyes and tossed a pair of scissors to Rand. "Use those."

Rand shoved the protesting cowboy down with a hand placed in the middle of his chest and went to work. "Hold still!" he ordered.

"Holy cow, Boss!" the cowboy wailed. "I ain't wearing no underneaths!"

Rand went still and cast a helpless look in Gail's direction.

"Oh, for Pete's sake!" She stalked across the room, dragging the suture tray on its rolling stand, then bent and ripped a sheet from the shelf beneath the table, tossing it onto the cowboy's middle. She grabbed a scalpel, pushed Rand's hands away and grasped the waistband of the wounded man's jeans. With one deft stroke, she cut through it, belt and all, then drew the sharp blade down the leg. The cowboy's eyes were as big as saucers by the time she was done, the wound lay exposed, and she hadn't so much as nicked him.

"Man!" Rand exclaimed. "They said you were good."

She was already too absorbed in treatment to pay him any mind. The wound was deep and jagged and placed very high on the thigh, within a couple of inches of the bend of the leg. The femoral artery was definitely involved. She began talking as she worked, explaining each movement as it occurred. He gritted his teeth when she injected local anesthetic, but lay perfectly still as she probed and swabbed and cleaned. He yelped when she clamped the artery, but only because her hand grazed intimate territory. She shook her head and, with tongue planted firmly in cheek, told him that he was lucky not to be singing falsetto. He turned first white and then beet red, while Rand strangled on a chuckle.

With the important bleeding stopped, she applied a pressure bandage, peeled off her gloves, pulled on new ones, and went to check on the other victim, the cowboy called Punch. His arm was definitely broken, and he had at least a minor concussion, but there was no sign of internal injuries. She gave him a mild analgesic and quiet reassurance, then left him to tend his more seriously injured buddy.

First she made a thorough examination. Next she set up an IV. She had no blood on hand, but at least she could get some fluid and immediate medications into him to stave off shock and reduce his pain. She sent Rand out to telephone for an ambulance from Alpine, then set to work stitching up the wound. The artery, fortunately, had only been nicked and not torn in two. It was still tricky business, though, and the cowboy lost even more blood before she was done.

"He's going to need a transfusion," she told Rand when he reentered the room. "They'll have to do that in Alpine." She gazed at the pale cowboy on her treatment table, only then noticing that he was fairly young and good-looking. "You know your blood type, cowboy?"

"No, ma'am."

She clucked her tongue, her attention once again focused on her working hands. "Everybody ought to know his blood type. Saves time and trouble. No matter. You're in no danger as long as this artery stays closed. They'll have time to type it in the lab. You might not be so lucky next time, though."

"Yes'm," he mumbled.

She tied off and began cleaning up the area before applying a bandage. By the time she was finished, the cowboy was sleeping peacefully. She signaled Rand and tiptoed from the room.

"He going to be all right?" he asked the moment the door closed behind them.

She nodded and peeled off the top layer of gloves, her third set. "He's lost a lot of blood, but you got him here in time. Good thing you decided to bring him to me instead of waiting for me to get to him."

Rand shivered. "When I saw that blood pumping through his blue jeans, I knew we didn't have any other choice. I wasn't so sure about Punch, though."

"You did the best you could, given the circumstances," she assured him. "But when things calm down, I suggest you look into a course on first aid. Given the isolation of your ranch, you need to know more than the average person, like when to chance moving a patient and when not to."

"Sounds good to me," he said, nodding. "Just let me know when you want to start."

She did a double take at that, but on second thought, she silently admitted that she just might have to administer such a course herself. Who else, after all, was there? She put the notion aside for the moment, however, and went back to the compound fracture waiting in the next room. With the ambulance on the way, she chose not to attempt setting the bone, preferring to wait for an X ray. The limb did have to be isolated, though, and the break protected from further injury. This she accomplished swiftly and efficiently with a minimum of discomfort for the patient. She put an ice pack on the bump on his head and responded to his good-natured bantering in kind.

"Will it leave much of a scar, Doc?" he asked at one point.

"Maybe a little one."

"Aw, heck," he grumbled. "I was hoping for a big, sexy zigzag to show the gals."

"Well, maybe the scalpel will slip," she quipped.

"Don't you believe it," Rand said. "She's got the smoothest hand with that thing I've ever seen." And he told them how she'd sliced Gary's jeans off him with one long stroke. He was so complimentary, in fact, that Gail found her cheeks beginning to glow. She excused herself and slipped from the room to check on Gary next door. He was sleeping lightly and roused when she entered the room, but by the time she had finished taking his pulse, he was snoozing again. She let him sleep, confident he had no concussion and was in only the mildest stages of shock due to blood loss. Out in the hall, she crossed to the reception desk and sank down onto the secretary's chair, feeling deflated now that the adrenaline had stopped pumping. Only then did she remember that she had patients waiting in the lobby.

Quick as a cat, she leapt to her feet and hurried around the partition to the waiting area. "I'm so sorry," she told the four people sitting there. "A bull hurt a couple of fellows out at the Hartesite ranch. We're waiting on an ambulance now."

"They going to be all right?"

It was Mr. Cole, the older gentleman whose blood pressure she had been about to check earlier.

"Oh, yes, I think so."

"That one feller, Gary, was bleeding pretty bad."

"Yes, he was, but I've patched him up. Now we just have to replace some of the blood he's already lost."

"What about that other one, that Punch?"

"Compound fracture of the left arm, slight concussion. He'll be okay as soon as the bone's set."

Mr. Cole grunted, nodded and got to his feet. "You're a good doc," he said as he turned away. "I'll be along again when you're not so busy."

Gail's mouth fell open. She was so stunned she couldn't say a word as the other three got up and followed old Mr. Cole out. *You're a good doc. A good doc...* She hadn't known how much it meant to her to be accepted and appreciated by these people. She'd thought of this place mainly in terms of moving closer to her daughter, and of private practice merely as a means to that end, and suddenly she knew she'd sold the whole lot of it short. This place was suddenly dear to her. These people were suddenly important, her practice vital. She felt struck by the weight of a blessing she'd never stopped to weigh.

"He's right, you know," said a familiar voice behind her.

She whirled around, both chagrined and thrilled to find Rand standing close. "What?"

"You are a good doc," he said, "and you're pretty, too, smart, sweet—"

"Rand!"

"And feisty. Man, do I like a feisty woman!"

"You're being silly!"

He shook his head slowly. "Nope, just honest."

She stood there staring at him, not knowing what to say. Finally, he reached out and chucked her under the chin. "I like you, Gail," he said softly. "I like you a lot."

You won't when you know, she thought sadly, but when he reached for her, she went into his arms, wrapped her own around his waist and laid her cheek against his collarbone. Nothing had ever felt so good as being held close to him. For the first time in her life, she actually felt as though she belonged, and the thought that it couldn't last was bitter indeed. But what choice did she have? She'd already waited longer to claim her daughter than she'd ever meant to. And yet she couldn't help thinking how wonderful it would be if she could have it all—her daughter, Rand, the practice here in Marfa. Vain, vain hope. Impossible dreams. Unanswerable longings. Still, she let him hold her until they heard the whine of the ambulance siren as it came through town.

She was standing on the porch waiting for them when the ambulance turned into the lot. "Around the side," she shouted, waving her arm in that direction. "I'll open the door there."

The side door led into the treatment room. She had never yet opened it, but she slipped the bolts, pressed the toe latch and swung that door wide as the attendants opened the back of their van and unloaded the first gurney.

"Whatcha got this time, Dr. Terry?"

"A couple of beat-up cowboys. Bull got them. The one in this room had an opened femoral artery, but we closed it up again. He's going to need typing and transfusion. We've got a compound fracture next door."

The attendant whistled through his teeth as he pushed the gurney through the door, then he drew up short when he saw Rand standing across the room. "You again? You Harte-sites must be falling on hard luck."

"Nah," Rand drawled, "we just can't stay away from this good-looking doc here."

Gail felt her face flame hot. "Rand!"

Everybody laughed, including the cowboy with the stitched-up thigh, everybody but Gail. She rolled her eyes and marched out of the room before anyone could catch her smile.

When both cowboys were loaded into the ambulance and on their way, Gail closed and locked the side door again, then grabbed her purse and car keys from the bottom drawer of the reception desk, Rand at her elbow.

"Boss?" It was Evert.

"Yeah?"

"You thinking of following that ambulance into Alpine?"

"What of it?"

"Seems to me that blood ought to be cleaned up out of the truck while it's still sort of fresh is all."

Rand lifted his hat and stroked back his hair. "Reckon you're right, Ev. You volunteering?"

"If the doc wouldn't mind me puttering around this place, using the garden hose, maybe? There's blood needs to be cleaned up in here, too."

"Oh, you're right," Gail said, glancing around her for the first time. "Goodness."

"You two go on. I'll take care of it."

"You're welcome to whatever you need, Evert, but you don't have to worry about cleaning up this place."

"Nah, I don't mind. Y'all go on."

Gail looked at Rand. "We could be gone several hours."

"No problem," Evert said stubbornly. "I'll be here when you get back. Maybe I'll have me a bite to eat and a drink of something cool when I get through here."

Rand fished in his pocket and brought out a folded bill, which he pressed into Evert's hand. "Have it on me, Ev. Catch you later."

Gail took her extra key from the desk drawer and handed it to him. "Be sure to lock up before you go. I've got dangerous drugs in here. And wear gloves. Always wear gloves when blood is involved. When you're through just make yourself comfortable in my apartment.''

"I'll do that, ma'am. Thank you.''

"Thank you for cleaning up.''

"Yes'm.'' He doffed his hat awkwardly and shifted from foot to foot.

Gail grinned at Rand as they left him. "Kind of shy, isn't he?'' she commented as she opened the driver's-side door of her battered little car.

Rand was right behind her. "Oh, he gets that way around a pretty woman,'' he said lightly.

She rounded on him. "Will you cut that out!''

He cocked his head, and she watched his jaw firm stubbornly.

"No.''

Completely flustered, she gasped, stomped her foot and glared at him. She could be just as stubborn as he could! "You're just trying to get a rise out of me,'' she argued.

He stepped forward, placed both hands on the top of the car, effectively trapping her between them, and brought his face close to hers. "I can see you don't like being told you're attractive,'' he said softly, "but you might as well get used to it, pretty lady, because I'm going to keep right on telling you every chance I get. Just take it as your lot in life and learn to say thanks while fluttering your lashes.''

That image was so ludicrous she chortled.

He smiled, kissed her quick and put one hand on the top of her head, shoving her down and into the car. "Climb over,'' he ordered. "I'm driving.''

She glared, but she climbed over. He tossed his hat into the back, folded himself into the driver's seat, slid it all the way back, then held out his hand for the keys. She slapped them into his palm, eyes narrowed. "You really are a high-handed, presumptuous son of—''

"Yeah, yeah,'' he said complacently, fitting the key into the ignition. "And you're still too damned good-looking for anything less than kissing." *And a whole lot more,* his eyes said.

She swallowed any other smart remark she'd thought to make and sat back in her seat, gaze glued to the windshield.

He got the little car moving, first forward, then backward along the drive and out into the street. As it started forward again, chugging for all it was worth, he shook his head. "Honey," he said as casually, as if he'd said it every day for a year, "we've got to get you a real vehicle."

Honey. We. Gail closed her eyes and said not a word for the rest of the trip.

In Alpine, she was once again in control, writing up orders for X rays, transfusions and treatment protocols, while Rand cooled his heels. In due time, she set the bone in Punch's arm, placed a few stitches and applied a temporary cast, using strips of plaster-infused gauze. By the time she was through, Gary had been successfully transfused and sedated. He was sleeping the experience off in a private room. She had Punch put in with him, filled up with painkillers and sent off to dreamland after promising to see them both in the morning.

Rand was waiting right where she'd left him. He took one look at her and fastened his hand around the top of her arm, saying, "You need a good dinner and a couple of hours of relaxation."

She frowned grimly. "Who gave you your medical degree?"

"It doesn't take a doctor to see you're tired and hungry. Besides," he added, grinning, "I've been trying to buy you dinner for two weeks."

She had to smile, she just had to, and the thought of going home to another meal alone was particularly repugnant at that moment. She nodded and allowed him to pull her out of the building and stuff her into her car—passenger side, naturally.

They went to a little nondescript steak place that was really buzzing for a weeknight. She ordered the grilled chicken, despite the roll of his eyes, and clucked scoldingly when he ordered the T-bone. A baked potato, salad and a thick slice of Texas toast later, she was stuffed to the gills and groaning with it. Rand mopped up every morsel on his plate, finished her uneaten chicken and ordered dessert with his coffee. She couldn't even watch him eat it, though he took great delight in smacking his lips and humming delicious sounds while he demolished a big wedge of chocolate pie. When he was done with that, he drank a tall, cold beer, taking his time and savoring every drop. Gail could only shake her head.

Some ninety minutes after they'd first entered the place, they left again. Rand turned over the keys without complaint when she asked for them, and settled into the passenger seat, letting the back down into a semireclining position. It was dark already, and she turned on the headlights as she started back the way they'd come.

Some distance out of town, Rand suddenly sat up and clamped his hand down on her knee. "Pull over," he said, pointing to a wide space on the south side of the road.

She turned across the empty oncoming lane and guided the car to a stop. "What is it?"

"The lights," he said. "They're shining."

"What lights?"

He gave her a puzzled look. "The Marfa lights, of course! Haven't you ever heard of them?"

"No."

He shook his head, reached across the car and turned off the engine. "Well, they're just known the world over," he informed her. "We had a Japanese bunch out here filming them just last year. Come on. I'll show you."

He opened his door and got out. She did likewise, first shutting off the car lights. The silence enveloped her the moment she stood still by his side. She leaned her head back and looked upward. The sky was unbelievably black and strewn liberally with the brightest stars she'd ever seen. It was breathtaking, utterly breathtaking, but when Rand moved behind her and stretched his long arm out to point across the lighter horizon, she dropped her gaze to follow it.

"See 'em?" he whispered into her ear. "There!"

She saw a round, bluish light that shimmered and blinked before disappearing, but suddenly there was a pinkish one next to where the blue had been, glowing bright and then dim in the distance. The blue one winked on again, shimmered and went out, only to reappear in another place. "What are they?" she asked softly.

He dropped both hands onto her shoulders and said, "No one knows."

She twisted around to look up at him. "Oh, come on."

"No, really. No one's ever found anything, and lots of people have looked, including the air force and the border patrol."

"Well, it's got to be somebody doing it," she argued.

"Nope. Some folks suggested they were car lights coming off the Presidio highway, but they were first seen long before that highway was laid, way back in the 1800s."

"Are they visible every night?"

He shrugged. "Couldn't say. I'm not out here every night."

"You know what I mean."

He chuckled. "More nights than not, I gather. There are usually several cars pulled over here after dark. Come to think of it, though, this is pretty early for them."

Gail pondered all he'd said as she turned to gaze out over the dark landscape. Only the pinkish light was glowing now, and it seemed to be in a different place. Below it somewhere, another one winked and flirted and finally burned briefly, going from yellow to white to nothing in the space of a breath. "Swamp gas?" she wondered aloud.

Rand laughed. "In the middle of the desert?"

"Mineral deposits of some sort? Phosphorus, maybe?"

He shook his head. "I'm telling you, they've looked. They've been over that whole territory on foot. I'm told they've dropped markers from the sky and hiked out to them, but they've never found anything that explains this."

"It's a genuine mystery, then."

"An *old* genuine mystery."

"Gosh." She stared for the longest time, watching the lights flicker on and off, sometimes seeming to change shape as well as color. Then Rand slipped his arms around her waist, pulling her back against him so that her head fell onto his shoulder.

"Thanks for what you did today," he whispered.

His breath warmed her ear and sent shivers up and down her spine. She closed her eyes against the sensations and quipped, "Just pay your bill when it comes, cowboy, and I'm a happy woman."

"No, you're not," he said softly. "I don't know why yet, but you're not."

Gail straightened reflexively, gasping a deep breath. "Don't be silly," she said as lightly as she could manage.

He pulled her around to face him. "I hear it in your voice sometimes, see it in your eyes. It's like you've got all the pain in the world tucked away inside you somewhere, and every time your guard's down, it slips out."

"That's absurd," she began, but broke off the instant he laid his big, hot hand against her cheek.

"I've felt like that before, Gail," he told her gently. "I didn't want anybody to see it, either, but pain that big can't be hidden. It has to be beaten down and chipped away until it's manageable and finally gone. You have to fight it, defeat it. Sometimes it helps just to talk about it."

She felt panic rising in her, felt words climbing onto her tongue that must not be uttered. *You have my daughter! Your brother stole my daughter, and I want her back!* Instead she turned away, clamping her teeth against disaster and closing her eyes tight, her hands balling into fists. For a long moment, he neither spoke nor moved, but finally he sighed and stepped up close to slide his arms about her again, this time from the side.

"You don't have to talk about anything you don't want to," he conceded gracefully. "Hell, if you'll kiss me, you don't ever have to speak to me again."

She wanted to laugh and cry at the same time. Chuckles burbled up and tears gathered. Suddenly she wanted nothing so much as to feel his mouth on hers again. And why not? Shouldn't she take all that she could while she could? God knows it wouldn't last long, no longer than it took for her to figure out which one of his girls rightfully belonged with her. What could it hurt anyway, one kiss?

She knew she was rationalizing, but she honestly didn't care anymore. It had been so long since she'd wanted to be with a man, any man, so long since she'd felt like this, if she ever had. She turned and put her arms about his neck, pressing her body against him and going up on tiptoe, feeling the drag of clothing against skin, the jut of his belt buckle against her belly, her breasts flattening against his hard chest. He lifted his hands to her hair and brought his mouth down to hers, kissing her with such aching sweetness and tenderness that she began to quake against him as tears dripped from beneath her shuttered lids and rolled down her cheeks. She pulled away before he could feel them, burying her face in the hollow of his shoulder.

He kissed the top of her head and let his hand slip down to pat her bottom. Then he pulled the plastic-coated rubber band from her hair and threw it away, catching the silken fall in his hand as it tumbled free. He combed his fingers through it, whispering, "You have beautiful hair. I've been wanting to do this since I first laid eyes on you."

She laughed, the tears all dried now. "I hate it. I have no patience with it. I've wanted more than once just to shave my head and be done with it."

He tugged her head back, glaring down at her. "Don't you dare!"

That arrogance again! As if he had any right to tell her what to do about anything. She stepped back, whipping her head to free her hair from his hands. "And just what do you think you could do about it?" she demanded.

For a moment, his jaw hardened, sharpening the tilt of his head, but then his smile flashed white in the deepening night. "Guess I'd just have to change your mind."

It was a fairly reasonable answer, but she wasn't feeling even slightly reasonable. She was feeling edgy and... dissatisfied. She glared at him and shoved her hair out of her face. "Oh, really? And just how do you *think* you *might* manage that?"

"Like this," he said smoothly, reaching out for her.

Almost before she realized he had moved, she found herself pinned against him, her back bowed over his arm, his mouth hotly plundering hers. She had instinctively thrown her arms around his neck again at the instant of impact, and now she tightened them, her mouth opening to his tongue, her own rising to meet it in a duel that quickly became a dance of passion. She forgot the issue at hand, forgot the wide space beside the road where they were standing, the mysterious Marfa lights, all the reasons she shouldn't, couldn't, be with this man. She forgot for a moment that Carel Hartesite had ever lived, that she had ever hurt or agonized because of him, that he had stolen her daughter, that she *had* a daughter. She forgot to think and simply gave herself up to the irresistible pull of sensation, and in so doing, felt with every fiber of her being each and every scintillating instant of sensual pleasure.

She felt the swirl of his tongue inside her mouth, the velvet pull of it against her own, the pressure and slide and gentle suction of his lips as they mated with hers. She felt the strong arm in the middle of her back, the heavy warmth of the hand that cupped her bottom and held her against him. She felt the hard ridge beneath the fly of his jeans pressed to her belly. She felt the bite of his belt buckle, the buttons of his shirt against her breastbone above the softness of her breasts swelling against the brick wall of his chest. She felt the stiffer denim of his jeaned thigh between the softer fabric of her own, the strong muscle that flexed as he lifted his leg slightly to rub against her. She felt the liquid response of her own body, the melting hunger that was an emptiness where no emptiness had been before. She felt her own femininity, the very womanliness of her body, from the hair that lay against her scalp to the toes that curled inside her athletic shoes.

Even the drag of his beard against her cheeks was somehow exciting, the rub of his nose against hers, the occasional clash of their teeth as their mouths worked against each other, the quickness of their mingled breaths. Their bodies generated such heat everywhere they met! And all else was cool with the chill of night air. She wanted more of that heat, and she pulled her arms even tighter about the strong column of his neck, her hands splaying across his back and into the silky vibrance of his dark, wavy hair.

She heard the car horn and the hooting voices dimly, as if from a great distance. She didn't even connect them with Rand's sudden withdrawal or the curse words he muttered, until he combed his fingers through her hair and said, "We need a more private place than this." She knew then that they had been seen and that she had been so deeply tangled in the throes of desire that she wouldn't have cared if spectators had lined both sides of the highway—until he'd broken the kiss.

Kiss? Was that all they'd been doing? Just kissing? It had felt like so much more than that! It had felt like a prelude to a joining, the beginning of a melding. It had felt, still felt, like the most natural and yet the most exciting thing she had ever done. She was stunned by the sheer intensity of it, compelled by the residual desire. She was . . . happy, happy from the inside out, despite the dissatisfaction, despite all the *shouldn'ts* and *couldn'ts* and *must nots,* and she didn't want to lose that. She didn't want to lose a moment of it, because she knew that it couldn't last.

"We'd better get back, sugar," Rand said gently, his hand clasping hers. She nodded, smiling, but didn't budge. His grin was quick, certain, pleased. He slid his free hand around to the back of her neck and pulled her against him once more. "Ah, what you do to me!" He chuckled as he stroked her hair. "You'd better drive again. I feel a lot more light-headed now than I ever have on alcohol."

She laughed as she pulled away from him, knowing what would happen if she stayed close and that she ought to be glad Evert was waiting for them back at her place, that their tenuous moment of privacy was spent. She was disappointed and pleased and hopeless and hopeful all at the same time, and she knew that she would decide later not to see him like this again—and ignore that decision again. It didn't seem to matter. She was happy for this moment, and that was so much more than she'd had in so very long. How could she not take it and savor it, at peace for once, even if only because she was too tired and too bemused to fight?

Chapter Seven

It was touch and go, and he knew it. He'd called her twice since she'd patched up the boys, and both times he'd heard the ominous wavering in her silence when he'd reminded her of the upcoming birthday party. Still, it was absurd, this nervousness of his. He was forty-one years old, for Pete's sake, experienced, intelligent. He had been reasonably satisfied with his life for a long time now. He had the girls, and he had Belle, and he had the ranch. And it wasn't sex. Sex was easy enough to find if a fellow was determined. He was, on occasion, determined, but sex had never quite been what he wanted it to be. Then again, his brief marriage had not been what he'd wanted it to be, nor the two or three other relationships he'd attempted, either. What made him think that it could be different with Gail Terry? The woman was as prickly as a horned toad one moment—and hot as fireworks the next. Just thinking about her did strange and exciting things to his body. And she might not come. He had to live with that possibility. She might not come.

He fought the urge to check his wristwatch for the umpteenth time in the past quarter hour and put on a false smile for the couple strolling toward him through the sand, long-necked bottles of beer in hand.

"Quite a party," the gentleman said.

It was what he said every year, what they all said, but this year Rand couldn't be sure, not until *she* showed. He kept his smile in place and extended a hand and an arm, the hand for the gentleman, the arm for the lady, whom he hugged with practiced ease. "Glad y'all could make it. Belle will be so pleased."

"I been meaning to talk to you 'bout that new bull," the man said.

But the sounds of tires on gravel snatched Rand's attention away. "Another time, if you don't mind. Soon." He was already walking away, hurrying with long strides toward the pickup he'd sent out Bones in, what seemed like hours earlier. The lights shut off and the engine rumbled to a stop. He heard the creak of a door and picked up his pace. She came around the front end of the truck just as he got there. He wanted to put his arms around her and pull her hard against him, fit her tall, slender body to his. He restrained the impulse, only allowing his hands to catch hers and hold them.

"That's quite a traffic jam you've got out there," she said. "My car must be parked two miles down the road."

"That's why I sent Bones down to wait for you. You're late, by the way." He knew he was grinning like an idiot, but he couldn't seem to stop.

She smiled, glad to see him. "Doctors are always late, didn't you know? Comes with the job."

He slid a hand up her arm to her elbow, turning her toward the house. "Emergency?"

"Nothing serious." She laughed. "A distraught mother came banging on my door just as I was about to leave. Her four-year-old had shoved several kernels of popcorn so far up his nose they couldn't get them out again. I had to calm her down and extract the kernels. Then we had a little nose-bleed to deal with. All my emergencies should be so serious."

He shook his head in that way adults do when they're mystified. "Kids. I remember once Mary Grace stuck a piece of cold cereal in her ear. Must've been there for days, weeks, maybe! I know we were all worried she was losing her hearing. Anyway, I took her in to Doc Garlock. He shone that light in there, said it looked like some strange growth and sent us on to Alpine. So here I am, sitting in this surgery waiting room, worried sick, and out comes this doctor with this little flesh-colored thing in a tweezers. 'Here you go, Hartesite,' he says. 'Here's your growth. Near as I can tell, it came in a box.' I don't know if I was more embarrassed or relieved." He shook his head again. "Yes, I do. I was relieved. And we didn't buy cold cereal again for years!"

"How old was she?" Gail enquired. He could tell from the shine of her eyes that she was absorbed in his little story. He wondered about that child she had lost, how old he or she might have been, how it had happened. There was so much he didn't know about her, but now was not the time to ask.

"About three, I guess," he answered. "She was always up to something, that girl, gave me more sleepless nights."

"And you've loved every minute of it," Gail said, looking up into his face.

"Um-hmm." He didn't realize they'd stopped walking until he caught himself bending his head to kiss her, and only then because Beth Purdy called out a greeting. He pulled up short, lifted a hand in halfhearted greeting to Beth and smoothly turned Gail away. He didn't want to share her just yet. He walked her over to a metal tub filled with ice, beer and sodas, one of many placed around the house and patio.

"What's your pleasure, ma'am?"

"Any old cola will do."

He bent, dug one out and handed it to her, wiping his wet, cold hand on his thighs as he rose. She popped the top and took a long drink, giving him a moment just to look at her. She was wearing half boots with stacked wood heels, and jeans that conformed nicely to the shape of her long legs and slender hips. She'd found a jacket, a tailored brown tweedy thing dotted with little rust-colored bits. She wore it over a cream white sweater with a cowl neck. Her golden hair was caught up in a sleek fall at the back of her head with the long, curved, comblike contraption the girls called a banana clip. Soft wisps had escaped to float about her face, highlighting her fine bone structure and those unusual gold-and-green eyes. It was her mouth, though, that always seemed to compel him. When she lowered the soda can and smilingly licked drops of cola from her lips, he felt himself go hard as stone.

Damn! He'd never wanted to kiss a woman so badly in his life. Kiss, hell. He wanted a lot more than kisses. He was worse than a randy schoolboy around this woman! To keep from embarrassing himself by reaching for her in front of all the people milling around, he slipped his fingertips into the front pockets of his stiff new jeans and dropped his head, using his hat brim to block his gaze until he could get his unruly body under control. She nearly undid him when she stepped forward and laid a slender hand upon his arm.

"Something wrong?"

"No! No, of course not. I was just trying to think what I have to do next."

"The busy host," she said warmly. "Well, don't mind me. I'll just look around for a while, then pay my respects to Miss Belle."

He wasn't about to part company with her, wasn't about to let her out of his sight. Thinking quickly, he said, "Actually, I could use your help, if you don't mind. I've got to get dinner dished up pretty soon, or it'll be midnight before we get that band wound up and the dancing going."

"Well, let's go," she said. "What do you want me to do?"

He turned and began strolling toward the house, explaining all that was going on out back. "Well, there's the charcoal pit. I've got the boys raking it periodically to keep the coals hot and cook the side of beef turning on the spit above it. And let's see, Camelia's putting together a Houston-sized salad in a scrubbed-out oil drum. Oh, and the gas grill for the toast ought to be firing up about now. Then there's corn on the cob and baked potatoes. We've wrapped them in foil and lined the edges of the coal pit with them. I never could tell when those were done right."

She laughed, a rich, full-throated trill of husky chuckles. "There's a major secret working here, Rand. You squeeze them, and if the potato caves and the corn spits, they're done."

"Well, let's get to squeezin' then," he said, catching up her hand once more and pulling her along at a quick pace.

They skirted the house. People covered the patio in the back and wandered the trails laid out in Belle's expansive rock garden, taking up space on the stone benches and the wrought-iron lawn chairs. The wooden benches lining the picnic tables laid out in long rows were occupied, too, by chatting, drinking, laughing people. Lanterns glowed from carefully spaced spots on the tabletops, and colored electric lights created a fan-shaped ceiling overhead. Children ran amok in the sand, squealing and sliding and catcalling to their friends. Rand stepped over a prickly pear cactus, veered around a clump of ocotillo and crunched across a bed of pink gravel, Gail right behind him.

"This is beautiful!" she said. "Why didn't I notice it on my way to the bunkhouse that day?"

He shrugged. "It's not much to look at in the daytime, I guess. Sort of blends into the landscape. Mother likes it that way. She used to keep some roses out here, but she dug them up after Daddy died. I always figured it was her way of dealing with her grief."

"Will roses really grow out here?" Gail asked doubtfully.

He sent her a quick look to show that he was answering in all sincerity. "Sure, if you water and feed them. These cool nights and sunshiny days produce prizewinners, if you have the patience to deal with them."

"Hmm."

She seemed to like that idea, and he made a mental note of it.

They wound down a packed pathway to the rear of the garden, where a big camp kitchen had been set up. A huge stone-lined pit curbed with cement glowed with one hundred fifty pounds of hot charcoal briquettes. Foil-wrapped ovals rimmed the cement curbs, and a side of beef on a long spit sizzled above them. On one side of the pit, a grill made of a big, barrel-shaped metal drum cut in half lengthwise and fit with propane burners slowly toasted inch-thick slices of buttered bread sprinkled lightly with chili powder. Next to the grill, Camelia was tossing salad in the other half of that cut drum, using her hands. Serving tables had been set out, covered with crisp white linen and laid with every conceivable necessity, from flatware to condiments and catering pans heated with little cans of fuel. Already better than three-dozen people were lined up, plates in hand.

"Meat's done, Boss," called the cowboy at the spit handle. Another sharpened two wicked-looking knives against each other, while a third stood ready with a stainless-steel serving pan some two-and-a-half feet in length. Others were stacked nearby.

"Carve away!" Rand said with a wave of his hand, then led Gail to a corner of the pit. She bent over and began to squeeze the foil-wrapped vegetables gingerly. Rand couldn't help admiring the view while she worked.

"These are perfect," she announced. "Hand me one of those pans and a hot pad."

He obliged her, squatting with the pan across his knees while she carefully picked the foil packets from the coals.

When the pan was filled, he decided they'd done their share and called over one of the cowboys working within the kitchen blockade. He handed over the pan and nodded at the pit. The cowboy transferred the pan to a serving table and quickly returned with another, while Rand ushered Gail to the side, saying, "Let's get us a bite to eat before the rush starts. I'm hungry enough to eat a horse." He called to Camelia in Spanish, ordering two plates to be filled and carried to a spot he'd already scoped out among the dining tables.

"I thought we were needed here," Gail said as he steered her with a hand pressed to the small of her back toward the spot he'd picked.

"Looks to me like they've got everything under control. Let's eat."

Apparently willing to stay at his side, Gail stepped over the bench and seated herself, asking, "Where are the girls?"

"Oh, they're about, busy as lizards on the run, no doubt."

"I'd like to see them," she said carefully, softly.

He was touched, honestly touched. "You'll see 'em. Night's young. Besides, they wouldn't dare miss the singing."

"The singing?"

He settled himself next to her, being sure they met at shoulder and thigh. "You know, 'Happy Birthday.'"

She braced her elbows against the rough tabletop and laced her fingers together. "Ah. That reminds me, where's Miss Belle?"

"In the house, of course. These things have a pattern, see. First there's the eating. Then Mother makes her entrance and there's the singing, followed by the holding of court—"

"What?"

He laughed. "You'll see. She'll set up there on the patio— in her wheelchair this year—and everyone will file by and pay their respects, which she'll accept as graciously as a queen. And then we'll dance."

"So after the singing, everyone wishes Belle Grace a happy birthday and hits the dance floor."

"Something like that." He laid his hand on her knee, a move greeted with only the slight arching of one slender eyebrow. He leaned close, intending to nuzzle her ear, but a plate of food appeared in front of him, courtesy of a grinning Evert. Rand cleared his throat and straightened, reminding himself once again that they were very much on view.

Evert served Gail with a little more finesse, plunked two beers in frosty bottles and two sets of flatware wrapped in heavy paper napkins onto the table, then smiled and left them.

Gail sniffed the thick, piquant sauce ladled over her sliced beef and smiled. "My arteries may protest, but my stomach's rejoicing."

He laughed and fell to eating, pausing only now and again to answer a greeting or remark. The table where he and Gail sat filled up fast, but Rand kept his head down and tried not to draw conversation. He introduced Gail as Dr. Terry to all who made it clear that they hadn't yet met and ignored the rest, all except one particular fellow. That one strolled by with his plate piled high and sent Rand a wink.

"That's a good-looking woman you got there, Hartesite."

"And don't you forget it," Rand shot back, bending his attention to his plate. He wasn't about to let no smooth-talking ranch hand horn in on his woman. Well, maybe she wasn't exactly his woman—yet—but he'd damned sure staked a claim, and he meant for everyone to know it, even if it did paint her cheeks red to hear it. As casually as possible, he dropped his hand to her knee again, and found hers there waiting for him, palm up. Thrilled, he squeezed it tight, no longer interested in his food or this party or anything but her. He'd never been so aware of a woman in his life. She was a magnet, a lodestone, and he was made of metal shavings apparently, because he felt as if every cell in his body were straining toward her. He wanted nothing so much as to get her in a dark corner alone, as if he could find an empty one on the whole spread that night.

Duty, nevertheless, intruded. As the food on plates dwindled, conversation buzzed louder, and Rand could not hope to avoid it all. Gail didn't seem any more inclined to join in than he did, but inevitably one or the other of them was tapped from time to time for comment. Mostly, however, they sat quietly, thigh to thigh, their hands linked beneath the table. Eventually he draped his arm about her shoulders, and as the evening wore on, she seemed to lean closer and closer into the curve of his arm. Finally, he had only to turn his head to nuzzle her ear. He couldn't resist, despite the very public setting, and found himself charmed by the delicious fruity fragrance of her shampoo.

He had the notion that if he put his tongue to the sensitive flesh behind her ear, he'd taste strawberry and apple, maybe even peach. The idea, the urge, was driving him crazy. His mouth watered. His nostrils flared. His heart beat a swift, steady tattoo, his groin knotting painfully. His muscles tightened with the effort *not* to pull her closer still. He shut his eyes and saw her bending over the fire pit, her bottom rounding nicely, a perfect fit for his hands—

When the applause began, he jerked mentally as well as physically. Sweat had beaded inside his hat, and he could feel it trickling down the center of his back. Though it was cool out, he was burning inside and momentarily disoriented. He knew where he was, but the applause held no real significance for him until his foreman laid a bony hand on his shoulder and bent to speak raspily into his ear.

"It's time, Boss. Miss Belle's waitin'."

His mother! He pushed up to his feet, pulling Gail along with him, because it simply didn't occur to him to leave her behind. He stepped over the bench, his hand at her waist to steady her as she did the same, and then they were hurrying through the throng that milled between the rows of tables.

Belle Grace was sitting in the center of the patio in her heavily padded wheelchair. Two of her oldest friends and both of the girls flanked her. She was wearing a long denim skirt that showed only the bottoms of her pearl-white boots, and a red tailored blouse beneath a colorful quilted jacket overlaid with a heavy squash-blossom necklace of intricately worked silver and smooth turquoise stones the size of quarters. Matching earrings hung from her earlobes, and on her hands and wrists she wore every diamond, opal, onyx and sapphire that she owned. It was a wonder she could lift her arms. The tail of her concha belt trailed down her leg, leaving no doubt that she was worth a fortune in precious metals and stones just as she sat.

The girls were similarly arrayed in tight, colored jeans and bright shirts with cut cuts. They wore matching boots of blue leather inlaid with bright yellow. Hand-tooled belts wrapped their waists. Chains were strapped around their ankles and insteps, as well as the crowns of their felt hats. Silver tipped their collars and sparkled at their cuffs and, at least in Mary Grace's case, hung from dainty earlobes. Rand thought he'd like to see Gail turned out in such finery or, better yet, in nothing at all, then colored to the tips of his ears at the thought. Suppose his girls could read his mind, or worse yet, Gail herself could. He should have known that it would be his mother who would notice his heightened color.

"Something wrong, Rand?" Belle asked as they drew near. Her eyes flitted from his face to Gail's and back again.

He made himself relax, much as he'd done as a boy when confronted with his mother's temper. "What could be wrong?" he said jovially. "I've got all my best girls right here in one spot."

Belle's gaze went pointedly to Gail, and Rand felt Gail stiffen at his side. A secretive smile tugged at Belle's usually stern mouth.

"So I see. Hello, Doctor. I hear you've worked wonders again."

Gail smiled, but Rand knew that she was feeling terribly self-conscious. "Actually, the wonder is that Rand got Gary to me in time," she said smoothly.

Rand decided that a rescue was in order. He clapped his hands. "Let's get this show on the road, hey?" He raised his hands over his head and clapped them again, turning toward the tables. Someone let loose a shrill whistle that riveted all attention on the patio once more. Rand stepped aside, put his hands to his hips and smiled. "Well, y'all know why we're here," he said loudly, gesturing at Belle. "She's not her usual frisky self, but—"

"Who's not?" Belle interrupted, to much laughter.

Rand shook his head. He should have known she'd cut up at that. He raised his voice a notch. "All right, all right, I stand corrected. Here she is, as feisty as ever and twice as formidable, at seventy-four, God love her! Happy birthday, Belle."

General applause followed. Then Bones stepped forward and swung his arms in the grand gesture reserved for concert conductors, and the whole body of celebrants hit the first note of the traditional song.

Belle tilted her head and smiled her gracious smile, elbows propped on the arms of her chair, hands lying gracefully in her lap until the last note wafted away on a soft desert breeze. Then she lifted her arms in an expansive manner of acceptance, and the crowd surged forward like stampeding cattle. Rand pulled Gail out of the way as the girls dropped hugs on their grandmother's neck and eager well-wishers surrounded her chair. Belle's two friends immediately waded into the fray to impose order, and in no time at all, a long, snaking line was organized. People shuffled by, nodding and bowing, looking for all the world like a stream of supplicants petitioning their queen. It never ceased to amaze Rand, this effect his mother seemed to have on people.

Gail began to chuckle. "Holding court," she said.

Rand nodded and put his hands on her shoulders, watching the spectacle over the top of her head. "Just like I told you."

She tilted her head back, her smile lying upside down. "Well, I say, more power to her."

"Oh, Lord, no!" he exclaimed. "She'd have me scraping and bowing next."

"The mighty Randal Hartesite, bowing and scraping," she said. "Somehow I don't see it."

Mighty? he thought. Was that how she saw him? If she could feel him trembling inside just now, she'd revise that opinion quick. Nevertheless he stood a little taller after that.

They began to catch the overflow from the reception line. One chatty person after another seemed intent on bending his ear. More than once he thought they'd be separated by the press of the crowd, but somehow he managed to keep a hand on her at all times, ultimately threading his arm through hers and around her waist to keep her close. When the band started setting up on a platform built next to the patio, the crowd thinned a bit, and Rand took advantage of a moment of relative privacy to drag Gail back into the shadows at the end of the house.

"Is it just me, or does everybody seem awful pushy tonight?"

"It's just you," Gail said flatly.

He couldn't see her face, but after a moment he could hear her begin to snicker.

"I'm sorry, I couldn't resist."

He laughed, keeping his voice low. "Guess I've been a little clingy tonight."

"A little?"

He'd have been real worried if he hadn't heard the smile in her voice. "All right, so I've been all over you like paint on a barn. I can't help it. I just want to be alone with you somewhere. Anything wrong with that?"

"Not at all wise," she murmured, but her arms were sliding about his waist.

He lifted his hat off and wrapped his arm around her shoulders, the hat in his hand shielding their faces from any too-sharp gaze, but just as he brushed his lips across hers, he felt a tug on his elbow. He straightened instantly and glowered down at the intruder. That bright-yellow hat could only belong to Mary Grace. He disengaged himself, feeling Gail's arms fall away, and tried to mask the impatience he was feeling.

"What is it, honey?"

"Can we dance now?"

"The band isn't even tuned up yet."

"But someone's got to tell them."

"Let your grandmother do it."

"She's gone walking with some of her friends."

"Walking?" Gail exclaimed.

"Well, I mean, they're pushing her chair."

Rand sighed, exasperated. "Go on. I'll be there in a minute."

Mary Grace reluctantly shifted away. "Don't be long. We want to dance."

"In a minute!" It came out sharper than he'd intended. She turned in a huff and stomped away, but when he reached for Gail again, she put up her hands.

"You've got guests waiting, Mr. Hartesite."

"I'm beginning to think this party was a bad idea," he grumbled.

"You wouldn't want to break with tradition, now would you?"

I'd break with just about anything to get you alone for a single hour, he thought, but he wisely kept his mouth shut.

She took his hand and led him back toward the light. He went peaceably, resigned to his fate. Mary Grace was standing next to the bandstand, her arms folded petulantly, but she brightened noticeably when he appeared.

Rand caught the eye of the band leader and gave him a nod. He said a quiet word to his companions and two fiddles began tuning, while the steel-guitar player made some minute adjustments in his slide. The drummer bopped his sticks in the air, whacking out the beat for a tune audible only inside his own head. One of the two guitarists played with the levels on the soundboard, and the lead stepped up to the microphone.

"Testing. One, two, three, testing." A speaker squawked almost painfully, and levels were adjusted a little more carefully. By this time, the patio was ringed with expectant dancers. After a moment, the guitarist nodded to the lead, who went smoothly into his act.

"Welcome to the Hartesite Ranch y'all!" A cheer went up, accompanied by whistles and hoots. "Ain't this a grand party?" More cheers. "It's scoot-your-boots time, boys and girls! A-one, a-two..." As he counted off the beat, couples stampeded the patio. The band swung into the music.

Rand turned to Gail, a question in his eyes, but she wasn't even looking at him. She was frowning at someone else. He followed the line of her vision and saw that she was staring at Mary Grace and her partner. Rand found that odd. "You know that kid?" he asked.

She sent him a slice of her frown. "Kid? That doesn't look like a kid to me. Don't you think he's a little old for her?"

Now Rand was frowning. "It's not like they're dating or anything. I mean, he's not even old enough to drive yet."

Gail did not seem to relax. "No?"

"Well, not till summer."

"She's just thirteen, Rand."

"Thirteen going on thirty," he muttered, wondering if he'd been a little lax in policing the girl. She appeared...very accomplished out there on the dance floor. He watched her performing a complex crossover movement and wondered where the heck she'd learned it. He'd taught her to dance, but he hadn't taught her *that*. He wasn't even sure he could do it himself. How'd they keep from knocking their hats off? Hey, they were really pretty good.

Gail poked him with her elbow. This time when he looked down she was smiling mistily. Now, what had brought on that change? Once more he followed her line of vision, and spied Carel Belle inching her way around the dance floor with old Mr. Garth.

"Isn't that sweet?" Gail said softly.

Rand saw the stilted smile on Carel Belle's face and knew the wrong girl had been talked into that "sweet" dance. Old Garth would occupy her for every song and Carel Belle was too nice to switch partners. He knew the old guy just wanted attention, but Carel had to have *some* fun out there. Rand grimaced, knowing what he had to do. "You stay right here," he told Gail. "I mean it, don't go anywhere." He stalked off in Carel Belle's direction, knowing full well that he was leaving a perplexed Gail behind.

He cut in on the old man firmly but smoothly. Garth yielded without a murmur. Carel Belle smiled up into his face gratefully. He winked, liking that smile and feeling ten feet tall. He wasn't dancing with Gail, but this was definitely the next best thing. "Let's show these stumblers a thing or two, huh?"

"Yeah."

He picked up the pace, sweeping her around and around in tight circles until she giggled. He caught sight of Mary Grace again. "Hey, do you know that crossover thing?" he asked Carel Belle.

"Sure. We learned it in cheerleading practice."

"Wanna try to teach an old dog new tricks?"

"You've gotta duck you head down," she said. "You're too tall." She put herself in position without breaking stride or rhythm. Side by side, they crossed arms and held hands. "Here goes." She pulled back on his hands, then threw her arms up, carrying his with them, and slipped underneath, crossing over in front of him.

In short order, she'd made the pass three of four more times. Then it was his turn. He saw quickly that he'd have to shorten his steps a bit in addition to ducking his head, but the first pass went smoothly enough, and by the third, he definitely had the hang of it. Soon they were crossing over quick as could be, and he was spinning her back and forth in between. She was good, every bit as good as Mary Grace. By the end of the song, they were getting as much applause as the musicians.

He gave her up to a croaky-voiced eighth grader, and as he departed, he bent down and whispered in her ear, "Next time just say no, sweetie."

She nodded, and her eyes twinkled. "Thanks."

He strode back to Gail, grinning. She was talking to Beth Purdy. He interrupted without apology, saying that he believed this was his dance. She gave Beth a smile and put her hand in his. As he led her out onto the floor, she informed him that she didn't have much experience.

"I don't know any fancy footwork. About all I can manage is your basic two-step."

"Suits me to a tee," he said, "so long as I get my arms around you."

She dropped her jaw. "Mr. Hartesite, I do believe you're flirting."

"Yes, ma'am. How'm I doing?"

She put her head back and laughed.

"That good, huh?"

He pulled her into his arms, marked the time and stepped off. After one initial bobble, she fell into step with him. Moments later they were moving smoothly around the perimeter of the floor. Her gaze flickered up and down several times, telling him that she had something on her mind. He smiled to himself, wondering if he was getting to know her ways some, and prodded her into speaking. "What's on your mind?"

Her next glance was startled, but she quickly averted it. "I was just wondering..." She bit her lip.

"Go on."

"A-about the girls just now. I-it's none of my business, of course, but..."

"Say it."

"Well, it seemed to me that you rescued the wrong one."

"Did I? Maybe I'd better explain then. Mary's starting to test her power over the opposite sex all right, but she's got a real strong sense of self-worth, and she'd expect any fellow interested in her to do a good bit of groveling and pleading for her favors. That boy's not the groveling, pleading sort, and even if he was, Mary's got no problem saying no. Carel on the other hand, couldn't hurt the feelings of a mass murderer, and that old man she was dancing with was bound to ruin her good time by keeping her busy all night. Now which one would you have rescued?"

She smiled apologetically. "The wrong one, obviously. Thanks for explaining."

"Thanks for caring."

She turned her face away at that and, after a moment, laid her cheek against his shoulder. He pulled her closer still, so close that he was thrusting his knee between hers with every step. It felt so good to have her this close that he didn't even let her leave the floor after the music ended. When the band segued into a slow, easy number, he silently rejoiced and swept her into the steps before she could make any protest. Not that she seemed of a mind to.

Heat had radiated through her body like a wave roiling across the parched face of the desert. She was aching to peel the blasted wool jacket off, aching to press herself even closer to the hard contours of Rand's chest. She closed her eyes and let him guide her in the languid, seductive dance, barely even aware of the music, let alone the crowd of couples milling about them. Undoubtedly, coming here like this tonight had been a mistake. She should never have allowed him to monopolize her as he had. She should never have allowed herself to play the role of girlfriend. Somehow, though, she couldn't make herself think of that. She couldn't make herself think of anything but Rand Hartesite.

He was a good man, a good father. She felt claimed, owned, safe. She knew, with the clarity of mind necessary to her profession, that she ought to be frightened, and she very well might be once she had put some distance—and perspective—between herself and this compelling man. But not yet.

It was slow, sweet torture for Rand. The friction of their bodies produced a ridiculous amount of heat and shortened his breath well out of proportion to the pace. Worse, he had a terribly difficult time keeping his hands where they were supposed to be. He wanted to knead and press and rub; he had to keep telling himself that they were in a public situation. When she sighed and laid her head on his shoulder, her lips grazing the side of his neck, it was almost his undoing. He wanted, very badly, to drag her back into the shadows. He wanted to drag her off to bed. He did *not* want to be interrupted, so when he felt the weight of a hand on his shoulder, he groaned inwardly and prepared a withering glare for whoever was idiot enough to cut in on him.

He was shocked to find that the hand on his shoulder belonged to Bones and that Bones's thin face was wrinkled in concern. Rand went still, holding Gail in his arms against him.

Bones leaned forward and said softly, "You better come quick, Boss, you and the doc."

Gail jerked, but it was Rand who demanded, "What's wrong?"

"She took a spill somehow," Bones said sorrowfully. "Tumbled right out of the chair."

"Belle Grace!" Gail whispered.

And Rand knew in that instant that it was so. Suddenly he was cold, so cold.

Chapter Eight

For a heartbeat, Rand stood rooted to the spot, his strong arms wrapped about Gail's body. It was as if he had withdrawn somewhere within himself, and then his gaze shifted to hers, read what he wanted to see there and abruptly slid away. Suddenly she was being pulled across the patio, her hand in Rand's, his long, sure strides carrying them quickly through the dancing throng. At the patio's edge, as if by mutual agreement, they began to run. Bones trotted awkwardly beside them for some yards, explaining breathlessly what had happened. Someone had been pushing Belle's wheelchair across the rough gravel walkway that curved in front of the house. Somehow the wheels had locked and the chair had pitched forward and sideways, spilling Belle Grace onto her side. Those with her had tried to help her up, Bones said, but the pain had been too great for her. A call for help had alerted him to the problem, and he had gone straightaway to Miss Belle's aid, but she had bade him just to find Rand and the doctor.

That in itself was alarming. A woman as stubborn and proud as Belle Grace Hartesite would have wanted to recover her dignity first and deal later with any but the most unbearable pain. Gail couldn't help thinking of the scar tissue that had weakened the surrounding hipbone. A rebreak in the area only now truly healing could prove extremely difficult.

The girls were there when they arrived. Mary Grace was on her knees in the gravel, clutching her grandmother's hand, while Carel Belle stood white-faced, wringing her hands. Belle Grace lay very much as Gail had first seen her weeks ago, this time, however, not on a smooth plank floor but on rough, sharp gravel. She made an attempt to mask her pain, but the set of her jaw and the grimness of her mouth betrayed her.

With hardly a pause, Rand went down on one knee beside her. "Mother!"

"Get me out of here, Rand," she said sharply, querulous in her pain and embarrassment.

He sent a pleading look at Gail. She nodded reluctantly, saying, "She can't stay here. The question is, do we wait for something solid to move her on?"

"We do not!" Belle snapped.

"I can carry her," Rand said to Gail.

She bit her lip, but could see that it might be best. "Come around to this side. We want to keep her weight on her good hip, so you'll have to carry her almost like a baby, cradled against you, her chest to yours. Think you can do that?"

He was already crouching beside Belle. Gail moved away to give him room. Very carefully, he scooped his mother into his arms, gently rolling her weight onto her good side. He brought her across his knees and then to his chest. She was pale, her jaw clenched so tightly that no one would have been surprised to hear the bone snap, but when he asked if she was all right, she nodded curtly. He got his feet solidly beneath him and pushed up to his full height, no small task, given that Belle was a big-boned woman who bordered on six feet herself. They had gathered quite a crowd by this time, and Gail forged a path for them, shepherding Mary Grace and Carel Belle before them.

When they reached the house, they found that Bones was already there, holding wide the paneled door. "My kit's in the car," she told him succinctly. He nodded and was gone, his crablike walk rapidly carrying him toward the truck at the end of the drive.

Gail and the girls stepped right into a large, rustic room done in pale woods, adobe and cushy tan leather. Gail noted details fleetingly. A wall of glass looked out onto the gaily lit patio, now abandoned by all but a few oblivious couples. A large woven carpet in shades of gold, brown and turquoise lay on the bleached plank floor. All in all, the impression was one of cool, classy ranch-style comfort with a decided Southwestern flavor. It was a room Gail would have liked to linger in, had her attention and concern not been for Belle Grace Hartesite and her family. Rand was even then moving sideways through the door, his mother clutched against him.

He swept past Gail and the girls to move swiftly but carefully down a long hallway opening off the living room and fronting the house. Gail fell in behind them, very aware of the girls treading practically on her heels.

"Is it her hip?" Mary Grace inquired.

"Probably."

"She's hurting," Carel Belle said in a small, tight voice.

"We can take care of that as soon as Bones gets back with my kit."

"Is she going back to the hospital?" Mary Grace asked.

"Very likely."

"Is it bad, then?"

Gail paused long enough to grip the girls' hands and give them a squeeze. She was thinking, *I want to comfort them always.* She said, "There's no way to know that now. Our first priority is to make her comfortable, then we can determine treatment."

"Is she going to die?" Carel Belle's tremulous voice reached out to Gail at the same time as her trembling hands.

"That woman's too strong to die of a broken bone!" she assured them both. "But she hurts like the rest of us, even if she is too stubborn to admit it, so it's up to us make her comfortable. That means we have to put aside our own feelings for now and concentrate on hers. All right?"

First Mary Grace and then Carel Belle nodded. Gail slipped an arm around each of them, knowing that it was presumptuous, but unable to resist. She ushered the girls down the hall after Rand and his mother. They hurried past a formal dining room and an enormous kitchen, followed by a number of closed doors and an enclosed staircase, immediately after which they turned a sharp corner. They passed one more closed door and came to another at the end of the hall. The room was dark, but Rand's voice came to them from the shadows.

"Get the light."

Mary Grace bolted the last few steps and reached around the door frame to flip on the overhead light, revealing a smallish room done in strong shades of blue, green and yellow. The bed itself was a full-sized four-poster of dark rosewood covered in improbable yellow ruffles. The walls were electric blue, stenciled with daisies, the draperies and carpet as green as grass. Hand-crocheted doilies covered the tops of the nightstand and mirrored dresser, as well as the arms of a small wing chair upholstered in a bright floral pattern. Exactly opposite the bed in the exact center of the wall hung the only picture. Gail knew at a glance that it was a portrait of Rand's late father. The photo made her halt uncertainly in the doorway. He looked uncannily like Carel in a cowboy hat, with the addition of years and pounds. His dark hair was combed with gray at his temples. Little wrinkles fanned out from the corners of his eyes. His smile was broad and spoke of an easy nature, his jaw not quite as square as Rand's, his nose a blunter version of Carel's. He was not as handsome as either of his sons, but his eyes radiated sincerity and an innate sense of humor. She liked him on sight and sensed immediately that his and Belle's had been a true love match.

Carel Belle hurried to throw back the covers of the bed, and Rand laid his mother gently upon the crisp white sheets beneath. Professionalism took over as Gail pushed her way to the bedside and bent over her patient. A few pointed questions and a brief examination assured her that the problem was indeed that previously broken hip. She instructed the girls on how to remove Belle's boots without causing further pain, then set Rand about the task of locating something simple and comfortable for his mother to wear, while Gail herself removed Belle's jacket. By the time they had made her comfortable and Rand had selected a white silk pajama set from the dresser, Bones had returned with the medical kit. Camelia came in behind him.

Gail performed a more thorough examination, satisfied herself that her original diagnosis was correct and that Belle Grace was in no danger of shock, then administered a strong painkiller. Camelia said that she would help Belle change her clothes and sit with her while Gail conferred with the family, but Belle was having none of that. She demanded to know if and when she was returning to the hospital.

Gail made a quick decision, then looked to Rand. "If you agree, I'd as soon let her rest here until tomorrow."

Belle sighed and visibly relaxed, as if the decision had been made. Rand, however, did not immediately commit himself.

"Would it be too much to ask that you stay the night?"

Stay the night here with him and her daughter? Daughters? It was Belle who made up her mind.

"Yes, stay, Doctor. Otherwise our guests will all leave, and we can't have that."

"You could be close in case she needs you," Rand added.

Gail nodded. "All right, if you have the space."

He smiled gratefully. "You can sleep in my room. It's close. I'll bunk in the guest room upstairs."

"Outside, all of you," Belle said, slurring her words slightly. "We've company. I just want to sleep."

"I stay with her," Camelia announced firmly.

Belle did not object, and it seemed a reasonable arrangement.

Gail looked to Rand and the girls. "There's a party going on out there," she said. "Everyone's going to wonder what's happened and how she is. All she needs right now is rest. I think we should do as she asks."

Rand reached for her hand, but his gaze was on Camelia. "We'll be close if she needs us."

"I will come right away if she seems worse."

He nodded, then signaled the girls. "Come on. Hit that dance floor."

They each paused by the side of the bed and kissed Belle's pale cheek, whispering their good-nights, before slipping from the room. Rand stood looking down at his mother until she opened her eyes.

"Don't worry about me, Son," she said raspily. "Do what you must, and there's no reason not to enjoy yourself while you're at it."

He chuckled and brushed his lips across her forehead. "Ever the realist, Mother."

She made no reply, just closed her eyes again and seemed to sleep. He and Gail tiptoed from the room. When they were a safe distance away from the door, he stopped her. "What do you think?"

She sighed inwardly, hating to tell him what she was thinking. "I'm afraid she's rebroken that hip."

"And that's bad, isn't it?"

No use trying to finesse this one, she decided, looking up into discerning gray eyes. "Yes," she said, "it's bad. It probably means that the bone wasn't mending to begin with as well as we'd hoped. It may also mean that it *won't ever* mend as it should."

"Meaning?"

"Meaning that she may require surgery."

He put his head back and exhaled deeply, as if greatly relieved. "You can fix it, then."

His reaction was both stunning and sweet. Was his confidence in her truly that great? She hated to disabuse him of that notion, but of course she had to. She placed a hand on his shoulder. "Not me, Rand, but possibly someone else, an orthopedic specialist, maybe."

"Specialist," he echoed dully, then his eyes sparked with blue. "But she'd want you to do it—I know she would. I certainly do."

She shook her head. "I'm not qualified for that sort of thing, Rand. We may be looking at a complete hip replacement here, and I'm barely familiar with the procedure."

"What are you telling me?"

"That you'd better prepare yourself for sending her to El Paso or even San Antonio."

He looked shocked. He lifted a hand to the crown of his hat as if trying to decide whether or not to remove it, then let his hand fall again to his side. "She won't go," he said simply.

But in this, Gail knew better. "She may not have any choice, Rand. It may be her only chance for walking again."

He sucked in a sharp breath, his gaze bouncing off the walls of the hallway. "How long?" he finally asked. "H-how long would she have to be gone?"

"Two to four weeks," she told him softly. "Complete recovery would take ten or twelve, more if there are problems."

He closed his eyes. "Damn."

"But the success rate with hip replacement is very, very high," she assured him swiftly, "a-and we may be able to perform some of the therapy here at home. I-I'm sure I could pick up the necessary skills rather quickly. That would reduce the time she would have to spend in the city."

"You'd do that, wouldn't you?" he said softly, placing his hands at her waist and stepping close. "You'd learn how to perform the physical therapy just so we could get her home sooner.''

She thought in that moment that she'd do anything in the world for him, and she opened her mouth to tell him so. Then she remembered that she had once felt the same way about his brother, and because she had, she dared not feel that way for this man. She countered the sudden sense of loss by telling herself that a daughter, or daughters, had resulted from her feelings for Carel Harte and that soon now they would be reunited. She resolutely pushed away questions about why she had delayed revealing herself thus far.

"I . . . I take the practice of medicine very seriously," she began. "A dedicated physician will naturally adjust to the needs of her—"

"Shut up," he said, curling his fingers beneath her chin and tilting her face just so.

She knew immediately what was coming, knew she shouldn't allow it, and did absolutely nothing to stop it. She merely watched as his mouth slowly descended, then closed her eyes, her focus blurring, and parted her lips beneath his. It was the softest, sweetest, gentlest thing she'd ever known, that kiss, and wrapped in it were promises galore, promises she had no right to, promises she could not possibly claim. But, oh! They were such beautiful promises, and she wanted so very desperately all that they pledged. That, of course, was impossible, but she could dream, couldn't she? She could pretend, just for a little while, just for tonight.

Sliding her arms about his waist, she leaned into him, tilting her chin upward and deepening the kiss of her own accord. He rewarded her with a groan that rumbled deeply within his chest. Then his arms clamped her to him. When his tongue touched hers, she shivered in anticipation of the invasion to come. He didn't disappoint her, filling her mouth with a velvet, questing thrust that caused her nostrils to flare and her breasts to swell as she pressed more firmly against him, keenly aware of a deepening need beginning to yawn within the private recesses of her body. She knew all the physical effects of sexual arousal, of course, right down to the substances released in the brain as a result, but she was shocked to realize that she had never before experienced all those effects. She couldn't have, for she had never before experienced anything like what she was feeling now. It was as if her continued well-being depended upon the joining of her body with that of the man in her arms, as if only by joining with him could she be whole.

This new knowledge was devastating. Not that she hadn't known all her adult life that she was somehow lacking, incomplete. She had assumed, however, that reunion with her daughter would take care of that, and now she had to acknowledge that she might have been hoping for too much there. Meeting Mary Grace and Carel Belle had evoked a fire storm of emotions in her that she had yet to quell, and she knew that she would never be truly happy without her daughter in her life, but nothing and no one had ever made her as aware of her solitary existence as Randal Hartesite. She wanted him. She wanted him in her life. She wanted him in her bed. She wanted him *inside* her, body and soul.

And she couldn't have him. That was the dark despair hovering over this new discovery.

She was almost grateful when the judicious clearing of a throat penetrated the fog of need and sensation swirling about her. Just as she had deepened the kiss, she now broke it, gently disengaging herself and nodding at Bones, who was standing at Rand's back. Rand himself seemed unaware of the presence of a third party, until Gail's nod alerted him. Only then did he actually release her and whirl around, sweeping her behind him in a sweetly protective gesture. But he needn't have protected her from Bones. Quite the opposite, in fact. The older man's color had risen alarmingly, his face pulsing dark red with embarrassment.

He couldn't quite seem to look Rand in the eye as he scuffed his feet and said, "Ever...everybody's asking 'bout Miss Belle. There's a rumor going 'round that her heart's giving out. I-I figured you'd wanna make some kind of announcement."

Rand bowed his head, sighing. "You figured just right, Bones. Thanks. I'll be right out."

"I'll go with you," Gail said quickly. "It can't hurt to have a physician supporting you when you make the announcement."

He folded her hand inside his. "Thank you, darlin'. I appreciate that."

A feeling swept through her, so warm and full and poignant that it clogged her throat and misted her eyes. She could only smile and nod, her hand clasped in his.

They walked together through the house, across the living room and out onto the crowded patio. The band was still playing, but the lively music seemed oddly discordant as few dancers twirled and scooted around the floor, while the majority of people stood in groups, buzzing with whispers.

Rand tugged her along behind him as he wound his way through the clusters, putting off the questions that came his way from all sides with a raised hand and terse shakes of his head. When he stepped onto the bandstand, pulling Gail up after him, the music abruptly stopped. After a quiet word with the lead singer, Rand approached the microphone, Gail's hand still entwined with his. He made short work of the announcement, confirming that Belle had very likely broken her hip again, but that the injury was far from life threatening and eventually she would be up and about, her old self once more. He assured everyone that Belle Grace was resting comfortably in her own bed. He closed by saying that the next few days would determine her course of treatment and that their prayers for a swift recovery would be appreciated. He then decreed that the party must go on, just as ordered by Miss Belle only moments earlier. He then requested a specific tune.

The band obediently began to play an unabashedly romantic song. Rand hopped down from the bandstand, then turned back and opened his arms to Gail. She went into

hem willingly, her breath catching as he slowly lowered her
body to his. She wrapped her arms around his neck, not
caring that they made a spectacle of themselves, and slid the
last few inches down his tall frame, creating the most in-
cendiary sparks to fly between them. He pushed his hat back
and lowered his head to lay his cheek against hers. His hand
fell upon her shoulder and slid down her arm. Lifting her
hand away from his neck, he clasped it and began to dance.
There were no grand, sweeping movements this time, no new
steps, just his body pressed tightly to hers as they swayed to
the music, their feet carrying them no farther than the same
square yard where they had begun. They might have been
the only ones there, the only two people on the face of the
earth. Certainly they constituted their own special world,
where they stayed throughout the evening.

Occasionally someone would walk by and tap Rand on
the shoulder, thanking him for a pleasant party and wish-
ing his mother well. At times, when they weren't dancing,
Rand was even obliged to return a few words. Somehow,
though, the gradual decline of the evening escaped them, so
that when they looked up at last from a quiet spot beyond
the dining tables, they were both surprised to find that only
they and the cleanup crew remained. It seemed early still, so
naturally Rand consulted his watch, only to exclaim, "Good
grief, it's nearly three a.m.!"

She wouldn't have believed it if he hadn't shown her, but
the moment she realized the truth of the matter, she knew
she had been terribly remiss in her duties. She moved toward the house at once. "I have to check on your mother."

"Of course," he said, "and then we should both turn in.
The sooner we get her into Alpine tomorrow, the sooner
we'll know what we're up against."

He escorted Gail into the house, which was now dark and
silent. Hand in hand, they tapped lightly at Belle's door,
then tiptoed inside and made a quick assessment. Belle
Grace seemed to be sleeping peacefully, and Camelia snored
from a comfortable position in the wing chair next to the

bed. They tiptoed out again, each relieved, and abruptly encountered the girls in the hall.

"How is she?" Carel Belle whispered.

Gail surrendered to impulse and stepped forward to place a comforting arm around the girl's slender shoulders. She looked achingly young with her hair down and her bare feet poking out from under the ruffled hem of her nightgown. Mary Grace, by comparison, seemed years older in a large, worn football jersey that revealed long, shapely legs. Gail suspected the jersey belonged to Rand and wondered if there were two of them or if Carel Belle simply preferred less revealing nightwear. She smiled down at the girl. "Your grandmother is resting easily. I hope she will do so for some time yet, but if she wakes up in pain, I'll be here to help her."

"Don't worry, honey," Rand added. "Dr. Terry's going to take good care of her."

"That's a promise," Gail said, and to her surprise and delight, Carel Belle slipped her arms around her for a hug.

"Thank you," Carel murmured, and put her head back to smile up at Gail.

Is it her? The thought leapt unbidden into her mind, bringing both warmth and a chill; warmth because it was a spontaneously affectionate act on the part of a girl who might well be her daughter, a chill because she feared the consequences if Carel Belle was her *only* daughter. Instantly it seemed insupportable that she might have to claim only one of them, especially when she recognized the concern and unease in Mary Grace's suddenly rigid stance. Gail instinctively reached out to the other girl, laying a hand upon her shoulder.

"I don't want you to worry, either," Gail told her, but Mary Grace flinched from her touch, muttering. Gail saw Rand's hand shoot out toward the girl, as if to scold or draw her back. Quickly she intercepted his hand and wrapped her own around it, pushing it down again and saying evenly, "It's late. We all ought to be asleep."

Rand sent her an enigmatic look, but immediately adopted a lighter attitude. "You two go on back to bed. I'll be up in a minute. I need to get a few things out of my room and show Dr. Terry where she'll be sleeping."

"You'll come say good-night, won't you?" Mary Grace asked.

"Sure thing, but you go on and get settled in."

Carel Belle pulled back, bade Gail a soft good-night and slipped up the stairs. Mary Grace hung back a moment longer, her gaze going between Gail and Rand in the darkened hall before she turned away and followed her sister. *She doesn't like seeing me with Rand,* Gail thought. Well, she wouldn't have to worry about that for long. He would no doubt turn his back on her the moment he learned who she was in relation to *his* girls. Both thoughts saddened Gail deeply, but she forced them away and followed him quietly a short distance to his bedroom door.

It felt terribly intimate to be standing in his room, but Gail took a long moment to satisfy her curiosity. It was a larger room than Belle's and airier, with bleached woods and cool neutral colors. Pictures of his parents shared space on his cocoa beige walls with those of the girls. Gail drank them in, feeling her throat close up and her eyes tear as she viewed them in various stages of development. In the earliest photo, they were perhaps two and dressed identically in pink gingham dresses with full skirts stiff with frothy petticoats. They had been very alike then, of the same size, their dark hair pulled back with big pink bows. Even then, however, they had not been identical. It was oddly easy to pick out which was Mary and which Carel Belle, and yet they might indeed be twins. Over the years, they had changed subtly, each assuming her own shape and size and look, but Gail kept coming back to that pink gingham, trying to see them through dispassionate eyes. Could they both be hers? It seemed incredible, but she knew suddenly how very much she hoped it was so. Having them both would somehow compensate for losing Rand—and yet, might they not work out something? She never wanted to deprive him or Belle Grace of the girls' company and love or vice versa, but that didn't mean he would want to see Gail herself.

"Well, I guess I'm ready," he said, pulling her out of her reverie. She turned to find him standing with toothbrush, comb, razor and shaving cream in hand. She saw no evidence of pajamas or anything else that he might wear to bed. She stopped herself from wondering if he slept in the nude. He gestured toward the bed, a large, rugged thing with a headboard that seemed built of rough fence posts. Lying upon the colorful spread, which looked like nothing so much as an enormous saddle blanket, was a soft white T-shirt and a navy blue velour bathrobe with red piping. "Thought you might like something to sleep in," he said in an oddly constrained voice. "I could always get you something of Mother's or the girls' if you'd prefer."

She didn't prefer. She very much liked the idea of sleeping in Rand's shirt, of snuggling into his bathrobe, climbing into his bed. She knew they would all bear his leathery, musky male aroma and that she wouldn't sleep a wink for it. "This is fine," she said lightly, walking over to finger the soft, thin fabric of the shirt. It had obviously been worn often and long. She fought the urge to pick it up and hug it to her, to bury her nose in its soft folds. Only with an effort of will did she turn away again, smile and bid Rand a goodnight.

He stood for a moment longer, his eyes telling her how very much he wanted to stay, but to allow that would be utter insanity. She knew that with the least encouragement, he would cross the room and take her in his arms, but she thought of Mary Grace and Carel Belle and purposefully dropped her gaze, her hands linked primly. He turned and left the room, closing the door softly behind him.

Gail crossed her arms, hugging herself, and moved once more to the wall of framed photos opposite the bed, her hungry gaze devouring every detail of the children depicted there. One—or both—of them was her daughter. She had to remember that. Whenever she thought of loving Rand Hartesite, she had to remember why it must never be.

Chapter Nine

She drifted somewhere between sleep and wakefulness, blissfully aware of the soft, silky feel of Rand's T-shirt against her skin and his faint but precious fragrance upon the pillow she clutched to her cheek. She did not dream, but she thought of him, wondering if he thought of her. Her body tingled in places. She could not quite subdue it, perhaps because she was lying in his bed, wearing his shirt, smelling the unique cologne of his body. He seemed so very close, almost a part of her. Almost.

Oddly enough, she didn't want to sleep. She wanted to lie there and absorb as much of him as possible. She didn't want to miss a moment of this strange awareness, for somehow her senses were heightened. And because they were, she heard the faint moan.

Belle Grace. Gail sat up, snapping into full consciousness, and flipped the bed covers back. Her bare feet hit the floor even as her hands reached for Rand's warm robe. Shrugging into it, she opened the door just wide enough to slip through and hurried toward the room at the near end of the hall. She did not knock, choosing instead to carefully open the door and step inside. Likewise, she did not reach for the switch to the overhead light, but padded quietly to the bedside and fumbled with the small lamp there until a gentle, golden glow illuminated the woman on the bed. Loyal Camelia snored on in her chair, while Belle gazed up at Gail grimly.

"You're in pain," Gail said softly. "I'll get something."

"Wait." Belle's hand shot out and fastened around Gail's. "I need to know what's going to happen."

Gail smiled comfortingly. "I can't tell you that, ma'am, because I don't know yet. We have to get some X rays first."

"But what do you think?" Belle persisted. "It's the old scar tissue, isn't it? My hip isn't going to heal on its own."

Gail sighed and resisted the impulse to smooth Belle's yellowing hair away from her face as Rand would have done. "That could be," she admitted, "but there are ways to deal with it."

"What ways?"

"We won't know until—"

"The X rays," Belle said, resignation heavy in her voice.

"I'm sorry, that's all I can tell you now, but I promise you that we will get you up on your feet again, one way or another."

Belle nodded, and Gail was astonished to see tears gathering beneath her quickly lowered eyelids.

"It's not for me, you know," Belle said in a near whisper. "I've had a good life, all told, a good man, sons, grandchildren. But Rand... Rand's had only the girls, really, and the three of them need me. You see, there isn't anyone else. There's never been anyone else."

The words slipped out before Gail could check them. "What about his wife?"

"Lynette?" Belle all but snorted. "They weren't married long enough for it to matter. There wasn't anything between them anyway. He only married her to please me."

He hadn't loved her then? Gail had to bite her lip to keep from asking. Such questions went well beyond the duties of a physician, but the relief of pain did not. She contented herself with a lifted brow, then turned away to move to the medical kit, which she had left on the dresser. Quickly she prepared a syringe and grabbed an alcohol prep. A few minutes later, she switched off the light and slipped out of the room, leaving Belle Grace resting comfortably once again. She pulled the robe more tightly about her and moved confidently through the darkened hall, sure of her way—until she was brought up short against a warm human wall.

She almost bounced off, would have if a pair of strong arms had not quickly caught and held her. She knew instantly to whom those arms belonged. "Rand!" she gasped, her voice low and breathless.

"I thought I heard someone."

"Yes."

"You've been with Mother."

She nodded, aware that her heart was thudding almost painfully inside her chest, and cleared her throat before saying, "She was in pain, but she's comfortable now, probably sleeping again."

"Good," he whispered. "Thank you. Again."

She shook her head, achingly aware that his arms were still about her, that her hands rested high upon his naked chest. It was quite a fine chest, all firm flesh and sculpted muscle furred lightly across the breast with crisp, dark hair that dwindled away down his middle, leaving an expanse of flat, bare abdomen above the waistband of his jeans. She realized that she ought to say something, but the only thought that came to mind was singularly inappropriate. It was none of her business if he had loved his wife. It was absolutely perverse of her to hope that he had not. Why should she? What difference could it possibly make? As if to show her, his hands rotated and splayed against her back as he brought her an inch or so closer.

"What are you thinking?" he asked softly.

But she had no answer for him, no *safe* answer. He didn't seem to require one. His hands moved up her back and down again as he stepped closer still.

She sought his face in the dark with her hands and found it. He turned his lips into one palm, pursing them against it, then nipping her skin with his teeth, telling her what he wanted in no uncertain terms. It was what she wanted, too, what she needed from him. He slid his hands up to her shoulders and curled his fingers around the soft, rolled collar of his robe, easing it away from her neck. His fingertips brushed her through the thin fabric of his T-shirt, igniting desire as they moved downward, parting the dark velour and loosening the careless knot at her waist. He slid one hand beneath the robe to encircle her waist with his arm and cupped her bottom with the other, pulling her against him, belly to belly. She could feel the hard ridge of his zipper pulsing against her and began to melt inside, while sliding her arms around his neck.

Her eyes closed as his mouth melded with hers, moist and warm and soft. She pressed against him, reveling in the feel of her unfettered breasts conforming to his chest with only the T-shirt between them. He crushed her hard against him, thrusting his hips at the same moment that his tongue filled her mouth. She went up in flames, standing on her tiptoes and plundering his mouth as thoroughly as he did hers. She burned with a scalding, liquid heat that seemed to have melted a hole at her core, which only he could fill.

Never taking his mouth from hers, he lifted her against him and took one long step, placing her back to the wall and holding her there with his big, hot body. That pressure was marvelous, but it was not enough to vanquish the flames licking up inside her. She moaned with frustration and felt as well as heard his answering growl as it rumbled up from his chest and poured into her mouth. He seemed bent on pressing her into the wall, but then his mouth left hers and fastened on the sensitive flesh beneath her chin, nipping and licking down her throat as his hand slid down her side to her thigh, then dipped to the back of her knee, lifting her leg, opening her to the thrust and grind of his hips. Mindless with need, she wrapped that leg around him, and when he raised the other, it followed suit as if of its own accord.

He brought his mouth back to hers, his hands pushing up beneath the hem of her T-shirt. His fingertips skimmed her torso, leaving gooseflesh in their wake. Then his hands cupped the weight of her breasts, and she felt his fingers trembling as they brushed over her nipples. Her nipples peaked, her breasts swelling and lifting. She put her head back, breathing hard, her fingers combing upward into the thick hair at the back of his head. It was then that he bent to bring his mouth to her nipple, biting it gently through the fabric before sucking it into his mouth. She lifted her forearm to her mouth to stifle the cry she felt building and held his head against her as she did so. His hand kneaded her breast beneath the fabric, while his mouth pulled at her nipple from the outside and his hips ground against her, sending through her concentric ripples of pleasure almost too sharp to bear. She felt as though she were climbing toward some never-before-achieved pinnacle of sensation. She was hot, her panties damp, her head beginning to swim as tremors shuddered through her.

Rand tugged at her breast, then raised his head to bring his mouth to the shell of her ear, his tongue swirling around its rim. "You're killing me, Gail," he whispered raggedly. "I've got to get inside you."

She nodded without really knowing what she was doing, what she was agreeing to, until she felt his left hand fumbling with his jeans, his right holding her breast. Panic welled up, but before she could react, the light flashed on overhead, blinding her.

Rand jerked back, his hands going to her waist to hold her steady as he pushed free. Somehow she was standing, her feet on the floor, the wall at her back. "Damn!" he said, and then "Mary Grace! Mary— Hellfire!"

Gail turned just in time to see the flip of a shirttail and the flash of bare legs fleeing up the stairs. Mary Grace! Mary Grace had seen them, right there in her own house. Shame flushed Gail's face pink as she realized just how much more the girl would have seen if she'd made her entrance even moments later.

Rand looked down at Gail, frustration and concern carving wrinkles into his sun-browned face. "I've got to go to her," he said apologetically.

She shook her head. "No, let me, please. I think she needs a woman right now, someone to help her understand, a mo—" She broke off, swallowing the rest of that dangerous word. Without waiting for his reply, she pushed away from him and hurried toward the stairs, pulling the robe closed. She reached the top of the narrow, carpeted stairs just as a line of light at the bottom of one of three doors that faced the landing flickered off. She chewed her lip, mentally grasping for the right words as she moved silently toward that door.

A light tapping brought no response, so Gail took a deep breath and simply opened the door.

"Go away!" wept a trembling voice from out of the darkness.

Tears. Fear. Gail recognized both and knew how to treat them. She searched the wall for a light switch, found it and flipped it.

Mary Grace was curled up on her rumpled bed, her face hidden by the fall of her hair. Her shoulders shook with silent sobs. Gail swept the room with a gaze, taking in the scattered clothing, the walls postered with images of country-and-western singers, the stuffed animals and the dolls, the bright pinks and lush reds of the walls and linens, which contrasted starkly with the white enameled French-provincial furniture. It was the room of a girl who had become a teenager in one mad rush of puberty. The teenager had won supremacy, but there remained something of the little girl, too.

Gail knotted the belt of the robe and walked to the bed, sinking down on its edge. "I really should thank you," she said softly, bluntly. "I might have made a terrible mistake down there if you hadn't come along."

Mary Grace sniffed and turned her face into the crook of her arms.

Gail stumbled on. "Unprotected s-sex is never wise, b-but it's hard to remember that, you know. Feelings overwhelm you sometimes w-when you like someone very much."

Mary Grace bounced up into a sitting position, her eyes dribbling tears, her mouth twisted angrily. "You're going to take him away from us!"

"No. I'm not."

"Why don't you just leave him alone then? He has everyone he needs already!" Mary Grace cried.

"What about you, Mary Grace?" Gail asked gently. "Do you have everyone you need?"

"W-what?"

Gail risked reaching out, her hand falling upon the girl's knee. "I want to be your friend, sweetie. I want to help you grow—"

"You want him!" Mary Grace cried. "I know you do!"

Gail blinked at the vehemence and the desperation, recognizing something of herself there, something of the abandoned little girl she had been but Mary Grace would never be. Never. She laid her hands on both sides of Mary's head and made the child look at her. "All right," she answered honestly, "but I tell you something now, something you can believe. As God is my witness, what I want most is for all of you to be a part of my life—you, your sister—and Rand."

Mary Grace shoved her hands away. "Well, I don't want you," she shot back, "so just leave us alone!"

Gail recoiled, pain wrenching her heart. It was silly of her, of course. Mary Grace didn't know what she was saying, who she was rejecting, but Gail knew, and felt as if the knowledge might slice her in two. "I-if you want me to stay away from Rand," she said in a choking voice, "I will. Then maybe we can be friends, you and I. That's all I want, really, a p-part of your life."

But how could Mary Grace understand, when all she felt was a threat to the continuity of her family? She saw Gail as an interloper, as competition for her uncle's affection. If only she knew! If Gail could have been sure of Mary's reaction, she'd have unburdened herself then and there, not even knowing if she was this girl's mother. Only by dint of will did she refrain, only by telling herself she had to know for certain before she could come to Mary Grace or Carel Belle as a mother to a daughter. Only then could she honestly ask for the acceptance she so desperately craved.

"Just go away," Mary Grace said tiredly, confusion marring her smooth brow.

Gail wanted so much to take her in her arms, but she wisely stood and folded her hands. "Of course. I-I'll send your... Rand to you, if you like."

Mary Grace nodded, pushing her hair away from her face. Gail attempted a smile, knew that it was dismal and abandoned it.

"Good night, dear," she whispered. "Sleep well." She bit her lip as she turned away, aware that she had to hold the tears at bay a little longer yet.

This shouldn't be so difficult. Gail stared at the telephone and told herself yet again that she had a right to know. *Then why not do it openly?* her conscience asked. *Declare yourself, tell your story, ask for blood tests. Within forty-eight hours you'll know which of them you gave birth to—or if you could have possibly given birth to both of them.*

"And what about Rand?" she asked herself aloud. "What would that do to him?"

But he would have to know sooner or later, and when he knew, he would undoubtedly feel betrayed, so she had lost him already without ever having *had* him. Yet, she shied away from the idea of hurting him. He didn't deserve to be hurt, and he didn't deserve lies and pretense, and he didn't deserve to lose one or both of the girls he had raised as daughters. Still, she or they belonged to her, and she couldn't just walk away empty-handed after all these years. Didn't she deserve someone of her own sometime? And didn't her daughter or daughters deserve to know her? But what about Rand?

It seemed that she had locked herself into a vicious circle with no way out.

She closed her eyes, sighing on a prayer. "Oh, God, what's the right thing to do? What's the best thing for everyone?"

She didn't know if He listened. So much of her life, He had not seemed to know that she existed. Nevertheless, a decision formed itself inside her mind. She would find out first if she could possibly have given birth to both the girls. Someone had to have known if Carel had been involved with another woman when he had lived with Gail. She had to know. They hadn't lived in a vacuum, after all, and every university had its own version of Peyton Place. Besides, she wasn't completely without resources.

Making a decision, any decision, was something of a relief. She opened the center drawer of her desk and extracted an address book bound in red leather, then reached into a lower drawer for three others held together with rubber bands, which she slipped off and tossed aside. Using a pen and a blank sheet of paper, she began thumbing through the oldest of the books, noting names, addresses and phone numbers of anyone who had known both her and Carel, however tenuous the connection.

When she was finished, she had listed eight names. All the addresses and phone numbers would be out of date now, but at least they were a place to start. She knew the drill all too well. She went over the names carefully, remembering as many details about each person as possible. She could recall this one's mother's name, that one's brother's, and then there were a couple whose entire families she had known and remembered. One was her first-semester roommate, Faye Anderson. Not that knowing Faye's family had done Gail much good, since Faye had not returned to school after they'd both dropped out that second semester, she to bear her child, Faye to tour Europe. Still, it was worth a shot.

After several minutes of racking her brain, she opened her current address book and looked up the number of the private investigator who had located Carel's family for her. She punched in the Dallas number, her heart pounding and her mouth dry. The familiar voice of his secretary greeted her after a few rings. As soon as she made herself known, the secretary put her through. Hearing the confident, matter-of-fact voice of the investigator soothed her enough to get through the interview. Only after she'd hung up did the doubts assail her again.

What now? What if he found out for her which of the girls was hers or that both of them were? What would she do then? What *should* she do? "Oh, Rand," she whispered, "forgive me. I never wanted to hurt you."

She closed her eyes and thought again of what she had said to Mary Grace. She wanted *all* of them in her life. It was true, of course. It had always been true. But she knew it was impossible without continuing to live with lies. She just wished the truth didn't hurt so much.

After a while, she pulled her spine straight and carefully wiped her nose and eyes with a tissue from a box on the corner of her desk. As always, she had work to do, and as always, the work would see her through the emotional difficulty that seemed to plague her. She took a deep breath and reached for the spiral file that held in alphabetical order the records of her professional contacts. She flipped through it and found the names and numbers of two excellent orthopedic surgeons.

She called the one in El Paso first, simply because he was closest, but his office informed her that he was vacationing in London and wouldn't return for nearly three weeks. They referred her to an associate, but Gail had heard that he disliked face-to-face encounters with his patients and tried to confine his involvement to the operating room—which was not a recipe for success with someone like Belle Grace. Gail called the San Antonio number and fared better, securing an initial examination for the following afternoon. The orthopedist got on the phone while his receptionist made arrangements to have Belle accepted at a local hospital. He asked a number of pertinent questions about Belle's case. Gail informed him succinctly, promising to send copies of her medical files and a typewritten diagnosis with the patient. By the time they were finished, the receptionist was ready with the details of Belle's hospital check-in and the name of a private ambulance service.

Gail made the final call, arranging for the ambulance to meet Belle and Rand at the Alpine hospital in the morning and deliver them to the hospital in San Antonio some six hours later. The orthopedist would arrange tests to confirm Gail's diagnosis that afternoon and call on them with the results early in the evening. Surgery would likely take place a day or two later, and Belle could come home within a week or two, providing physical therapy was available. Gail wished now that she had not made that promise to Rand to oversee Belle's physical therapy, but a professional promise was sacrosanct. Problem was, she hadn't meant it as a professional promise but as a personal one, the more fool she. Nevertheless, she would hold to it. She simply had to avoid Rand in the process—if that was possible.

Rand was waiting for her when she stepped into the cool hallway of the hospital. His dark head bowed, thumbs hooked in his pockets, he had the appearance of a man who had been pacing, but then his head jerked up, and a smile lit his face. Gail's heart turned over, but she did her best to ignore it. He didn't make things easy, though, coming forward with outstretched hands and that warm expression in his grayish blue eyes. He folded her close before she could think of a way to stop him, sighing as he hugged her.

"It's been a long day," he said softly. "Glad you came."

She could only stand there stiffly, fighting the emotions he stirred in her. "Yes, well, you knew I would." She tried to sound professional, but sounded strident even to her own ears.

He loosened his hold enough to frown down at her. "What's wrong?"

"Nothing." She tried to shrug him off, but he locked his hands in the small of her back, an eyebrow lifted skeptically.

"Don't give me that. You avoided the issue last night, but you haven't been the same since Mary Grace caught us together. What did she say to you anyway?"

She dropped her gaze. "Didn't she tell you?"

He gave her a you-know-better-than-that look and said, "I can always ask her again, or I could go to Carel Belle. Despite the differences in their personalities, they almost always confide in each other. I just hate to drive a wedge between them over this. I will if I have to, though—it's that important to me. *You're* that important to me."

"That's just the problem," she said, carefully extricating herself from his hold.

He brought his hands to his waist. "I don't understand. Are you saying the problem is that you've become important to me?"

Gail took a deep breath. "Mary Grace is afraid that I'll become more important to you than she and Carel Belle are."

"Well, that's nonsense," he said, every syllable clipped. "Those girls have been everything to me since I first held them. Nothing and no one could ever replace them in my heart or my life. But one thing doesn't have anything to do with the other. I trust you told her that."

Gail shook her head. "I just told her that I want to be her friend, and that..." She gulped, averting her gaze, and hurried on. "I told her that I wouldn't see you anymore."

"You *what?*"

She heard the disbelief in his voice, but kept her gaze on the floor. "I told her I wouldn't—"

He closed his hands on her upper arms and shook her so that her head flopped back, bringing her gaze to his. "You can't do that!"

Anger blazed. Why was he making this so hard? "You don't have anything to say about it," she told him flatly, only to wince at the wounded look that came over his features.

"The hell I don't! I'm in love with you!"

Her mouth fell open, incredulity rocking her. In love with her? In love with *her?* "You don't mean that. You don't know me well enough to—"

"What do you think that was last night?" he interrupted angrily. "You think that was just sex?"

She lifted her chin, even though it was wobbling. "No, not *just* sex, though primarily."

"You can't believe that!" he said, reaching for her again and hauling her up close. "And I can't believe you're *not* feeling some of what I do! I've been with women who felt nothing for me but desire, and that was *not* what we had last night, not by a long shot."

Gail licked her lips, trying to think beyond his declaration of love to what had to be done. Finally she closed her eyes, as if closing out the sight of him could soften the agony of what she was going to say. "Look, Rand, we're adults, you and I, but Mary Grace and Carel Belle are not. They're at that difficult time of adolescence when they veer back and forth between a kid's emotions and a teenager's confusing needs. We have to put the two of them first."

"Granted," he said, sliding his arms around her, "but, dammit, Gail, we're entitled to some personal happiness, too, aren't we? Aren't we?"

She looked up at him, wanting so much what he offered, but knowing that she couldn't ever really have it. "Not at the expense of someone else, not if it hurts m—your... daughters. I'm sorry, Rand, but I think we'd better not see each other, at least for a while."

He released her abruptly. "I can't believe you're saying this, doing this."

"Eventually you'll see that it's the only way," she told him softly.

"You're making too much of this!"

"I don't think so, and I can't take the chance that I am."

"I'm their *father*. You said as much yourself. Can't you trust me on this? Can't you accept that I know them better than anyone?"

She shook her bowed head, before peeking up at him and whispering, "I'm sorry."

He glared at her for a long moment, a number of emotions flashing across his face—disappointment, longing, anger, determination. "I won't let you do this," he said roughly. "I've waited my whole life to feel this way about somebody. I won't let anyone mess this up, not even you." With that he pushed past her and out the door she had just entered.

She wanted to cry, wanted to grieve, but it wasn't over yet, and she first had to see that it was. But not now. She couldn't do anything else to convince him now. All she could do was tend to business, and that meant tending to another Hartesite, Belle Grace.

She walked listlessly to Belle's room, tapped once on the door and went in. "Good evening, ma'am."

Belle Grace frowned at her from the bed, then determinedly put on a pleasant face. "Come in, Doctor. I assume you've come to tell me who'll be wielding the scalpel and when." She folded her hands across her middle, looking tired and ill. "Can't be soon enough for me," she went on. "This being laid up is wearing."

Gail smiled in understanding. "The doctor is in San Antonio. An ambulance will come for you early tomorrow morning, and the orthopedist will see you later tomorrow afternoon. The day after tomorrow or the next, he'll perform the surgery. Then a physical therapist will help you adjust to the new hip. God willing, you'll be home again within two weeks."

"Sound so simple," Belle murmured, "but I doubt that it is."

"Hardly."

The older woman nodded. "Do me a favor, will you?"

"Just ask."

"Convince Rand to stay here. I won't need him in San Antonio, and he'd only fret."

Gail swallowed a lump in her throat. "I don't think I can do that, Miss Belle. You're going to need support, and if you were my mother, I'd want to be there."

"But the girls," Belle argued. "How will they manage without the two of us? Camelia has her hands full, and she drives like a snail. Bones will be more than busy with Rand gone. He doesn't have time to get the girls to and from school, let alone cheerleading practice and football games."

Gail bit her lip, an idea coming to her. Oh, it was audacious. It might even be foolish. But after that disturbing scene with Rand, it was something to hold on to, a way to further her connection with the girls—and a way to help, too. She tried to keep her voice even and unemotional as she put it to Belle Grace.

"I might be able to help after all, Miss Belle, if you think...well, that is, I have an extra room at my place, and since I'm right there in town, it'd solve everyone's problems. I-I'd enjoy the company so much, and..." She couldn't think of anything else to say. "Well, I'd be glad to have them stay with me while you and Rand are in San Antonio."

She held her breath, waiting for Belle Grace to think over her offer and respond. She had the terrible feeling that Belle

ould see straight into her mind or, at the very least, her
eart, which was beating like a trip-hammer. Belle nar-
owed her eyes shrewdly, making no move and no sound,
ust staring at her as if studying an insect. Finally, she re-
axed, the tension in the muscles of her face, neck and
houlders easing incrementally. She folded her hands and
miled.

"How very generous of you, Doctor. Are you certain they
vouldn't be an intolerable inconvenience, however?"

Gail resisted the impulse to swallow hard. She was being
ested somehow, she knew it, so she kept her voice light as
he replied, "Nothing I couldn't handle, I'm sure."

Belle nodded slowly. "Rand won't mind," she said,
icking at an imaginary piece of lint on her blanket. And
hen she fixed Gail with the most astonishingly bright smile.
'Perhaps it's time you and the girls got to know one an-
ther better."

Her meaning hit Gail like a ton of bricks. Belle knew that
Rand was in love with her, or thought he was, and she was
iving them her tacit approval by agreeing to leave the girls
vith Gail while she and Rand were in San Antonio. And
Jail dared not react with the shock or mingled sadness and
oy that she was feeling. Her face felt as stiff as a board as
he nodded and reached into her pocket for the envelope
ontaining the pertinent papers, but she managed to smile
s she explained in detail the arrangements that she had
nade.

Chapter Ten

Gail put her forehead to Carel Belle's and giggled like a schoolgirl. It was delicious, so delicious, to be making friends with her daughter. She felt certain that Carel Belle was her daughter, but then she felt equally certain that Mary Grace was her daughter, too, despite the fact that Mary Grace glowered at the two of them from her place in old Doc Garlock's worn recliner. She hadn't warmed up at all in the two days since an equally glowering Rand had taken himself off to San Antonio to pace by his mother's bedside. For that was what Belle Grace had informed Gail he was doing—pacing and muttering and occasionally blowing up at one of the nursing staff. Belle Grace had sounded pleased when she'd said it—had practically chortled, in fact—but Gail couldn't see anything funny in Rand's sour mood—just as Mary Grace didn't see anything funny in Gail's spilling hot tea down the front of a white cotton shirt.

"Well, I'd better get this into some cold water," Gail said, sobered by thoughts of Rand.

"Want me to help?" Carel Belle offered engagingly. "I help Camelia with the laundry sometimes."

Gail smiled and cupped the dear child's cheek with her palm. "No, thank you, sweetie. The pizza ought to be about ready to come out of the oven, though. Can you keep an eye on that?"

"Sure."

Was it her imagination, or was that the gleam of hero worship in Carel Belle's hazel eyes? Only, it would be heroine worship in this case, wouldn't it? Gail refused the urge to kiss that sweet face and hurried toward her bedroom, where she stripped off the blouse and the sturdy cotton bra that she wore beneath it. She went into the bathroom and ran the sink full of cold water, then submerged her ruined clothing in it, scrubbing furiously at the stains with a bar of soap. When the spots lightened, she left them to soak and returned to her bedroom to pull on a slinky peach-colored bra and a big, sloppy, airy sweater. As she walked into the living area, she heard the beginning hum of the buzzer on the oven and smiled as Carel Belle jumped up from the couch to answer it.

Mary Grace, who sat with her back to Gail's bedroom door, said acidly, "You make me sick, fawning all over her. Let her old pizza burn! *I* sure don't want any of it!"

Carel Belle only then glanced in Gail's direction, and instantly her face flamed red. Then her gaze dropped guiltily, as if she had been the one to display such patent dislike. Gail stepped out to rescue her, smiling understandingly and nodding in the direction of the open kitchen at the end of the long room. Carel Belle hurried away and shortly the buzzing ceased.

Gail mentally girded herself and walked around Mary's chair to the sofa. "What's the matter, Mary Grace? Don't you like pizza?"

Mary Grace shrugged, but the veneer of bravado that she wore was painfully thin, her discomfort at having been caught venting her spleen just as painfully obvious. "I like

Camelia's cooking,'' she said petulantly. ''I want to go home.''

''Of course you do,'' Gail replied calmly, ''and you will just as soon as Rand returns from San Antonio.''

''Isn't Grandmother coming home with him?'' Mary Grace demanded angrily, punching down the foot of the recliner so that the back propelled her forward and onto the edge of the seat.

That anger, Gail knew, was simply a cover for panic.

''Yes, certainly,'' she soothed, ''and before you know it she'll be up and around, good as new—well, better, actually, since she won't have a bad hip any longer.''

But Mary Grace was not about to be mollified. ''I don't know why she had to go off to San Antonio just to get her hip replaced anyway,'' she grumbled, ''when El Paso's so much closer!''

Gail sighed, nearly at the end of her patience. ''We've been all through that, dear. You know perfectly well why—''

'''Cause you made her!'' Mary Grace bawled, coming to her feet. ''It's all your fault! Everything! I hate you! I hate you!'' She ran from the room, stumbling over the rickety side table flanking the chair.

Gail closed her eyes, despair filling her. When she opened them again, it was to find Carel Belle standing before her, one hand wearing an oven mitt.

''I don't know what's wrong with her,'' Carel Belle said, tears spilling from her eyes. ''She's not normally so awful!'' She collapsed in a heap at Gail's side, sobbing.

Gail felt her own eyes filling, as she reached out to bring the girl at her side into her arms. ''It's all right, honey. understand.''

Carel Belle pushed her hair out of her eyes and looked up hopefully. ''You do?''

''Oh, yes. Indeed I do. She feels threatened, as though her safe little world is about to destruct, and that's terribly frightening, even if your particular world isn't all that wonderful. I know from experience. I went into a panic every time I had to change foster homes, and I covered my panic with anger, just as Mary Grace is doing now."

Carel Belle's gaze grew solemn and thoughtful. "Foster home," she said softly. "Is that where the state puts you when you don't have anyone to take care of you?"

Gail took a deep breath, knowing that she had a decision to make—whether to answer the question dispassionately or reveal her own unhappy and uncertain childhood in detail. She still could not quite fully suppress the childish shame she had always felt over her background, to have been abandoned by those who were most expected to love and care for her, and yet this was her time to get to know her daughters and help them get to know her. She looked at Carel Belle's sweet face and knew she could trust her to understand. She could not be so certain of Mary Grace, but it would be beyond foolish to try to hide her background; she had already told Rand. She took Carel Belle's hand in hers.

"I never knew who my father was. I'm not sure that my mother even knew. She was not... She was not what you might call *respectable,* and when I was still a little girl, she gave me up to the state."

Carel Belle screwed up her face. "I think my grandmother's the most respected woman in the county, and I always figured my mother must've been something like her. I know they say she killed herself, but...that doesn't mean she was bad, does it?"

"No," Gail said, squeezing her hands.

Carel Belle nodded, apparently satisfied. "That's what I thought. I don't know why. Something deep inside me just knows what kind of woman she was."

Gail hugged her close. "I hope you never believe otherwise. You have to know that she wanted you very, very much."

"Didn't your mother want you?" the girl asked softly.

Gail tucked the dark head beneath her chin. "No, I guess she didn't."

"Didn't you have a grandmother?"

"No."

"An uncle or somebody?"

"Nope. No one."

"That's so awful! How did you ever stand it?"

"Well, you just do, that's all. You dream about being somebody and having someone of your own, someone to love you no matter what, and you just hold on to that with everything you are."

"You're somebody," Carel Belle said, pulling back to look up into Gail's face. "You're a doctor, even!"

Gail laughed. "So I am."

"And we do love you," Carel Belle continued. "I do. Uncle Rand does, I know."

"Did he tell you that?"

The girl bit her lip, finally giving her head a reluctant shake. "But he does—I know he does." Then, seeing the expression on Gail's face, she added, "Don't you want him to?"

Gail's eyes instantly teared again. The lie was right on the tip of her tongue, but she was so sick of the lies, deathly sick of the lie she was living. She composed herself. "Yes, I want Rand to love me, but loving someone when you're an adult is pretty complicated."

"But if he loved you and you loved him, you could get married and then you could be, like, our stepmother. Then we'd always be—"

Gail laid a finger across Carel Belle's lips, shushing her. "You mustn't count on that, sweetie. Just know that you and your sister have become very important to me. You must trust me in this, dear, because the thing that would make me happiest—I need you to believe this—is that you and your sister...remain some part of my life. In fact, I think that's all I could really ask of life."

"But—"

"Shhh. Listen, while we're sitting here being silly our pizza is getting cold. Go and see if you can coax Mary Grace to join us, while I slide the pizza back into the oven and throw together a salad, all right?''

Carel Belle nodded reluctantly and got up off the couch. ''I still say that he—''

''Please!'' Gail laughed, her hand over her heart. ''I'm starving!''

Carel Belle huffed, but she said nothing more. Instead, she stood looking down at Gail for a moment. Then she bent and kissed her gently on the cheek, before turning and marching out of the room, her dark hair swinging about her shoulders. Gail leaned forward, her elbows on her knees, and covered her mouth with both hands. Dear God, what was going to happen to them all?

Rand hung up the phone and scowled in frustration, his fingertips sliding into the front pockets of his jeans.

Belle Grace chuckled from her hospital bed. ''What is it now?''

''She won't even talk to me on the phone! I thought leaving the girls with her would show her that they'd get along, that she's being silly about this thing, but no matter what I do, she won't even talk to me! Damn that stubborn woman!''

Belle waved a hand dismissively. ''She's an independent woman, Rand. You've known that from the beginning. From what you tell me of her background, she's used to being alone. Give her some time. Just don't rush her so much.''

''It's got nothing to do with me rushing her! She's convinced we're hurting Mary Grace somehow. I've tried to tell her that Mary's just high-strung and used to getting her own way, but she won't listen.''

''Yes, and if I know Mary Grace, she's not doing a thing to change Gail's mind.''

''You'd think she'd lighten up just for my sake,'' Rand grumbled. ''She knows how I feel about Gail.''

"Maybe, maybe not," Belle said thoughtfully. "Have you told her?"

Rand shrugged uncomfortably. "Well, not flat out, but... Hell, she caught us in the hall the other night! She's not stupid."

A grin split Belle Grace's face. She wrestled it, coughed and finally gave in to a hearty laugh. "Oh, I never thought I'd see it," she said at last. "You moonin' over a female!"

Rand colored from his neck up. "Aw, Mother, you know darned well that I've ... well, that I've ..."

Belle sobered, her gaze falling to her hands. "I never expected you to live like a monk, Rand. You're not that sort of man. But you're not the sort your brother was, either, thank God. You're a man of honor and deep feeling that is only now beginning to be tapped. You're like your father," she said softly, closing her eyes, "so like your father. You'll love once and only once." She opened her eyes and impaled him with that sharp look of hers, the one that brooked no argument. "You simply cannot let her get away. You'll regret it all your life if you do. It's time someone had a blunt talk with Miss Mary."

Rand sighed and nodded. "I'll give her a call tomorrow. Not that I think she's likely to listen to me."

"I agree," Belle said, "so I'll call her myself."

Rand was shocked and very deeply touched. "Mother. You'd do that for me?"

Belle was not pleased, and it showed in the tightening of her mouth and the stony paleness of her eyes. "You think I want to see you unhappy?"

"No, of course not, but—"

"But I let you marry Lynette," she said brutally, "knowing that you didn't love her, that she didn't love you."

"There were plenty of reasons for me to marry Lynette!" he snapped.

"To please me," Belle insisted flatly, "to make up for what your brother had done, to give her a home. Yes, I gave myself all those reasons and more at the time, but the most important reason, the only legitimate reason, was lacking, and I knew it. I knew it, and I let you do it, anyway. I have a lot to make up for. I think it's time I started."

"Mother, the decision to marry Lynette was mine. I married her because I felt sorry for her and because I felt attracted to her and I thought that would lead to love. It was my own mistake."

In a gesture quite foreign to her, Belle Grace reached out her hand for his. "Don't let that stop you, Rand. Don't let the fear of another mistake stop you from going after love. I won't, and if I did, I wouldn't be worth a bucket of mud as a mother or a person."

Rand started to laugh, gently, poignantly, Belle's hand clasped in his. "Mother," he said, "I haven't told you very often how much I love and admire you."

"Oh, pish!" She jerked away, huffing quite unconvincingly. "If you're going to get maudlin, you can just go. But pass me the phone first. I have a call to make, and then I'm going straight to sleep. They want me walking down the hall tomorrow, can you believe that? A new hip only yesterday, and I'm expected to sprint up and down the hall. They don't know their business here the way Gail knows hers, I can tell you. Next they'll have me running a marathon!"

Rand dropped the phone onto the bed beside her, chuckling silently. Then he bent and kissed her hard and quick right on the mouth. She scowled her most intimidating scowl, her lips drawn into a tight, puckered pout. He didn't mention it, but he saw the tears standing in her eyes when he turned to go, saw them and understood them and let them comfort him as he headed for a lonely bed in an impersonal motel room.

But it wouldn't always be this way. It couldn't be, because he very much feared that his mother was right. He was the sort of man to love once and only once.

* * *

Gail sighed, stretched and smiled, her hands falling on the shoulders of the two girls. "You were an enormous help this afternoon. Thank you both."

Carel Belle laughed and clapped her hands. "I had fun!"

Gail leaned forward, smiling into her eyes. "You know, so did I. It's nice to work together, isn't it?" She swung her gaze to Mary Grace, doing her best to share the praise. "It was so wonderful not to have to answer the telephone! And you know, Mr. Cole told me I have the best-looking two receptionists around."

"Big deal," Mary Grace grumbled. "Are there any others?"

Gail had to think. "Well, maybe at the old hotel or the courthouse. I don't know about that real-estate office just outside town."

"How about the bank?" Carel Belle asked.

Gail just stared at her, then quickly looked at Mary Grace. For an instant, their eyes held, and Gail saw nothing but the animosity Mary Grace had radiated since the night of Belle's birthday party. Then something changed. Something moved behind those eyes, and suddenly a glint of amusement entered them. Gail was astonished to find that she could read the girl's thoughts. For a heartbeat, she held her breath, but then she and Mary Grace said together, "Nah!"

Everyone laughed. Gail ushered the girls down the hall to the apartment door. Her heart was light and her spirits high. That had been the first pleasant moment that she and Mary Grace had shared, the first unguarded response, the first moment of any intimacy.

They pushed the door open and squeezed through three abreast, giggling and squirming and scraping their thighs on the doorframe. They stumbled into the short hallway. Carel Belle remarked that she needed to wash a few a things.

"We'll do a load later," Gail said. "How about we eat out tonight? I have to make a run into Alpine to the hospital. We can do our laundry there, then try this little steak place where Rand and I—'' She broke off abruptly, feeling Mary Grace stiffen beneath her arm, but the girl relaxed and a sheepish smile curled her lips.

"I know just the place you're talking about," she said, "but if it's all the same to you, I'd rather have fried chicken."

"Or a sub," Carel Belle added. "There's a sub shop across from the college."

Mary Grace didn't seem opposed to the suggestion, but Gail didn't want to take any chances. "You two decide," she said brightly. "Makes no difference to me."

They stepped into the end of the kitchen next to the dining table and turned toward the living room, stopping in their tracks. Rand was sitting in the recliner, his hat resting on his knee. He rocketed up, hat in hand, his gaze moving uncertainly over each of them. Then the girls were running toward him, squealing like freed pigs. He caught each one in a long arm, folded them in and pecked kisses on foreheads, chins and cheeks.

"Oh, I've missed you!"

"How's Grandmother?"

"On the mend! Sends her love."

"We worked in the office today."

"Team lost Friday night."

"Worked in the office, you say?" He came up out from under hugs and kisses to look longingly at Gail. The girls at once traded gazes and disappeared, mumbling about hair and bathrooms and objects forgotten. Carel Belle was the first out of the room. Mary seemed to stall, her eyes going from one to the other of them repeatedly, and then she put her head down and hurried out.

Gail watched them go with both chagrin and gratitude. She could not help thinking that her time with them was almost gone, or how wonderful Rand looked standing there turning his hat in his big hands. She managed a smile. He swallowed. They both started talking at once.

"How is Belle?"

"I hope you don't mind—"

A stilted laugh. A hand lifted in gracious invitation. He took a deep breath and began again. "I hope you don't mind me letting myself in. The door was open, and I figured it'd be better meeting you here than in a busy office."

She nodded. "Business has picked up considerably. I don't know how I'd have managed without the girls." But of course she would have to. Somehow. At least for a time. That thought made her feel better, so that she lifted her chin and relaxed a bit. "How is Belle?"

"Fine. Really, she's doing well. The worst day was the day after the surgery, and you were right. She needed somebody there. These past couple of days, though, I've been pretty much cooling my heels and drinking bad coffee. Guess I got on her nerves. She sent me home for a few days. I'll be going back early next week, after I take care of a few things at the ranch. Shouldn't be too long after that before I can bring her home, and damned if the doctor there doesn't say she'll be walking good as ever. 'Course, she won't have much strength, and she will be needing therapy." He looked down, licked his lips, then went on. "What I was thinking was that maybe you could go with me to get her, and the therapist there could show you what needed to be done. That is, if you're still willing—"

"Oh, certainly," she interrupted, and then remembered that she'd pretty much decided to beg off. Ah, well. Too late for that now. Still... "I, um, don't know about going with you... My practice is pretty solid these days. It would be hard to be away, but I will call the therapist and have her give me explicit instructions. I, um, do have some expertise in the area. It should only be a matter of knowing which exercises to employ."

His disappointment was palpable, so much so that she wished she could put her arms around him. She stood there awkwardly with him, the silence drawing out, and then Mary Grace skipped into the room, pulling on a sweater, her hair combed smooth. Her gaze skittered around the room

nd came to rest briefly on Gail before switching to Rand.
he smiled brightly and completely confounded Gail by
aying, "We're going into Alpine for dinner. Wanna
ome?"

Rand's head came up so quickly that Gail wondered that
he bones didn't snap. He looked at Mary Grace, then he
ooked at Gail. She jumped into the breach immediately.
'You're probably exhausted after that long drive back from
an Antonio."

"No, I'm fine," he insisted.

"Uh, we were thinking carryout or e-even subs."

"Definitely no steak," Mary Grace said with a wave of
er hand.

"No problem," he said. "Can't be worse than what I've
een eating."

Carel Belle slipped into the room then, eyes only for her
ister. Mary nodded once, and Carel brightened instantly.
'Great!" she said. "Everybody ready?"

Gail could only blink and tamp down her misgivings,
ware that she had been neatly maneuvered into a corner—
y Mary Grace, no less!

"Don't you need to get your purse or something?" Rand
sked innocently.

"Oh. Uh, just let me get my wallet and...comb my hair."

He nodded and folded himself back into the recliner, de-
ositing his hat on his knee once more. "Take your time."

Gail moved swiftly to her bedroom. Once there, she
ipped off her lab coat and T-shirt and yanked on a pale-
ink silk shirt. Kicking off her shoes, she wiggled out of her
oft, worn jeans and into crisp new ones with straight legs.
Quickly she threaded a narrow black belt through the tight
oops at her waist and buckled it, then sat down on the side
f the bed to pull on the new black, round-toed boots the
irls had helped her pick out. Next she ripped the rubber
and out of her hair and dragged a brush through it three or
our times, tossed it back out of her way and clipped on
mall silver earrings shaped like closed eights. She shrugged

into her jacket, dropped her wallet into the pocket, took a deep breath and walked calmly into the living room.

The girls were sitting on the couch. Carel Belle threw an elbow in Mary Grace's direction, and both came to their feet. Cued to her presence, Rand stood, too, and casually turned. His eyes went wide, and a grin split his face.

"Well, look at you! All you need now is a hat."

Gail managed a chuckle despite the hammering of her heart. "I don't think I'm quite ready for the hat. I'm still getting used to these tight jeans. I like the boots, though. The man who fit them to me said I had the right kind of feet for them, whatever that means."

"Should've known you'd be a natural," Rand said softly. "You look good, hon, real good. But you always do."

Gail could not derail the thrill that coursed through her. She mumbled a thanks and turned her attention to the girls. "Well, are we ready?"

"Do we have to go in your car?" Mary Grace asked, her face screwed up.

"Oh. Well, I guess it would be a tight fit."

"Like those jeans," Rand muttered, adding in a louder voice, "we'll take the truck."

Gail nodded and led the way, aware of a happiness she hadn't felt before, the sheer joy of being with those she loved most—all three of them. If she had doubted her feelings for him before, she had only needed Rand's sudden reappearance to let her know that she did love him. No matter how foolish it was, she loved the brother of the man she had borne a daughter, possibly, very likely, two. She couldn't help being happy to see him, and if—when—the time came that she could not, well, she'd survive. She always managed to somehow.

The drive was cheerful and quick, everybody talking at once and laughing. Rand entertained them with stories of Belle Grace and the San Antonio hospital. The surgeon, he declared, knew his stuff, but he wore the most atrocious hairpiece imaginable. "An Elvis wig," he said, "that looked like he'd dusted the furniture with it. The day of surgery, he met Mother in the hall just outside the operating room, and she told him to tack a hundred bucks onto the bill and buy himself a good hat."

Gail gasped. "She didn't!"

"She did."

The girls howled and started telling Belle stories. "Remember when Margaret Tillmon went over into Mexico and got that awful face-lift? Everybody was talking about it for weeks, but Grandmother never said a word. Then she saw Margaret in the grocery store, and stupid old Margaret had the nerve to ask Grandmother what she thought about it."

"Oh, no," Gail moaned.

Mary Grace grinned. "Grandmother asked her what corpse they'd gotten that face off of."

"Oh, no!"

"Oh, that's nothing," Mary Grace said. She turned to her sister. "Remember the time Bonnie went into El Paso and got her hair permed?"

Carel Belle screwed up her face. "Ugh! It looked like steel wool!"

"Bonnie's mother kept telling everybody how much it cost, bragging like," Mary Grace continued. "Well, she told Grandmother." She passed a look to her sister, who finished the tale.

"Grandmother, cool as anything, sticks her nose in the air and says, 'She could've got the same thing free by sticking her finger in a light socket.'"

"Bonnie didn't get any more perms," said Mary Grace flatly.

Gail's mouth was hanging open. "Poor little girl!"

Carel Belle hung her chin on the back of the front seat. "Bonnie's always bragging about how much her stuff cost."

"And she's always got to be the first one to get anything new," Mary Grace said.

"There's a little competition here," Rand explained. "When the school decided the girls ought to skip fifth grade—and they were the ones who came to me with it, mind—well, Bonnie's mother went and *demanded* Bonnie be bumped up.''

''She failed,'' Mary Grace said succinctly.

''Had to repeat sixth grade all over again,'' Carel Belle confirmed.

Mary Grace had the last word on the matter. ''Put her right back where she started,'' she said, folding her arms neatly.

Rand just shook his head, and Gail mirrored him. He winked and grinned, as though they were two indulgent parents listening to the adolescent chatter of their children. The idea had been hovering in the back of her mind ever since he'd said that he loved her, but that moment was the first time she'd allowed herself to think it: They could be two indulgent parents listening to their children. Now that Mary Grace was coming around, all she had to do was keep her mouth shut and let nature take its course. She didn't doubt that Rand would get around to asking her to marry him if she just gave him the encouragement he was seeking. He never had to know that she had a prior connection to ''his'' girls. No one ever had to know. Except that she already did, and she wasn't at all sure that she could live with that secret. Oh, but it was tempting! To have them all, the girls and Rand, too.

She wondered if he could see the temptation in her eyes, because he reached over just then and covered her hand with his where it lay against her thigh. Her hand turned palm up of its own accord and her fingers interlaced with his. For a moment, the connection vibrated soul deep. She closed her eyes, overwhelmed with the richness and complexity of it. Like the emotional equivalent of sex, it was supremely intimate, utterly enthralling, electric, and the most ultimately satisfying experience she could imagine. Then Mary Grace sat forward again, chattering blithely about the play day planned for a Saturday three weeks hence.

She wanted to know if Rand thought she should ride Buttermilk, her mare, in the barrel race, or if the gelding might be ready, and suddenly Carel Belle was talking about some boys at school who were team roping and how they'd beaten the best time at national finals. Gail sat silently, clasping hands with Rand, and listened to the conversation buzzing around her, but the only words she could really identify were those that were running through her mind.

Mine. Mine. They could all be mine.

Oh, dear God, help me.

Chapter Eleven

When the phone rang at the reception desk, Gail almost apologized to the patient whose leg she was examining and excused herself to answer. Then she remembered that she no longer had to answer her business phone herself all the time. The girls were always eager to help out during the late afternoon, and Gail was grateful for the respite. Having them there had shown her how overworked she was when she handled the office alone. More than that, however, it showed her how very much she had missed over the years that she had lived alone.

They had passed a pleasant three days since Rand had returned to San Antonio, but she would be lying to herself if she said that she hadn't missed him. Still, she was thrilled with the way things were going between her and the girls, particularly Mary Grace. The animosity that Mary had exhibited previously seemed to have vanished, and Gail could only assume that it had something to do with a telephone conversation the girl had had with her grandmother almost a week earlier. Gail wondered what Belle had said to Mary, and what she might have said, instead, if she had known that Gail was the girl's mother come to reclaim her.

The door opened and Carel Belle stuck her head through. "Could you come to the phone?" Her smile was clearly audible in her voice. "Call's from San Antonio."

Rand. Gail kept on doing what she was doing, determinedly tamping down her eagerness. "In a minute. I have to finish here."

"Okay." The door closed.

Gail took her time, cleaning and treating the spider bite, then instructing her patient about at-home care. Only after he had repeated her instructions back to her did she excuse herself.

She stepped out into the hall. Through the opening in the partition, she could see two patients in the waiting room, reason enough to tell Rand to call back later, but she didn't. Instead, she walked into the office, punched the blinking button and picked up the phone. "Hello."

"Hi."

That single syllable held a wealth of emotion. Gail pulled a deep, silent breath, steeling herself against the tenderness and longing he evoked in her. "How's your mother?"

"Homesick."

"I can imagine."

"No more than me, though," he said softly. "I miss you and the girls."

She had to bite her tongue to keep from telling him how much she missed him, too. Instead, she asked how Belle's therapy was going.

"Pretty good, I reckon. Mother's worried about how weak she is, but the therapist says it's to be expected, given her age and all."

"I'd say so, yes."

"Well, don't say so to Mother," he said, chuckling. "She about took that therapist's head off for 'as good as calling her old,' according to her."

Gail laughed. "Sounds like she's on her way to a full recovery."

"Hope so." He paused a moment. "I'm on my way somewhere, too."

"Oh?" She heard the note of intimacy in his voice and felt her heart start to pound with unusual force. "Where's that?"

"Fort Davis."

"Ah." Fort Davis lay some twenty-one miles to the north of Marfa in the Davis Mountains. She'd been told that the tiny town enjoyed the finest climate in Texas. She knew she shouldn't ask, but she had to. "What's in Fort Davis?"

"Best restaurant in the whole area."

She drew her brows together. "You're going to Fort Davis for something to eat?"

"Yep."

She gritted her teeth, truly wanting not to ask, but unable to help herself. "When?"

"Saturday."

Saturday. She tried to keep the hurt out of her voice, but knew she'd failed. "I thought you were coming home Saturday."

"I am."

When he chuckled, she got suspicious, and her eyes narrowed. "Before or after Fort Davis?"

"Before, of course. Why would I want to go to Fort Davis to dinner without you?"

It was absurd how relieved and pleased she was. "I wouldn't know," she said tartly, but she was smiling.

He was quiet a moment before he said, his voice a silky whisper, "You will go to dinner with me on Saturday, won't you?"

It didn't matter that she shouldn't. She couldn't have refused him if her life had depended on it. She cradled the phone with her hands as if cradling his face. "What should I wear?"

"That's up to you."

"You said it was a nice place."

"It is. It's part of a lovely old hotel there, a real show-place in its time."

"Guess I should wear a dress, then," she said, deciding that it would be something very special.

"In that case, I guess I'll have to slick up," he replied.

She lifted her eyebrows. "Oh? Does that mean you'll actually be giving up your jeans?"

He laughed. "Hell, no. It means I'll have to find a dark pair and starch 'em."

"*Starch* them?"

"Sure, it's what all the best-dressed cowboys wear."

"And you'll starch them yourself?"

He laughed again. "They wouldn't be fit to wear if I did. Nope, I'll have to leave that to Camelia. She puts a knife-edge crease on 'em that'd cut glass."

"Sounds dangerous to me," Gail quipped.

"Oh, I'm a dangerous man," he teased. "Haven't you learned that yet?"

"Yes." She didn't say anything else. She didn't have to. The silence this time was thoughtful. When he finally came back, his voice was soft, with just a touch of bitterness in it.

"It wasn't just Mary Grace, was it?"

"Wh-what do you mean?"

"Whatever stands between us, it's a lot more than Mary Grace not wanting to share me. It's him, isn't it?"

She sat up straight, her heart plummeting. "W-who?"

"Whoever broke your heart.

She closed her eyes, feeling a burn in her chest. "I-I don't know what you mean."

"The hell you don't. Who was he, Gail?"

"This is absurd," she said, trying to make light of it and failing miserably.

"Whoever he was, he really did a job of it, didn't he? But that wasn't me, Gail. I don't know why you have to hang me for his crime."

Her throat constricted as if she could feel the rope tightening around her neck. "It's not that, Rand. I swear it isn't. I-I'm just a careful person. I don't want to make a-another mistake. You can understand that, can't you?"

"Maybe," he said. "Maybe I could if you'd tell me about it."

Panic made her speak more quickly and forcefully than she should have. "W-what's to tell?"

"How you met, who he was, what happened, why you broke up."

"Rand, it happened so long ago..."

"Did you tell your ex-husband about it?"

"No."

"So he didn't even know what he was fighting," Rand said angrily.

"It wasn't like that!" she exclaimed, desperate to make him understand. "I've told you about my marriage. We were friends. We made a mistake thinking we could be more. Once the novelty of living together wore off, he began to resent sharing so much of his time with me, and vice versa. That was enough to destroy the relationship because there simply wasn't anything to hold it together. I never loved my ex-husband the way I love—" She swallowed the next word, appalled that she'd almost told him what he shouldn't know, but what he assumed was even worse.

"Who, Gail?" he demanded. "You never loved your ex-husband the way you loved *him*, the man who broke your heart, the one who ruined you for every other man?"

"No!"

"Then who, dammit?"

"You!" she screamed, and then, realizing what she'd done, she slammed the phone down. Not that it would help. Oh, God, not that anything would help! What had she done? She folded her arms against the desktop and laid her head on them, waiting for the tears. Only she didn't really feel like crying. She felt...glad...free...right. When the phone jingled, she grabbed it up before it could finish the first ring. "Rand?"

"You hang up again and I'll be knocking on your door by midnight," he promised flatly.

She smiled. "You can't get here by midnight. It's too far."

"Don't you remember? My truck can fly, sugar." His voice dropped to a husky whisper. "I think I could fly all by myself right now."

She squeezed her eyes shut, deeply moved, and *then* the tears started. "Oh, Rand," she murmured.

"Just trust me not to hurt you, honey. Can you do that?"

"Rand," she said, "you don't understand. You're the one I don't want to see hurt."

"Gail, sweetheart, you couldn't possibly—"

"Yes, I could! Just because I don't want it to happen doesn't mean that it won't!"

He made an exasperated sound, then said, "Okay. I've been duly warned, but that doesn't change anything for me."

"It should!"

"Well, it doesn't. I'm in love for the first time in my life, and I wouldn't change that even if I could."

Despite everything, despite the catastrophe she could see coming, that was the most welcome thing she'd ever heard, and she couldn't let it go without response. "Me, too," she squeaked.

"All right, then," he said, his voice gone all soft again. "I'll see you Saturday."

"Saturday," she confirmed, because it wouldn't do any good to tell him no now and because she wanted to be with him so very much.

"I wish it could be sooner," he said, "but it can't, *and* I'd better let you get back to work."

Work! "Oh, my gosh, I forgot! I've got patients waiting!"

He laughed at that, a rich, deep, rolling sound that warmed her all the way through.

"Just tell them it's my fault."

"I will not!"

He laughed again. "Better not keep them waiting any longer, then."

"No, better not," she agreed. Yet she didn't hang up.

"I'll see you soon," he promised, "just not soon enough." He broke the connection then, without saying goodbye.

She held the telephone receiver to her ear a few seconds longer, before laying it gently on its cradle.

He wrapped an arm around each of the girls, getting and giving hugs and kisses. "Oh, I've missed y'all!" he said. "I've missed my girls!" All the while, Mary Grace and Carel Belle were rattling on about a dozen things apiece, bouncing up and down and giggling.

After two or three minutes of effusive greeting, he gave each one a last squeeze and stepped free of them, advancing purposefully on Gail. Her hands wringing nervously, she watched him come, of two minds, as usual, but of one heart. She expected a peck and a cheeky grin in front of the girls. Instead, he took her in his arms and did it properly, making such a thorough job of it that her cheeks were flaming by the time he released her. The girls were looking around the room, pretending not to be watching. Carel Belle was trying not to smile, but Mary Grace was utterly expressionless. Gail flashed a look at Rand, wondering if they should worry about Mary's reaction or lack of one. He just winked and clapped his hands together.

"Well, we'd better be moving, girls. Your grandmother is anxious to see you, and by this time I figure she's needing rescue. Camelia was clucking over her like a mother hen when I left the house."

They were already running to the truck with their bundles and bags. They'd accumulated quite a bit of clothing and such during the previous two weeks. Gail had made more than one trip to the ranch to retrieve various articles, the desperate need of which had not been anticipated on the trip before. Now the girls were hauling them out to the truck with an eagerness that couldn't be denied. Gail bit her lip, wondering if they were so anxious to put her behind them or merely concerned for their grandmother. Rand took advantage of their activity to steal another kiss, then pulled her down onto the couch next to him, his arm draped about her shoulders.

"They give you a hard time?" he asked.

"Oh, no. Not at all. They were angels, both of them."

"Both?" He raised an eyebrow skeptically.

She felt oddly defensive. "Honestly. In fact, they were such good company, I'm going to miss having them around, especially at the clinic. They were a great help."

"They can be pretty good company," he admitted. "So you're going to miss them, huh?"

"Very much."

"Good." He clapped her on the knee and grinned.

Good? She might have pursued an explanation for that comment, but he abruptly changed the subject.

"Man, I'm glad to be back!" he exclaimed. Then he settled his arms around her and pulled her close to his side, his long legs crossed. "I'm looking forward to this evening," he said, nuzzling her ear. "Camelia's already pressing my new jeans."

Gail had to swallow away a tremor in her throat. Did he know how he affected her? He had to. She thought of the girls running back and forth with their stuff and tried to defuse the situation with humor. "*New* jeans," she quipped. "Goodness, I didn't know we were going black tie."

He laughed. "Hey, nothing is too good for my darlin'."

Mary Grace appeared in the doorway then, impatience stamped on her face. "You coming?"

He uncrossed his legs, releasing Gail smoothly, and stretched both arms along the back of the couch. "Haven't you and your sister forgotten something?" he asked pointedly.

Mary Grace glanced at Gail, turned around in the doorway and motioned her sister to her. Meanwhile, Rand got to his feet, and Gail stood with him. He stepped back, and Carel Belle came forward to wrap her arms around Gail and kiss her cheek.

"Thanks," she whispered. "I had a good time."

It was all Gail could do not to clasp the girl to her and weep, but she managed to keep the goodbye to one good squeeze and a kiss on the cheek. "I'm so glad you stayed with me. You were such a help."

Carel Belle smiled and stepped back. Mary Grace came forward then and wrapped Gail in a rather tepid embrace. "Thanks for letting us stay," she said blandly. "I'm glad we could help you."

Gail wanted to shake her and demand that she show her some of the warmth and openness they'd shared the past week. Instead she hugged Mary Grace and tenderly kissed her cheek, saying, "Come again anytime, sweetie, anytime at all."

"'Kay." Mary Grace danced back out of her grasp, smiling and giving her a little wave. "'Bye."

"'Bye," Carel Belle echoed.

Gail followed them to the door, feeling abandoned and lonely. "Goodbye." She watched them get into the car, then turned around and found herself once more in Rand's arms.

He held her against him, leaning back to smile. "I'll see you about six."

She could only nod, wanting desperately to hold all three of them with her. Then he stepped away and was gone. It was just past noon, and six seemed very far away. Had it been only a little more than two weeks since she'd last had empty hours to fill? It seemed like a lifetime ago, and yet the loneliness was all too vivid.

She puttered around the house for a while, dusting and polishing and straightening. About two she made herself a cup of hot tea and sat down with a medical journal. An hour later she gave it up and ran herself a bubble bath. Her hair piled loosely atop her head, she soaked for a long time, then began a languid but thorough preparation for her evening out.

When he knocked at her door, fifteen minutes early, she was ready and waiting. She felt her skirts swish against her legs as she walked across the floor, an utterly feminine sensation. Rand took one look through the opened door, pushed his hat back and took another, his gaze moving over her with swift, hot approval. Gail smoothed the black knit, long-sleeved, closely fit body of her dress all the way to the dropped waist, then fluffed the soft, billowing layers of cranberry red chiffon that overlaid the short skirt. She'd worn the thing only once before, to a charity function, and had been conspicuously uncomfortable in it, but somehow it felt just right tonight, especially when Rand eyed her like that.

"Lord help me," he said, staring at her legs.

She was wearing black silk stockings and black satin high heels. Together, they made her legs look and feel yards long.

She had used more makeup than usual, mascara and red lip gloss. Her hair was a sleek fall of gold combed from a side part and tucked behind one ear, exposing a cluster of shiny black beads clipped to the delicate lobe. In addition to the earrings, she had on a narrow, black enamel bangle bracelet etched with silver. The overall effect, she felt, was one of elegant simplicity, and it seemed to have the desired result. He was still staring.

"This is not fair," he said. "How am I supposed to play the gentleman with you looking like that?"

"Well, you're looking pretty good there yourself," she returned, indicating his black Western-style suit. "What happened to the jeans?"

He grinned and resettled his black felt hat. "Oh, I thought the occasion called for something a little spiffier than starched denim." That included a white shirt with thin black stripes and a string tie, black boots polished to a hard shine and a narrow black belt with a small, rectangular silver-and-gold buckle. Very polished. Very handsome.

She picked up her little black bag from the coffee table and put her hand in his. He drew her out into the soft evening light and helped her into his mother's late-model luxury sedan.

The drive was fascinating. They went rather quickly from the broad plain of the desert floor to a setting that was almost alpine. Cactus mingled with evergreens on the lower slopes, as incongruous a sight as she had ever seen, but dwindled as they moved higher. The mountaintops of the Davis range were not craggy and sharp like those of the desert ranges. They were instead smoothly rounded, thickly grassed and peppered heavily with spruce and cedars, most not much taller than a man, and other trees that she could not identify. Black cattle wandered the slopes and along fence lines, so fat and glossy that they resembled large, plush toys. Moreover, the air had such a sweet, fresh smell to it that Gail felt compelled to lower the window and inhale deeply, her head falling back upon the seat.

"That's the cleanest smell," she remarked idly.

"Should be," Rand said. "It's the cleanest air. That's why they built the McDonald Observatory over on Mount Locke to the northeast there."

"I remember reading about that."

"We'll go over there one of these days, if you want. They let the public in during the daytime."

"All right."

It occurred to her that she was making plans with a man with whom she had no real future, but she didn't want to think about that. She just wanted to enjoy the drive.

All too soon, however, they were slowing as they pulled into Fort Davis. "That's the courthouse," Rand said, pointing to a dollhouse of a building with a silver dome. "Fort Davis is the seat of Jeff Davis County. 'Course, there's only one other town in the county, and that's Valentine, over to the northwest. It's not much more than a wide space in the road, really, but you can send your mail over there in February and get a Valentine postmark. I do it for the girls every year."

"That's sweet."

"I'm a sweet guy, in case you haven't noticed."

She just smiled. As if she could have missed that about him. They drove slowly through the picturesque little town. The two or three informal blocks of the main thoroughfare were stocked with touristy shops and restaurants and the wonderful old hotel that, altogether, seemed to take up half a city block. Rand showed her where the Butterfield Overland Mail Route had run and pointed out the old adobe station a bit farther up the slope. They then drove on to the far edge of town and turned in at the Fort Davis National Historic Site. The gate was closed, so they couldn't go down to the visitors' center, but they sat in the car and looked through the gently waning light at the neat white buildings laid out in exact patterns at the base of a rocky cliff.

"I thought it would be walled in," she said.

"Nah. The mountains to their backs was sufficient." He went on to explain that stockade walls wouldn't have kept out a determined Apache or Comanche anyway. "The plains Indians were brilliant strategists," he said, "fearless fighters. The same could also be said for the Buffalo Soldiers stationed at the frontier fort."

She had heard the term "Buffalo Soldier" before but wasn't sure what it meant.

"They were black, mostly Union veterans of the Civil War," Rand told her. "Seasoned soldiers, for the most part. Some say they got the name because their hair reminded the Indians of buffalo hide, but more likely it was a term of respect. The soldiers at Davis were considered enemies deserving of respect for their tenaciousness and skill. Some other day we'll come up and take the tour. It's mighty interesting."

Some other day. More plans. She tried not to wonder if they'd ever see those future days.

He headed them back toward the tiny "downtown" area, where they parked in front of a closed real-estate office. Rand held her hand as they walked across the dusty street to the hotel restaurant, which was attached to the hotel via a small bookstore and a gift shop. The evening was cool, but pleasant and clear. The town was quiet to the point of silence, and deeply peaceful.

He slid his arm around her as he ushered her through the rustic plank door. They were seated immediately at a table with crisp linens and given menus that offered a surprisingly sophisticated list of entrées. The friendly waitress made recommendations at Rand's request, and they finally made their selections.

Each and every dish had been prepared to perfection. Every bite deserved savoring. Gail and Rand traded tastes and smacked their lips comically over the many complementary flavors. After the entrées, Rand could not resist a thick slice of chocolate pie, half of which he fed to Gail with the same fork he used to eat his portion.

They lingered over the meal, sipping steaming cups of rich coffee after the dessert. Occasionally, someone Rand knew would stroll by. He was friendly, but politely refused to let himself be engaged in conversation, his hand curled over Gail's possessively. She felt warm and well fed and cherished.

When good manners made it impossible to put off vacating the table any longer, they rose to pay the bill. Afterward, they wandered through the bookshop. Gail noted that all the titles had to do with the West or cowboys or Texas in general. Rand told her that they could look around as much as they wanted, even go into any open rooms inside the hotel, saying that the proprietors maintained a generous open-door policy. They meandered down a hall lined with cookware, passed a potting shed and appreciated a room full of exotic glassware, most of it imported from Mexico or produced by local craftsmen.

They retraced their steps to the potting shed and let themselves out through a screen door into an informal courtyard. The air was heavy with the perfume of roses and pine. Arm in arm, they strolled lazily beneath the shade trees and past a short bench, gazing upward at a rich, navy blue sky. They entered the hotel through a back door with a welcome sign over it, then passed a small office and an old-fashioned soda-and-coffee bar, the floorboards creaking companionably. They stepped into the lobby. It was decorated with luxurious hand-dyed carpets, comfortable old-fashioned furniture, Victorian-style wall coverings and softly hued paintings in elaborate frames.

The reception desk was caged into a corner by the door beyond the exquisitely turned staircase. The woman at the desk nodded, smiled and went back to her reading. Rand trustingly left his hat on the arm of a brass-and-ivory antique coat tree before guiding Gail into a cozy front parlor with a stately piano and a crackling fireplace as its focal points. A man and a woman occupied matching chairs at one end of a plush sofa, he with a newspaper held before his face, she bent over a paperback novel. Neither looked up as Rand and Gail moved out onto the enclosed veranda, where a foursome of guests played a board game at one wicker table and others rocked quietly in the serene night. Rand and Gail returned smiles and said nothing before walking back through the small parlor to the lobby and up the elegant sweep of stairs.

Only two doors stood open on the long upstairs hallway. They walked quietly toward the first and peeked in. They were treated to a garden display of florals from the wine red carpet to the ceiling moldings. A large bed with a brass bedstead ornamented with perfect copper roses stood in the center of one wall, its theme echoed in the spread and in the curtains that graced the tall, broad window, even in the small bath, where the wood sink was carved with roses and rose soaps rested in a decoupage dish of bouquets of flowers. Even the walls were painted a rich rose pink and trimmed with leaf green. It was a charming room with an old-fashioned feel, but what awaited them down the hall was a breathtaking step back into the past.

Cherrywood gleamed in the forms of an elegant sleigh bed set into a curtained niche in the wall, a small gateleg table and a tall armoire. The soft, buttery yellows and rich, glowing golds of the walls and lush, figured carpet seemed to reach out to them. Amber teardrops dangled from a pair of painted glass lamps. A brass fan stood before a flickering fireplace of cream painted brick. Needlepoint cushions adorned a pair of lyre-back chairs that flanked an ornate dry sink with fold-out mirrors and a lovely antique pitcher-and-bowl set. Everything about the room created the aura of a previous century, a time of elegance and romance and adventure. Gail could almost hear the rattle of harness and wheel as horse-drawn buggies passed in the street below.

"How lovely," Gail said with a sigh, walking to the center of the room.

"Incredible," Rand agreed, moving to stand behind her. She had the feeling he wasn't talking about the decor.

"I'd love to have that bed."

He slid his arms around her waist and pulled her back against him. "I'd love to have you in that bed," he whispered, "or any bed."

She closed her eyes, feeling slightly disoriented and set apart from the world outside. He bent his head, bathing the skin of her neck with his hot breath. She lifted a hand to cup his strong jaw and felt the nip of his teeth in her palm before he turned to taste the curve of her throat. Her skin prickled with sudden wanting.

All at once she was cold outside and blazing hot inside as he ran the tip of his tongue down the column of her throat and licked inside the neck of her dress along her collarbone. She gasped, and her head fell back upon his shoulder. He lifted his mouth to her cheek, and his hands rose to cup and knead her breasts.

The sensations were overwhelming, hot and cold flashing up and down, knifing and liquid all at the same time, culminating in the core of her being, the private chamber of her womanhood. She could feel herself growing damp with need, and resisted the telling impulse to clamp her thighs together in growing desperation. As if he'd read her mind and knew exactly what she was feeling and how best to breach her defenses, he dropped one hand to flip up her skirts and splay over the flat of her belly. She moaned and jerked her head to the side. He caught her mouth with his and thrust his hot, wet tongue inside. Her knees threatened to buckle. Her legs felt liquefied. He slid his hand down between them and cupped her, pulling her firmly against him.

She felt on the verge of collapse, held there against him with the strength and heat of his hands intimately cupping her body, his mouth fastened to hers, his tongue slowly thrusting in and out. Oh, how she wanted what he promised. It was so difficult to stand there, her body literally brimming with sensation, softening against his firmly muscled plains and ridges, his hands at her breast and between her silky legs, their mouths joined. She wanted that bed at her back and his body sinking into hers, to love and be loved, heart, body and soul. And the voice telling her that she was asking for the impossible was dim and feeble and far, far away.

Fortunately, the voices in the hall were not.

"I wish there were more rooms open."

"Yes, but at least you can see this sleigh bed. It's my favorite."

Rand was the one to react. He broke the kiss, growled something about timing and whirled away from Gail to literally slam the door in the faces of two shocked middle-aged women and their male companion.

"Well, I never!" said a muffled voice.

"It's obviously occupied," said another.

Heat pinked Gail's neck and flashed across her cheeks. She covered her mouth with her hand, mortified beyond words.

"They didn't see anything," Rand assured her softly.

She shook her head, unable to tell him what really appalled her, that without interruption he'd have had her on that bed in another two minutes, ready and willing, despite everything that stood between them, everything she knew and believed.

Rand stepped in front of her and lifted her chin with his hand, brushing her own aside. "Gail, listen to me," he said. "They didn't see anything, but what if they had? I love you and I for one don't care who knows it."

The sweet words stabbed straight into her heart, but she dared not return them. If he was disappointed, he didn't show it, but she caught the underlying note of frustration in his voice when he softly said, "We'd better go."

She nodded and slipped her arm through his. Would they ever be together? She knew she'd be foolish even to hope for it, but as was so often the case where Rand Hartesite was concerned, somehow she just couldn't help herself.

Chapter Twelve

Rand killed the engine, released his seat belt and turned slightly sideways in his seat so that he could look at her, at least until the lights shut themselves off automatically. Lord, she was beautiful! To his mind, no model or movie star could touch her, not for looks and certainly not for brains. A doctor, no less. Who'd have thought he would have the good sense to fall for a doctor? A doctor with a warm heart, too. It showed in the way she welcomed his girls into her home and affections, the patience she used with his mother, her obvious concern for each and every one of her patients, even in her determination—misguided as it was—not to get between him and Mary Grace. It showed in those big green-and-gold eyes of hers, so quick to fill with tears. She was everything a man could want, and he wanted her with a fervor that surprised even him. It was the one and only time in his life that he had ever known that a thing was unquestionably right between him and a woman. He was going to have to marry this woman, and that was not the first time the notion had occurred.

Just don't rush it, he told himself, even as he reached for her, leaning across the console to find her mouth. Damned bucket seats. He wished that he'd brought the truck, with its wide front bench, but he'd wanted to make this evening special for her. He wanted to make every evening special for her. He wanted to make her understand how deeply he loved her, how serious he was about this relationship. He wanted to make her shiver and moan and burn again, and he wanted to burn with her. Lord help him, had he really almost made love to her in a hotel room that he hadn't even rented? How much more likely was it to happen now with her bed just yards away? He knew she wasn't indifferent to the idea. That was her heart he felt beating like a big brass drum beneath the hand that had cupped her breast.

He broke the kiss, mentally cursing all car designers who schemed to keep apart people who so obviously needed full body contact. Dropping his hand to her thigh, he laid his forehead against her temple and blew into her ear, smiling when she shivered. He placed a kiss on her cheek and teased the corner of her mouth with the tip of his tongue, pleased when she turned her head to bring her mouth to his once more. Unable to resist such an invitation, he clamped his hand behind her head and plunged his tongue into her mouth. It was the most heavenly form of frustration he could imagine, and when he broke off minutes later, he was panting like a blown horse. He wasn't the only one.

After a few seconds, she took his hand in hers and squeezed it. "What a wonderful evening this has been," she said softly.

He smiled. "I'm glad you've enjoyed it, but I suspect the best is yet to come."

She lifted her gaze to his. "What do you mean?"

He lifted his free hand and skimmed her cheek with the backs of his fingers. "I want to make love to you, Gail, and I've got this notion that you might want the same thing."

Her gaze immediately dropped, and she shrank from his touch, saying, "It's not that simple, Rand."

"Why not?" he asked gently, not yet convinced that she meant to turn him down. "We're in love, and I think we have a good chance of staying that way."

"I've thought that before, though, Rand, and it didn't work out."

Him again, the heartbreaker. Rand knew a moment of hurt, anger and jealousy. Just the idea that she'd loved some other man enough to be so hurt by him was enough to set his teeth on edge, but being cast in the same role as that man who'd broken her heart was more than he could take. He put a clamp on his feelings, striving for the patience that had once come so easily to him. "I don't want to pressure you, Gail. I'd never want you to do something that you don't want to do, but—"

"It's not that I don't want to, Rand," she said quickly. "It's just that..."

"What?" he prodded gently, slipping his hand beneath her hair to fit it to the nape of her slender neck. "Why won't you tell me what happened with him?"

She closed her eyes, and he could feel her trembling, but he didn't expect what she said next.

"Shame," she whispered. "I don't talk about it because I'm ashamed of what I let him do to me."

Something inside him twisted, and he leaned close, his elbow on the console as he stroked Gail's arm reassuringly. "We all do foolish things, honey, but I'm sure if there's anything to be ashamed of, you're not the one to bear the burden of it."

She shook her head sadly. "You don't know," she murmured, turning her head to stare out the window into the black night.

He didn't know what to say to that, simply because she was right. He didn't know because she hadn't told him, but apparently that was about to change, for she took a deep breath and began to speak.

"I've told you how I grew up."

"Yes. You were alone."

"So alone," she said. "When I got to college, I didn't know anyone, didn't have anyone, but right away I met *him*. He was handsome and smooth, and he wouldn't take no for an answer. I guess I was flattered."

"Understandable," Rand muttered, wanting to hear it even if he didn't like it. Handsome, was he? Smooth?

"He sort of swept me off my feet," she said. "It was wonderful—until I realized I was pregnant."

Rand closed his eyes, no longer certain he even wanted to know. She had lost the child. He remembered her saying something about it that first day. "He abandoned you."

"Yes."

"And you lost the child, too."

"Y-yes, after she was born."

She. He thought of his girls, and his heart constricted. Her little girl had died from some disease or defect. No wonder she had gone into medicine. She probably wanted to save all the little children in the world. That also explained her thoughtfulness where his girls were concerned, and the value she placed on Mary Grace's feelings. He thought he was going to burst with the love he was feeling. He pulled her to him. "Oh, honey, I'm so sorry."

"You must think I'm terribly stupid," she said, sniffing.

"No, not at all. I told you, everyone does foolish things at one time or another. God knows I did, and I wasn't nearly as young as you were."

She wiped at her cheeks with trembling fingertips and looked up into his eyes. "What are you talking about?"

He hadn't intended to tell her; he realized that the moment he'd decided to do it. Why should he divulge anything? He wasn't proud of being dumb enough to marry where there was no love, but he'd learned a lesson, as Gail had no doubt done, too, and if the telling would help her to put her foolishness into perspective, then he'd gladly tell. He pulled back a bit, so that she could easily see his face in the gloom, and began choosing his words.

"I hope you know my mother well enough to understand what I'm going to say. I think you must, because, like you, she grew up without close family of her own, and I guess that's why family's so important to her now, family and . . . family honor, I suppose. I don't know any other way to put it. Somehow, though, I always knew those things about her, just as I knew that my father would find a way to do whatever he had to, whether it was working the ranch or seeing that we all had everything we needed or soothing Mother's temper.

"Anyway, my brother, see . . . Well, I don't know what it was about him. He was as slick as owl grease, sorry as wet powder, but he could make you smile even when you wanted to strangle him. He just had a way about him, and Mother doted on him, even though he disappointed her time and again, especially about not wanting to stay on the ranch. Then he got this girl pregnant." Rand heard Gail's indrawn breath and looked up. Her face was as white as the moon. He sighed. It was ugly, all right, as ugly as what that character had done to her.

"Go on," she whispered.

He licked his lips, surprised at how hard it was to tell. "Well," he said, "Carel had these big plans, see, and they didn't include a little preacher's daughter from Alpine and a shotgun wedding, but he was sort of on the spot, so when she told him about it, he agreed to meet her here in town and marry her. Instead, he went on his merry way to college in far away California. When he didn't show up, she called the ranch, and that's when we found out about it. She was afraid to go home again, and . . . well, it seemed like we owed her protection. A Hartesite had gotten her into the mess, after all, so it was up to a Hartesite to get her out of it."

"What happened to her?" Gail asked anxiously.

Rand took a deep breath. "Well," he said slowly, "it seemed to me that she had to be married so . . ."

Gail's hand convulsed in his. She rocked forward. "Oh, no! Don't tell me that Lynette was the girl . . . that you—" She seemed to choke.

"I know, I know," he said. "It was stupid beyond words, but she was a little thing, pale blond with great big eyes. I felt real sorry for her, and Mother . . . She was just crushed because it was Carel who had gotten her pregnant and run off. She just couldn't understand how he could not want his own baby. It was her grandbaby after all. So, we took her in. God knows she didn't have anywhere else to go. But she was so miserable, so hurt. And Mother, I can't tell you what it had done to her. She was devastated. Family's everything to her, and to think that Carel could shame us like that. I tell you, it was hard for both of them, and it seemed like it was up to me to fix everything, to make it all come out right somehow, like I did when Daddy died and I took over the ranch, so I sort of took over for Carel and . . . married her."

She pulled her hand from his and covered her face. "Oh, Rand!"

"I thought we'd come to love each other. I thought she . . . Hell, I thought she'd forget him and turn to me out of—I don't know—gratitude, I guess, but instead she couldn't seem to warm up to me. I thought that after the baby came . . . but it was only worse after that. The baby was stillborn."

"Oh, my God."

He shrugged at the tightness in his shoulders that remembering brought with it. "I tried to tell her that it didn't matter to me, but she knew the baby was the only reason I'd married her. After a few weeks, she left. I was more relieved than hurt. God knows, it was never a love match, so I didn't fight the divorce, but it was a pretty bitter experience, all the same. Eventually I put it behind me, but Mother couldn't seem to get over the baby's loss. I started thinking that maybe it was up to me to find somebody else and give her the grandchild she so desperately wanted. Then Carel came back with the girls."

"With the girls," Gail echoed softly, her voice oddly expressionless.

Rand rubbed a hand over his face, wanting to get it over with now. "He practically laid those two babies at Mother's feet," he said, careful to keep the bitterness from his voice.

"His ticket home," Gail whispered, "the one thing Belle couldn't have resisted."

"Right you are," Rand told her. "Still, I was willing to forgive and forget, too. They were such sweet little girls. Like Mother, they just wound me around their little fingers from the first. Carel didn't seem to have much interest in them, frankly, and I guess being back in the family's bosom wasn't everything he'd expected it to be. He started running around a lot and drinking too much."

Gail lifted her head, hands drifting down to her lap. She looked at him with the most agonized eyes. He felt a chill shudder through him. "He was driving drunk, wasn't he?" Gail asked dully.

Rand set his jaw and managed a cool nod. "They were on their way to El Paso, him and some friends. He lost control of the car for some reason. He and a woman were killed."

She closed her eyes. He leaned close and wrapped his arms around her. "Hey, now," he crooned. "It's all right. We've both been through a lot, but we've survived all that to find each other. That's the important thing, isn't it?"

"Yes, but... Rand, the girls...what if someone... Could you ever forgive—"

Tears shone in her eyes. He laid a finger over her lips, wanting to forestall those tears by cancelling her words. "I know what you're thinking. Mother and I have said it a thousand times. What if he hadn't brought them home to us before it happened? What if they'd been with him when he'd lost control of that car?"

"You don't understand," she insisted, tears spilling down her cheeks. "The baby I lost—"

"I know," he said gently. "At least I've had the girls. That was the one good thing Carel ever did. You don't know how many times I've thanked God that he brought them home to us. They've been the great joy of my life and Mother's, while you've had no one all this time."

She looked up at him then, her mouth hanging open, her eyes awash with tears and dribbling mascara. He smiled, loving her for her soft heart and the awe that seemed to fill her, as if he were some kind of hero or something, when all he was was grateful, grateful that he'd experienced fatherhood with two such extraordinary girls, grateful for the life he led, grateful for finally finding a woman with whom he could share it all. He kissed away her tears, kissed her tempting mouth, and then sat back in his seat, knowing for sure how he wanted it now, how he wanted her. He wanted it done right all the way down the line. He wanted to get down on his knees at the perfect moment and ask her. He wanted to see the joy light her face. He wanted to hear her say yes, with wedding bells and rockets and the whole bit. He wanted to know that she was his for no other reason than she wanted to be. He wanted her to know the same thing about him. And he wanted it all soon. Real soon. But not tonight. Tonight was for telling secrets. The day for asking her to marry him would come, and when it did, there would be nothing between them but the sweet truth.

He smiled and said gently, "I'll walk you to the door now."

Flowers. He had brought her flowers, and she couldn't imagine where he had found the bright bouquet wrapped in cellophane, which only made them all the more special. No one had ever brought her flowers before, and she couldn't help smiling even as alarm bells began clanging in the back of her mind. She hadn't seen him since their dinner at Alpine, four days ago, although he'd called her every night since. She was surprised he'd come, but happy inside. "How lovely!" she said, reaching out for the bouquet.

He yielded the flowers easily and swept off his hat, grinning ear to ear as he followed her into her apartment. "Hope you've got something to put them in."

"I'll find something," she assured him, glancing back to show him her smile again. It was then that she noticed he was holding something more behind his back. "Now what?" she asked, turning to face him.

"Just a little something," he muttered. He put a hand to his throat and swallowed hard.

And it was then that she realized he was wearing a bolo tie with a black onyx as big as a half-dollar in the slide. She gave him a good going-over, flicking her gaze down his big frame and up again. His belt matched his tie, the buckle a palm-sized chunk of hammered silver with the onyx in its center. His jeans were dark blue and as stiff as boards. His royal-blue-and-black canvas-striped shirt of heavy polished cotton looked new. His black boots were polished to a hard shine, and the black felt of his hat had been brushed scrupulously clean. What on earth was going on here? And what was that hidden behind his back? She lifted her gaze to his eyes and suddenly wished that she could send him right back out the door. It was there on his face, the raw desire that told her everything he was thinking.

She whirled away, her heart pounding, her thoughts skipping from idea to idea in search of one that would keep him from asking the question she could see in his eyes. She couldn't think of a thing that wouldn't hurt his feelings—or worse. Desperately she strode to the kitchen and busied herself finding just the right container for the flowers. Behind her, she heard the refrigerator door open and turned in time to catch him stashing a bottle of champagne. Champagne. Oh, God.

She carried the flowers to the living room, arranged them on the end table and popped down onto the couch, realizing only as he bent to take his place beside her that she'd left herself open. Abruptly she bounced up again.

He laughed as he settled into position, one long leg balanced upon the other, his hat perched on the arm of the sofa. "Will you sit down?" he said. "You're as nervous as a cat in a room full of rocking chairs."

He grinned and patted the seat next to him, but she noted that his hand was shaking and knew that he was every bit as nervous as she was.

Heaven help her, she did not want to do this. She did not want to hurt him. How had she let it come to this? She had known that it could come to a proposal of marriage, but so soon? She walked past him and sat down in the recliner, not daring to so much as look at him.

"I know I've told you already," she began brightly, "but it bears repeating. I'm so pleased with the progress your mother is making. She's working very hard and—"

He sat forward suddenly, his forearms balanced against the calf of his crossed leg. "She's terribly fond of you, you know. She wouldn't say so, of course, but I know that you can read her. You understand her. You understand us all."

She could feel her smile wilting and forcefully renewed it. "Well, I'm happy Belle is improving and . . . a-and . . . Did I tell you that I'm interviewing office help?" He nodded, but she hurried on anyway. "It's such a relief to have reached this point, to be able to afford the help. Don't think I've forgotten that I owe you for that. It was kind of you to—"

He got up and stepped in front of her, bending to scoop her out of the chair. He lifted her into his arms, ignoring her gasps, stepped back and dropped down onto the couch once more, arranging her on his lap. When she was leaning back against his arm, her own looped lightly about his neck, he ran a fingertip over her lips, then kissed her. After several minutes, he sat back and smiled at her.

"I want to ask you a question."

She closed her eyes. "Rand, please. Let's not—"

"Have you ever had an engagement ring?"

Her eyes snapped open. "What?"

He repeated himself very deliberately. "Have—you—ver—had—an—engagement ring?"

For a moment she could only stare, despair weighting her heart. Solemnly she turned her head side to side and whispered, "No."

"Well, you have one now," he told her softly, digging into his shirt pocket.

She slapped her hand over that pocket, trapping the fingers that delved into it. "Don't," she told him.

He froze, but then he relaxed, sighing. "I didn't do it right," he grumbled. "I should've let you pick it out. I should've gotten down on my knee and begged you—"

She pressed trembling fingers over his mouth. "No! Never say that. The woman doesn't live that you should have to beg... for anything."

He chuckled and opened his mouth to gently nip and suck her fingertips. She jerked them away, suffering more acutely than if he had slapped her.

"Let's start over, all right?"

She shook her head vehemently. "No. It... it's too soon or... It's too soon!"

She watched the nervous joy slowly drain from his eyes, leaving them dull and pained.

"Too soon?" he echoed. "I'll say it's too soon! You might at least let a man ask before you shoot him down!" He shoved her off his lap and sprang to his feet.

"Rand, don't!" she cried. "Don't make this more difficult than it has to be!"

He snatched his hat up and slapped it on his head. "Difficult? Sugar, you make turning me down look like child's play!"

Oh, he would be unreasonable about this! Couldn't he see that it was tearing her up, too? All she had wanted when she had come to this town was to find her daughter. Instead she had found the man of her dreams who was the brother of the man who had stolen her child from her, and two girls who could be that child, neither of whom she could bear to give up. And he thought this was easy for her! "You don't know what you're saying," she rasped.

"I know what *you're* saying," he retorted. In a voice just above a whisper, he added, "I thought you loved me."

"I do!"

"Do you?"

"Yes!"

He dug the ring from his pocket and held it out to her. Bleakly she stared at it. What a lovely thing it was, a classic, simple band of heavy gold with a solitary diamond rising from it. He must have paid a fortune for it, and she dared not take it. She dared not claim the beautiful thing that it promised, the priceless love that it represented. If only she could, if only she could forget who he was and why she'd come into his life. If only she could believe that he wouldn't hate her when he discovered the truth. She closed her eyes, too miserable for words, utterly lost. He said something under his breath that she knew was best not heard, then his footsteps clumped toward the kitchen. She heard him yank open the refrigerator door, and moments later he was standing in front of her again, the ring held under her nose with one hand, the other grasping the neck of the champagne bottle.

"Seems I have more use for the booze than this," he said bitterly, dropping the ring into her lap. "Let me know when the right time comes, will you? If it ever does, that is."

She picked the ring up, intending to give it back to him, but at the last moment, she couldn't quite let go of it. She folded it into her palm as he stalked away. She watched him go through the door, heard it slam behind him, and opened her hand to reveal the ring glimmering in her palm.

Easy? Oh, no. It was the hardest thing she'd ever done, refusing what he offered, but what else could she do? One day he would thank God that she had not agreed to marry him—and curse the day he'd first laid eyes on her. She took the ring between her fingers and held it up to the light, a perfect circle as endless as time, a precious piece of bril liance caught in a stone. She slid it onto her hand, knowing that she had to give it back, that even the pretense was foolishly dangerous. She thought of the phone call she'd received that very afternoon, the impersonal voice of the investigator telling her that the truth lay in Baja California with her old college roommate Faye. She would find the answers to her mystery there. Did she have one daughter or two? Had Carel done to some other poor woman what he had done to her? And why? Why?

He practically laid those two babies at Mother's feet.
His ticket home.

He had used them all, manipulating their lives with the ease of a puppet master until God or pure chance had removed him from the theater.

The investigator had said that her old college roommate, Faye, was married to an older man she had met in Europe, so she had indeed made that tour her mother had given as her excuse for not returning to school. Nevertheless, the investigator felt certain that only Faye could tell them what they needed to know.

She prayed that Faye could somehow tell her how she could have given birth to twins without realizing it. That would make up in some small way for what she had lost in Rand, but it would never be enough. She knew deep down that nothing would ever be enough. She thought of Rand, the hurt in his eyes, the way his hand had curled around the neck of that bottle of champagne. She prayed he'd have sense enough not to drink and drive, and it occurred to her that she hadn't heard the truck fire up. Maybe it wasn't too late to reason with him, to plead a case for sobriety.

Leaping up, she rushed to the door and flung it open. The truck sat just where he'd parked it earlier, but Rand—and the bottle—were gone, where, she couldn't say. She went to the truck and peered inside. The keys were in the ignition. Quickly she removed them and slipped them into the pocket of her lab coat. At least if he came back drunk he wouldn't be able to drive away in that condition. Maybe he hadn't gone far. Maybe he wasn't planning to drown his sorrow. He didn't normally take off on foot, but that didn't mean that he was planning to tie one on, did it? Maybe he'd stroll up in a moment, a sheepish smile on his face and an apology in his eyes. Maybe he'd say that she was right, that it was too soon to be thinking of marriage. Maybe he'd give her a few more weeks of his love.

She clutched the ring on her finger and climbed up onto the tailgate of the truck, telling herself that any minute now he would be opening his arms to her, pleading for a little more time. Just a little more time. Please.

It was dark when she slipped down and went inside, dark when she curled into a ball in the corner of the sofa and closed her eyes, too emotionally numb even to weep. "Oh, Rand," she whispered, "I do love you. I do."

Sometime later she jerked awake, heart pounding and eyes wide in the almost total black of night. Groggily she pushed hair out of her eyes. She remembered it all, Rand and the flowers, the champagne and the ring, the pain and the anger, sitting on the tailgate of the truck, hoping Rand would return, and getting down again to come inside. She remembered curling up on the couch, praying for time. *Just a little more time, Lord. Please give me a little more time.* What she didn't remember was falling asleep, and now she wondered what had awakened her.

"Ga-il!"

Rand. "Thank God!" she whispered, reaching for the lamp on the table to her left.

"Damn you! Where'm my *keys?*" He was bawling loud enough to wake the whole neighborhood and get himself arrested in the process.

She finally found the lamp and switched it on. Before she could get to her feet, he began pounding on her door. "I'm coming!" she called, hurrying toward the noise. When she opened the door, he literally fell through it, toppling onto the floor with a groan. "Rand!" She dropped to her knees, reaching for him.

He shoved her away, knocking off his hat in the process, and struggled into a sitting position, one knee drawn up to balance himself. "Damn. Where'm I?" he said, slurring the words.

Gail sat back on her heels, her eyes all but crossing as the alcohol vapor reached her. "On the floor," she said, waving a hand in front of her face. "What did you do with that champagne, bathe in it?"

"Trade it for um fif' a whizzkey."

"Good Lord, it's a wonder you aren't dying of alcohol poisoning!"

"Don' wan' die, jus' sztop thi'king…think-ing. Oh-h-h." He put a hand to his head and fell back on the floor.

"Looks like you're going to get your wish," she muttered, bending over to lift his eyelids and gauge his level of consciousness. His eyes rolled back in his head, then righted themselves, more or less. She knew he'd be snoring in three seconds if she didn't get him up. "Okay, cowboy," she said, tugging at his arms, "let's get you to bed."

"Bed," he echoed, suddenly launching himself upward again. "Why didn't you say so?"

Shaking her head, she took a fresh grasp of his arm and hauled him to his feet. He swayed wildly, arms flailing, then seemed to steady a bit. She slipped under his arm and wrapped one of her arms around his waist. "This way, hot-shot."

He draped his arm around her neck, crossed her chest with it and cupped her breast with his hand. "I've wan'ed take you t'bed for a long time!"

She could only smile as she guided him, stumbling, across the room. "Yeah, well, tonight I'm taking you to bed, and you can thank me tomorrow, if—by some miracle—your head's still attached to your shoulders."

He groaned at the mere mention of his head and pressed his free hand to its top. She bit her lip to keep from laughing outright. Thank God she had taken his keys! Otherwise she might be scraping him up off the highway between here

and the ranch. Oh, if anything should ever happen to him...
She turned off that thought and bumped open the guest
room door, hitting the wall switch to the overhead light
while trying to keep him steady on his feet. He spied the bed
and reached for it as if he could bring it closer with just the
desire and his fingertips. She led him to it, intending to turn
him and sit him on the edge. Instead, he lifted one knee as
if to crawl onto it, missed the edge and fell face first on top
of it, almost taking her down with him. She gasped, afraid
he'd passed out, but then he started to laugh and rolled over.

"Whew! Damn! Sof'er ona floor."

She didn't know whether to shake him or to laugh with
him. She settled for a cluck of her tongue and a reluctant
smile, then began stripping off his boots, belt and tie. He
was moaning in pain by the time she got the bolo over his
head. She left him with strict instructions not to move so
much as a hair until she returned, then hurriedly retrieved
the correct analgesics from her bathroom medicine cabinet
and a glass of water from the kitchen.

He was snoring softly by the time she got back to him, but
she knew that if she didn't get the medicine down him, he
would be in agony the next morning, an experience she
could only mitigate at best. Nevertheless, she felt compelled to try. By tugging and pulling and lightly slapping his
face while loudly telling him what she wanted him to do, she
finally got him up on one elbow, poked the pills between his
teeth and poured the water down him. He sighed, wiped his
mouth with the back of his hand and collapsed upon his
pillow, reaching for her and mumbling, "C'mere, baby."

She pushed his hands down and picked up the blanket
that lay folded at the foot of the bed. "Go to sleep," she told
him, spreading the blanket over him. He mumbled something unintelligible and rolled onto his side, sighing deeply.
Gail turned on the bedside lamp, turned off the overhead
light and came back to him for one last check. He looked
positively angelic lying there, his dark hair falling across his
forehead. She hoped he wouldn't be too miserable in the

morning. Dared she hope that he'd forget the whole evening and all that had transpired? It seemed no more foolish than everything else upon which she'd built her baseless dreams. At least he was here now.

She smiled and brushed the lock of hair from his forehead, bending to tenderly place a feather-light kiss on his temple. He looked so peaceful, so *perfect*. What she wouldn't give to keep him here always. Sighing, she moved away, but suddenly his hand shot out and clamped around her wrist. She caught her breath, her gaze flying once more to his face.

He stared at her with lucid, probing eyes, as sober as anyone could hope to be. "Why won't you marry me?" he asked roughly, pain flashing across his face.

Tears pricked her eyes, and she reached out instinctively to smooth the taut lines of his jaw. "Because I love you!" she whispered urgently.

For a moment he continued staring, but finally his face softened, and his eyelids first drooped, then fluttered down. She leaned over him until his breath sighed out and his chest began to rise in a slow, even, restful cadence. Only then did she leave him for the sleepless loneliness of her own bed.

Chapter Thirteen

She felt the faintest brush of skin against her cheek, and suddenly light was leaking beneath her closed eyelids. It was morning, very early, and she didn't want to get up—until she remembered Rand. Her eyes flashed open, and there he was, crouching beside her bed, his grin a mile wide.

"'Morning, beautiful."

She struggled up onto her forearm, pushing at her hair. His was wet, she noticed, and his face was cleanly shaven. He must have borrowed her razor, but she didn't bother pondering that as her attention focused elsewhere. His chest was bare, and when she peeked over the side of the bed, she saw that his feet were bare, too. Her gaze went immediately back to his chest. He was even broader in the shoulder than she'd remembered, and his well-developed chest tapered to a surprisingly narrow waist. She thought, inanely, that he ought to tailor his shirts to show off his muscular build more. She thought, too, how very attractive the triangle of crisp, dark hair on his upper chest was. Her mouth felt strangely dry all of a sudden. She licked her lips, searching for something sensible to say. The doctor in her surfaced.

"How are you feeling?"

"Better," he said, "now."

His gaze dropped pointedly to her hand splayed against the mattress.

She looked down to find the engagement ring sparkling on her finger. She sucked in her breath. How could she have forgotten? But the answer to that was blatant. She had forgotten to take off the ring because she didn't want to part with it, as she didn't want to part with him. Oh, what was she going to do? If she took off the engagement ring now, she would only hurt him again. She remembered the pain she'd seen in his eyes the night before, and she didn't think that she could bear to see it again. She licked her lips.

"Rand, I'm so sorry about what happened last night. I never meant—"

"I know, I know," he said, smoothing his hands through her hair. "That doesn't matter now. As long as you're wearing my diamond, I'm a happy man. I'll be happier when you put the wedding band with it, though."

Her heart swelled and swelled, until she thought it might explode with love for this man. Why couldn't she marry him? She could make him happy, she knew she could. She'd work every day of her life to see that she did. He never had to know about her and his brother. She could protect him from that. Perhaps she could even absolve her guilt by seeing to it that he never knew she had borne his brother a child—and by never knowing which of the girls was that child, her child. Did it really matter anyway? A child of the heart was as dear as a child of the body. She let her breath out in a long sigh and smiled up at him tremulously. "I love you so much!" she whispered.

He threaded his fingers through the hair at her temples and tilted her face. Gently, he brushed his lips over hers, once, twice. The third time they came to stay, slightly parted, his tongue flicking out to taste the tender insides of her lips before slipping between her teeth. Her bones melted as she sank back upon the bed. His hands moved from her face to the base of her throat then across her chest to the rising mounds of her breasts. She felt his fingers curl beneath the edge of her coverings as his mouth created a splendid pressure against hers, and then he pulled back, abandoning her mouth to plumb her gaze with eyes gone smoky gray.

"I'm going to make love to you," he said.

Her lungs seized, her heart seeming to turn over in her chest. She shouldn't. She knew she shouldn't. It was the very mistake she had made with Carel, giving herself too soon. But this was Rand, not Carel, and he deserved at least as much love and faith as his scoundrel brother had. He deserved so much more than that. *He deserves your honesty,* said a small, faint voice in the back of her mind, but she pushed it away, buried it beneath the layers of love that she felt for this man.

"Yes," she said, "Make love to me."

He pulled the covers back, flipping them over the foot of the bed onto the floor. He rose then and sat on the edge of the bed, his gaze skimming the soft, long-sleeved, knit nightshirt that she wore. It reached all the way to her ankles from a simple T-shirt neckline and was slit up the sides to just above the knees. He slid a hand into the nearest slit, smoothing it upward along the outside of her thigh and lifting the gown with it. His smile was slow and sure as he shifted his weight and brought his other hand into the action, sweeping her nightgown up to the tops of her legs. She lifted her hips for him, and then her shoulders as he pushed the gown up and over her head, the sleeves peeling up her arms as he pulled the garment free. He tossed it aside, then cupped her breasts with his hands from beneath, lifting and kneading them as he gently squeezed her nipples between thumbs and forefingers.

The sensations were unbelievable. Radiating from her breasts to her groin, they sparked heat in her belly and the most curious drawing sensation between her legs. She had never felt anything like it before, never *imagined* anything like it, and she knew instinctively, physiology be damned, that no other man could evoke such a response from her. No other man's touch would feel quite like his. Science obviously focused too little on the emotional, for she knew without any doubt that her feelings for this man were what made all the difference. It was as if her body recognized him as its mate simply because her heart told it to, and her brain, not to mention her mind, had nothing whatsoever to say about it. She marveled, aware of everything from the quickening of her breath to the softness of the morning light and the slick toughness of the calluses on his finger pads. Even the sensitivity of the skin on her back seemed heightened to the texture of the sheet upon which she lay. She was panting, her hands curled into fists at her sides, when he finally moved his hands to the waistband of her panties and dragged them down her body. Then he was on his feet and shucking his jeans.

Her mouth fell open. She had seen the human body in all its glory and in every guise, but nothing had prepared her for what she now beheld. To think that she did *this* to him. She wondered that he wasn't in pain, then a glance at his face told her that he probably was, and she lifted a hand to him. He took it and came back down to the edge of the bed, lifting it to his lips. Deliberately he licked along her forefinger before sucking it deep into his mouth. She gasped, amazed, as liquid heat erupted between her legs, and snatched her hand away. He grinned and bent to kiss her, his chest covering hers, so that she felt for the first time the drag of those crisp hairs against her peaked nipples. How could such a small thing elicit such shattering sensation, and how could the press of his lips and the flicking of his tongue enthrall her so? She felt drugged and keenly sensitive at the same time. Her arms seemed literally to float up of their own will and hook themselves around his neck. Not that she would willingly have hindered them. Quite the opposite. In fact, when he again pulled back, she tightened her hold, so reluctant to let him go that she arched up against him.

"Wait, love," he said roughly, prying her arms loose so that he could sit beside her. "Let me do this right." He slid his hands down her body to her waist, where they squeezed gently, his gaze traveling in their path. "You're almost too beautiful to be real," he told her. His hands continued their journey over her abdomen and down her thighs to slip beneath her knees. He lifted them and opened her legs. "Beautiful," he murmured, his fingers finding her and delving deep.

Within moments he had her thrashing with need and then exploding, sensation peaking again and again, so that her head swam and her vision went white, her body shivering with cycle after cycle of climactic pulsing. It was then that he moved between her legs and pushed upward, joining them and methodically driving her to new heights again and again, until she was utterly lost in a sensuous world of his making, with only him to anchor her, to keep her from flying to pieces like a Roman candle bursting against the black canvas of the sky.

Some time later, they lay side by side, limbs entwined, heads together upon her pillow. She was still trying to grasp the incredibleness of all she'd experienced, when he disentangled his hand and lifted it to her face, tilting it upward so that he could gaze down into her eyes.

"I'll always love you," he said. "Please believe that."

And in that moment, she did. How could she not after what she'd just experienced? She snuggled her head against his chest, his chin against her crown. "Thank you for this," she said softly. "I'd rather have this time with you than a lifetime with any other man."

He sighed, the breath from his nostrils ruffling her hair and warming her scalp. "How about this and a lifetime together, too?"

She smiled. "There's nothing I want more. Nothing."

He slid a hand down to cup her breast, and she lifted her mouth to his once more. The time for talk had passed for now. It was time once more for creating moments of passion that nothing and no one could ever dim.

Rand pulled the brush through his hair, wondered if he needed a haircut and turned his head side to side, tilting his chin as necessary to gauge the overall length. Behind him, Gail laughed and slid her arms around his waist, going up on tiptoe to lay her cheek against his. "What?" he asked the ponytailed reflection of her face.

"I never would have believed it if I hadn't seen it. Rand Hartesite is vain!"

He tossed the brush down beside the sink, turned and leaned back against the edge of the counter, his arms pulling her tight against him. "And why not? I've just made love to the sexiest, most beautiful woman in the world. That must make me pretty special."

She put her nose to his. "Silly goose."

"I think the proper term is gander."

"Silly gander." She pulled a face. "Doesn't have the same ring to it."

"Speaking of rings," he said, capturing her hand to show off the diamond she was wearing. "When do we put the other one on your finger?"

She smiled up at him despite the chill that passed over her. Could she really do this? Could she marry him without telling him the truth? She swallowed down her fears—and took the coward's way out. "We don't have to talk about that now, do we? Give me time to think about it and come up with a possible date. These things take time, after all."

He put back his head and groaned. "We aren't planning a huge, complicated wedding, are we?"

She laughed. "Hardly."

"Then what's the holdup?"

She rolled her eyes, babbling words that hardly registered in her mind first. "I'm a busy woman, Hartesite. Besides, you haven't even told your mother and the girls yet. What if they don't like the idea?''

"Oh, get real," he told her. "My mother's been singing your praises for months. Carel Belle adores you, and even Mary Grace is coming around."

He couldn't know how that warmed her, but she still held back instinctively. "All right, but maybe they have some ideas about how we should do it. We ought to ask, anyway, don't you think? A-and what about all your friends, not to mention my patients? Shouldn't we consider them as we make our plans?"

He shook his head, but he was laughing. "I can already see it. You're going to be taking a poll. How should sweet Dr. Terry and that lucky man Hartesite tie the knot? Details please. Well, let me cast my vote for *soon*. That's all I'm going to say on the matter. Have as much or as little wedding as you want, just have it *soon*. I'm tired of sleeping without you."

He punctuated that with a kiss, and she was convinced all over again that marrying him was the right thing to do. After he lifted his head, she smiled up at him dreamily. Could this really be happening? Could she really have the man whom she loved and her daughter—daughters—too? *Oh, God, please let it be true. Haven't I paid enough for past sins? Thirteen years without my child. All I want is to make him happy, to be a mother to his girls.* She turned off all the voices that argued happiness could not be built on lies and promised herself that their happiness would be built on love.

"It's so pretty, Gail!"

Carel Belle turned Gail's hand so that the diamond caught the light. "I'm so happy for you, for all of us!"

Gail slid her arms around the slender shoulders and squeezed them tight. "Thank you, darling. That means so much to me."

She looked over Carel Belle's shoulder at Mary Grace's carefully blank expression. Her heart turned over. Would

Mary Grace accept her? How ironic to think that her own daughter might be the one who could not abide her as a member of the family. The pain of that was searing, but Gail kept it carefully concealed. She watched Rand nudge Mary Grace with his elbow and wished that he hadn't. In fact, it might have been easier all around if he had not not come in early from the range this day. Had he not been there to greet her with open arms when she'd arrived to administer his mother's physical therapy she might have been able to more accurately gauge his family's reaction. As it was, though, all she could do was muddle through.

She shifted Carel Belle to her side, keeping an arm about the girl's shoulders as Mary Grace came forward. Mary Grace was the more outgoing of the two girls, but at this moment she seemed uncharacteristically shy. She didn't look up when she quietly wished Gail a happy life. Gail looked helplessly to Rand, but his expression did not change so much as a hair. He might have prompted the exchange, but he was clearly leaving it up to the two of them to work things out. At first, Gail didn't know what to do, but then she felt Carel's fingers lace with hers, and suddenly she understood how she had to react. She wrapped her free arm around Mary Grace and hugged her close, whispering, "I love you all so much."

Mary's arms came around her waist. "I'm sorry!" she squeaked, emotion ringing the resonance from her voice. Gail didn't have to ask what Mary was sorry for, and she didn't really care at the moment.

"No apologies, love. We all get scared sometimes, Mary. I hope you know that from now on anytime you're worried or upset or even just curious, you can always come to me. Always."

Mary sniffed, then lifted her head, laughing. "Will you make Uncle Rand let me go to the ballgame on Friday with a boy?"

"I will not!" Gail said flatly, surprised by the sudden turn in the conversation. "Not until you're sixteen, anyway."

Mary stomped her foot, shoulders slumping, but there was no rancor in it. Rand smiled at Gail, folded his arms, and said to Mary, "Told you so."

Mary stuck her tongue out at him, then laughed when he stuck his out at her. Relief washed over Gail in a giddy wave; then they were all laughing.

The laughter had hardly dwindled when Belle waved over the happy couple from her place on the sofa. *One more,* Gail thought, and she silently hoped that Rand was correct in his assessment of his mother's opinion of her. Just in case, she put on her best professional smile as they approached. "And how are you today, ma'am? Regaining your strength, I hope."

Belle waved that away with an imperious flick of her hand. "What I want to know from you, my future daughter, is why we don't have a date to work with. Can't plan a wedding without a date, and I mean to see to it that Rand has the sort of wedding this time that is fitting. I'm sure you get my meaning."

She shot a look at Rand, who warned, "Now, Mother."

Belle waved that off, too, giving Gail her full attention. "I was thinking after Thanksgiving," she said firmly. "The first week in December ought to do nicely, don't you think?"

"Why not before Thanksgiving?" Rand wanted to know.

"Be realistic!" Belle snapped. "Men are never realistic," she said to Gail. "They think they're so logical, but we women are the ones who think things through, aren't we?"

Gail disciplined a smile. "Oh, I'm sure you're right."

"Don't encourage her!" Rand cried. Then, seeing the sparkle in her eyes, he promptly backed off. "Great! They're already ganging up on me!" he complained to the ceiling, but Gail saw and reveled in the smile she saw lurking around the corners of his mouth. *My two women,* that smile said, *my mother, my wife.*

Gail felt a warm glow that began in her chest and spread slowly throughout her body. She made him happy. Somehow she made this wonderful man happy. She felt tears pricking the backs of her eyes and had to look away to hide them. It was as if the movement unstoppered her ears, for she suddenly became aware of Belle's low, drawling voice.

"Perfect place, of course, is the barn," Belle said decisively.

"I-I beg your p-pardon," Gail stammered.

Belle went on as if Gail hadn't even spoken, thinking aloud now. "We'll have to move all the animals well beforehand and clean it top to bottom, but then it should serve nicely, given a Western theme. Where, after all, do cowboys spend the majority of their time?"

"Bars," Rand ventured cheekily, "rodeo arenas, pickup trucks. I suppose a church would be the last place you'd associate with a cowboy. Somehow, though, when I think wedding, I just naturally think church."

"Smart aleck," Belle pronounced flatly. Then she turned a conspiratorial smile upon Gail. "I'm sure you understand, my dear, no church in the area is large enough to host a Hartesite wedding, and neither, as I pointed out, is this house. It will have to be the barn."

Gail's mouth dropped open. They were planning a wedding in a barn? "I don't think so." The words slipped out completely without her permission. Belle looked momentarily shocked, but Rand, who was now seated on the arm of the couch, put his head back and laughed like a man delighted with the turn his world was taking. Gail blanched, feeling the color drain from her face and hating it. She had alienated her future mother-in-law. She had blown it all with one muttered sentence, and the one person in the world who could rescue her was . . . rescuing her.

"Good night, Mother!" Rand scoffed. "You didn't really think you could bully her, did you? The lady is a doctor, after all, an educated woman with a mind of her own. Hell, the first time I asked her she turned me down, if you can imagine it." He grinned as if he relished that fact now, as if it hadn't pained him one bit. His eyes said he was proud of her, and it hit her suddenly that this man was truly committed to loving everything about her.

Too good, she thought, *too good for a woman who lies to him.*

The weight of those lies was suddenly insupportable. She closed her eyes and pushed it away with all her might. It was at precisely that moment that Rand got up, walked around his mother and sat down next to Gail, taking her hand in his.

"Okay," he said softly, "what do you want? How do you want to get married?"

I want to tell you the truth and have you love me still. She shook her head. Rand took it as a sign of uncertainty.

"Close your eyes," he said, his voice like satin on cotton. She closed her eyes because it was simpler than keeping them open. "Think about the perfect wedding, the wedding you'd have if only it was possible."

The night of Belle's birthday party popped into her head. She saw the colored lights strung over everything like a tent roof, heard the music playing and the low murmur of interesting conversation. She was wearing a form-fitting long-sleeved white lace on white shiny knit top with a high neck and a narrow skirt that flared into lacy calypso layers at the knee. Her hair was swept up loosely and crowned with a ring of flowers. Rand was at her elbow, dressed in black and a white, pleated shirt. They were both beaming. She chewed her lip, thinking. It would be awfully chilly at night at that time of year. They could light small bonfires or something and set up an elaborate buffet with sparkling white tablecloths and napkins. They could hold the ceremony in the middle of the dance floor with an arch of colored lights framing them. She wanted a piano with the band. She opened her eyes and smiled at Rand. He laughed and took her face in his hands and kissed her on the mouth.

The moment he released her, she spilled it all in a babble of freshly discovered details, too excited even to be embarrassed by what had been, all things considered, a rather hotly passionate kiss conducted in front of his mother and the girls. Not even the look that Belle traded with her granddaughters penetrated Gail's hazy dream of the perfect wedding with the perfect man. Soon, however, her enthusiasm infected Belle and the two called for paper and pens and began scribbling notes. Rand sat with his arm draped loosely about Gail's shoulders and occasionally put in his two cents' worth. The girls rhapsodized about a planned shopping trip to El Paso for bridesmaids' clothes. Gail thought about a nurse at the hospital that she would like to ask to be her maid of honor, then of all the people she would have to invite to the wedding. It was overwhelming, wonderfully overwhelming. She wouldn't have time to think about what she should be telling Rand. She *would* have the wedding of her dreams and the man of her heart. It was the happiest moment of her life.

He hadn't wanted the huge wedding with all the trimmings. If it had been left up to him, he'd have hauled her to the courthouse and gone home a married man, but the look on her face when she'd finally allowed herself to begin imagining what she wanted was enough to change his mind completely. If she wanted to roll out the red carpet for the whole damned county, they'd roll out the red carpet. Period. But it was beginning to sound like the first week in December wouldn't begin to give them enough time for what was developing. He sighed inwardly and smiled outwardly. He was going to be doing an awful lot of driving between the ranch and Marfa, but he wasn't the only one to come to that conclusion.

The moment the girls left the room, their attention span exhausted, Belle Grace lifted her chin and looked down her nose at him. That was the standard signal that a set-down was coming. He instantly bristled but kept his mouth shut out of automatic respect. She bowed her head, obviously choosing her words. "This is all so fine," she said slowly, "and I hesitate to speak out in this way."

"That'll be the day," Rand muttered, and Gail dropped a quelling hand on his knee, obviously concerned about what was coming but wanting to build a peaceful, loving relationship with her future mother-in-law. He covered it with his own much larger one and instantly thought of pushing her nightshirt up her thigh. It required considerable effort to drag his attention back to his mother's voice, but he managed to do so in time to catch her slant.

"Both adults," she was saying, "but Marfa is a very small town. People are bound to notice the comings and goings of their neighbors. It won't be long before talk begins, and the more notice you attract, the more talk will follow. Naturally you want to spend time together, but . . ."

Rand had heard enough. He glanced at Gail, saw that she had not missed his mother's thinly veiled meaning and instantly resented the stricken expression on her face. She wasn't ashamed of loving him, was she? Well, he wasn't having it, not from either of them. He set Gail's hand aside and got up. His movements were measured in a leisurely fashion as he took a step forward, turned to face his mother, and put his hands to his waist, leaning forward slightly in order to look down *his* nose at *her.* "Let me make this perfectly clear, Mother," he said to her gaping mouth. "I don't give a damn what the neighbors say about us—or anybody else, for that matter—and if you think I'm going to play the virgin bridegroom for even the next week, you are seriously deluded."

"Is that so?" Belle countered smoothly. "And what about the girls? Do you imagine they won't know where you spend your nights when you aren't at home?"

"Do you imagine they don't know *now?*" he retorted. "Believe me, for a long time they've been aware of the fact that I have a healthy interest in the opposite sex, and they can't possibly doubt the physical attraction between Gail and me. Why should they? I'm not hypocrite enough to try to hide it."

"But she's right," Gail said quietly, so quietly that it had about the same effect as a tolling bell upon utter silence. Rand found himself staring at her, his mouth settling into a frown. She reached out and laid a hand on his wrist, her sincerity absolutely compelling a hearing. "I love you," she said, a wealth of feeling invested in those three words. "But young girls sometimes think themselves in love long before the real thing ever happens. Do you want your girls sleeping with every guy that comes along professing love?"

That was a thought, he realized suddenly, that he'd been avoiding for a long time now, a year anyway, ever since he'd noticed Mary throwing back her shoulders and pushing out her chest when boys were around. He cleared his throat, then pulled in a deep breath, facing defeat with manly resignation.

"Hell," he said. But then a happy thought struck him, the perfect compromise. He tried to mask it with a glower, grumbling at his mother, "All right, so I won't be spending the night at Gail's house anymore." That did not mean, however, that he wouldn't be seeing the inside of Gail's bedroom anymore, quite the opposite, in fact, and Belle knew it. The glint in her eyes said so, and suddenly he was seeing his mother in a whole new light. Just for an instant, there sat the fetching young woman with whom his father had fallen irrevocably in love, the sultry female who had satisfied his dad's blatantly physical side, and there, just behind it came the devastating emptiness of loss. She missed him. God, how she still missed that man. How had she survived losing the love of her life? What would he do if he lost Gail somehow? He couldn't even think of it, wouldn't.

He pretended annoyance to hide the understanding and fear that had so abruptly taken him. "Well, if you two are through ganging up on me for now, we all have work to get done before dinner." He glowered at his mother, who wasn't buying a second of it, then turned slightly and curled a hand beneath Gail's chin, telling her with his eyes that he didn't

mean it before smacking her on the mouth. Gail smiled and
turned her head to follow him with her gaze as he left the
room. If he didn't lose the chill that had skittered up his
spine, at least he was able to ignore it.

Chapter Fourteen

For two weeks she careened between elation and despairing fear. She asked herself a dozen times how she could marry Rand with this awful lie between them, and then, she would ask herself, how could she hurt him. As the wedding plans progressed and it became obvious that his joy was as great as hers, she began to believe that it was going to be all right somehow, that she could live happily with her secret, convinced that she was doing the best thing for everyone. And yet, on occasion, in the dark of night, alone in her bed, Gail would think about the possibility of another mother out there. She could admit, in such moments, that the likelihood of her being the mother to both Mary Grace and Carel Belle were slim at best, and then she would wonder if that other woman ever thought of her child, if she searched and yearned, if she would show up on the Hartesite doorstep one day to reveal the whole ugly story and spirit away one of the girls. Which one? Gail would wonder. Which one would she lose? Could her old roommate Faye tell her, as the investigator seemed to think?

She had meant to go to Baja to find out what light Faye could shed on this mystery, but somehow it hadn't seemed important after she'd decided to marry Rand. She couldn't help wondering at times, though, if not going was wise. That other woman could show up and do what Gail herself had intended to do, take away one of Rand's treasured girls. Gail didn't think she could bear that, not for Rand, not for herself, not for any of them. So she would marry him. It was the only way. Wasn't it? Oh, if only she could tell him the truth! He had said that he'd always love her, but would he? Could he?

When she was with Rand, it seemed as if nothing bad could ever again happen to her, as if their love protected them both from all the horrors that the world held, but they were apart more than together. Rand was busy with the ranch after having spent so much time away while his mother was in the hospital in San Antonio, and Gail's practice had grown so fast that even taking on a full-time receptionist hadn't alleviated much of the burden. Still, she was thankful for the work, for it was in moments of privacy that the doubts plagued her, so many doubts that she knew finally that she would have to do *something*. She called the investigator and asked him to speak with Faye to find out what she might know. Perhaps Faye's knowledge, if she had any, would help Gail protect those she loved, her family, her precious family. That was exactly what was on her mind at the end of a long, busy day just before Thanksgiving when she let herself into the apartment, expecting nothing more than a solitary meal and a phone call. She did not expect to see Rand sitting in the recliner.

"Rand!" Delight rang through her voice.

"Hello, sweetheart."

He rose as she hurried toward him, and her heart lurched at the sight of him in jeans and boots and a shirt opened to the midpoint of his chest, sleeves rolled back to expose his strong forearms. She went into his arms and lifted her mouth for a long, welcome kiss, then stayed close to rub her nose against his when it was over. "Why didn't you let me know you were coming?"

He locked his hands together in the small of her back. "Oh, I just thought I'd surprise you with dinner. You've been working pretty hard lately, you know."

She smiled up at him. "How sweet."

"It's nothing fancy," he warned her, "just burgers and fries and salads, *and* I do have ulterior motives."

The smoky fire in his eyes told her exactly what those ulterior motives were. She snuggled close and slid her arms up around his neck. "Hungry?"

He shook his head. "Nope, not for food, anyway."

She grinned. "Oh, good," and suddenly she was being lifted off her feet. He swung her up into his arms and carried her around the sofa and into the bedroom. When he attempted to put her down, she clung and twisted against him, wrapping her legs around his waist. He laughed and tumbled with her onto the bed. Her hands went to his shirt front while his skimmed down her legs and tugged at her shoes. Getting undressed while maintaining as much physical contact as possible proved a delightful game, but the loving that came afterward was beyond description, especially when he joined their bodies while his eyes held hers and he told her how very much he loved her.

More than an hour later, they lay side by side, stroking one another's skin as the fires cooled and a strong sense of belonging and contentment enveloped them. Then the phone rang, and they both groaned, assuming that some emergency had arisen, the bane of every doctor's existance. Rand slid out of bed and into his jeans. "I'll set out dinner. Maybe you can eat before you have to go."

"Maybe." She reached for the phone as he padded from the room, but the voice that returned her greeting was not that of a patient. It was the private investigator.

"Hello, Dr. Terry. I have some information for you. I know who the other mother was."

Gail sat up in bed, the sheet clutched to her chest. Her heart was pounding so hard that she could barely speak for it. For one awful moment, she wanted to hang up the phone and pretend that he had never called, that both girls were undeniably hers, but then she thought again of some other woman showing up to claim her daughter, and she swallowed down her disappointment. "Wh-Who?"

"Faye Anderson Cochran herself."

Gail closed her eyes. She had suspected once she'd thought back over Faye's reaction to her own pregnancy, and yet she couldn't quite believe it. "H-How did it happen? Wh-when ... I mean, which one of us ... was first?"

"I can't tell you that, ma'am."

"D-Didn't you ask her?"

His voice softened. "No, ma'am. I never talked to Mrs. Cochran herself."

Gail put a hand to her head, confused and stunned. "What? But where did you get your information then?"

"From Mr. Cochran. His wife told him the whole story before she died."

"Died?" Gail nearly shrieked the word. "Faye is dead?"

"I'm afraid so, ma'am, cancer of some sort."

"Dear God!"

He delivered the rest of the information quickly, relating what Faye had told her husband, that Carel had flirted with her every moment Gail's back was turned, then how they had started meeting in secret, and how he had finally seduced her, swearing that he would break up with Gail, that he only needed time to let her down easily. When she'd revealed the pregnancy, he had seemed pleased and promised that he would take care of everything, but right away she had learned that Gail, too, was carrying his child. It was then that Faye had realized that he was never going to commit himself to her, that he'd never had any intention of doing so. When he'd offered to send her away to deliver the

hild in secret, pay her expenses and find a good home for
he baby, she had agreed. An attorney had shown up at the
ospital after the child was born, ostensibly to deliver the
aby to its adoptive parents. He'd even given her a glowing
eport of the couple who would raise her child. He'd also
iven her a sizable check and warned her to stay clear of
Carel and Gail. She had accepted the check and done as she
as told. Eventually she had married and helped raise her
lder husband's two youngest children, and then the can-
er had struck.

The investigator promised to send a detailed report and
ng off. Gail hung up the phone in a kind of daze. Faye.
Carel had impregnated Faye with the same deliberation that
e had impregnated Gail herself. He had needed a ticket
ome, and that second child was his guarantee. If anything
ad happened to one child, he'd have had the other, and of
ourse, they had been conceived so close together that he
uld always claim they were twins. That was even better.
e could give his mother back two grandchildren for the
ne she had lost. And to think that both she and Faye had
allen for that easy charm, that practiced sincerity, the false
romises! Worst of all, Faye was gone, without ever having
nown her own lovely daughter, for whichever girl it was,
e couldn't be dearer.

"Oh, Faye!" Gail whispered, drawing up her knees and
rapping her arms over her bowed head. She didn't realize
and was even in the room until he sat down on the bed next
her and took one of her hands in his.

"Bad news?"

She bit her lip and lifted her face, wiping at the tears. "An
d college friend d-died of cancer."

"Aw, honey, I'm sorry. Damn." He put his arms around
r and kissed her forehead. "Come here, let me hold you
r a little while. Dinner will wait." He eased her back on
e bed and lay down beside her, pulling her close. "Tell me
out your friend."

And she did. She told him everything, how stylishly she had enhanced her plainness, how she'd wanted to travel and see exotic places, how she'd liked bologna sandwiches with catsup and much preferred old Humphrey Bogarte movies to studying, how disappointed she had been about not snagging a steady boyfriend to take her to the school dances and football games. She told him everything about Faye except the one thing she wished was not true. She tried to tell herself that it was enough that he would never lose one of his girls to a mother come to claim her, that the truth could not bring back Faye and reunite her with the child she had borne. She tried to believe that she was doing the right thing by keeping those facts from him, by holding the secret close to her heart, but even then, when he began to slowly and gently make love to her again, she knew that the worst lies were the ones she was telling herself.

She would tell him the truth. She had decided once and for all on the morning she'd received the investigator's detailed report. How could she not? Hadn't the man proved how much he loved her? Shouldn't she trust in that love? Even if he couldn't forgive her, at least the truth would be out in the open and she could make some kind of relationship with her daughter. She toyed briefly with the idea of leaving Faye out of it and claiming both the girls as her own, but she couldn't justify that. The truth was the truth, after all, and she either made her peace with the truth, the whole truth, or she lived an agony of lies. She'd allowed herself to live in a fool's paradise for a time, because she loved Rand and the girls so much. But after the night Rand had comforted her about Faye, Gail knew she couldn't live a life based on a lie. She loved Rand too much. He deserved the truth. Besides, the truth wasn't just that she had given birth to one of the girls. The truth was that she loved them both and she loved Rand with all her heart. That had to count for something. She prayed that it counted for enough, and then she called Rand and asked to see him. After that, it was only a matter of maintaining her courage.

It was late in the afternoon when Rand opened the door to the waiting room of Gail's office. He was glad to see that it was empty and glad that she had called. They hadn't been spending as much time together the past few weeks as he had hoped, and he had suggested, lightly, that it might be wise for her to start looking at hiring an assistant or, better yet, a partner. She hadn't seemed really to hear him, but that was understandable, considering that she was planning a wedding while trying to stay on top of her practice at the same time. But it wouldn't be long now. With Thanksgiving at hand, he was starting to count the days instead of the weeks. He was hoping that he'd misread her and that she was going to tell him today that she was taking on a partner, but no matter why she'd called, he didn't intend to go home again until the wee hours. He just couldn't get this close and settle for a chat and maybe dinner, and he didn't for a minute think he'd have to. He strolled up to the receptionist, his hat in his hand, and smiled at the new girl.

"Oh, Mr. Hartesite, she's still in with a patient."

"Guess I'll just have to wait," he said with an exaggerated sigh.

She popped up off her chair. "At least let me put you in her office. She'll have my head if I make you wait out here."

He didn't tell her that he could just as easily let himself into the apartment, going along meekly instead to the cramped little office. He stood until she closed the door, then tossed his hat onto the sofa, walked around the desk and smoothed his hands over the back of Gail's chair. He liked knowing that she sat here, worked her. On impulse, he pulled the chair out and sat down, leaning back to prop his feet on the blotter on her desk. He put his hands behind his head and twisted slightly. His feet moved just enough to knock a sheaf of stapled papers onto the floor. Leaning forward again, he picked them up, glanced at the title on the

cover page as he handed them toward the desk, then froz
and brought them to his lap.

What was Gail doing with an investigative report on Fay
Anderson Cochran? It was probably medical stuff, he tol
himself, and as such legally private. But Gail was not Fay
Chochran's physician, and the name of the report's autho
was followed not by the initials defining a medical degree
but by that of an investigation agency in Dallas. That shive
of uncertainty he'd felt that day at the ranch returned. Ran
flipped the page and began to read, telling himself that h
had no right to pry into Gail's private business, even if the
were about to be married. Yet, he was unable to stop him
self.

Gail smiled perfunctorily and bade the day's last patien
farewell, both relieved to be done with the chatty olde
woman and regretful at having lost her final reason for de
laying her confession. The moment she had entered the hal
the receptionist had whispered that Mr. Hartesite waited i
the office. She had expected to find him waiting in th
apartment again, but she didn't suppose it mattered one wa
or another. She sent the girl on her way, instructing her t
lock the door on her way out, and turned toward the
fice. That hallway had never seemed so long before, her fe
had never felt so heavy, her heart had never quivered wit
such painful dread, but somehow, suddenly, she was stand
ing before the office door, pulling deep, fortifying breath
into her oxygen-starved lungs, trying to make herself read
for the knob. *I'll always love you.* The words whispere
through her mind, and she seized them mentally, wringi
courage and strength from their assurance. With a fin
breath, she forced her hand around the knob and turned i
a smile of greeting plastered upon her face. But Rand w
not there. At least it didn't seem so—until she pushed t
door wider and stepped inside.

He was standing at the window, his back to her, a foreig
stillness holding him like a glass cocoon. She knew i

tantly that something was wrong, and yet she could not quite accept that as truth. She so desperately needed to believe that all would be well that she refused to register what her senses were telling her. Instead she swept into the room, her smile broadening, skirted the desk and crossed to the window.

"Hello, darling." She lifted a hand to his shoulder, only to feel him shift away. Still she held on to the dream, ignoring the roll of papers clutched in his hand. That could not be the investigator's report. She had to tell him first. She had to remind him how much she loved him. She had to pledge eternal devotion and confess her profound regret at the lies she had let stand between them. She had to beg forgiveness and show him sincerity and respect and... She closed her eyes unable to deny the look of mingled horror, pain, and anger on his face. It was her worst nightmare come true, her deepest fear realized, and yet hope still lived.

I was coming to tell you," she said quietly. "That's why I called you. I couldn't go through with the wedding without—"

He cut her off. "Well, you don't have to worry about that."

No, God, please! She crossed her arms in an attempt to shield herself. "Y-you have to know how much I love you."

Rand didn't even acknowledge her declaration. He didn't care about that any longer, it was obvious.

"*He* got you pregnant."

She closed her eyes again briefly. "Yes."

For a long moment, Rand merely stared, but then he shook his head with such bitterness that it hurt her as physically as any slap. "You were the one thing in my life that *he* hadn't touched. Did you know that? Did you know how much I treasured that? *My* woman this time. Not *his*, mine!" he roared.

Gail covered her ears with her hands before she could stop herself, then abruptly dropped them again. "Rand, *please*. Let me explain."

He threw the rolled report onto the desk with such vio-
lence that half a dozen bits of paper fluffed up and wafted
to the floor. He rounded on her, rage now the predominant
emotion. "How can you explain this away? How can you
explain having *his* baby?"

"I was young and lonely and stupid, Rand! I thought he
loved me. I thought we were getting married!"

"I thought the same things about you," he told her
harshly. "Guess we both found out the hard way!"

"No! I still want to marry you!"

"Well, that's just too bad, isn't it?" he said.

She practically leapt at him, throwing her arms about his
shoulders in desperation. "You have to understand. He stole
my baby! I had to find my daughter, and after thirteen
years, I finally did, but there were *two* of them!"

"Why didn't you tell me?" he hissed, such pain clouding
his eyes that she couldn't bear to look into them.

"I couldn't! Not until I knew which one of them is mine.
They aren't twins. I hoped for a while that he'd kept one of
them from me, that they were both mine, but deep down I
think I knew that wasn't really possible. Then the investigator who sent me here told me that Faye might know the
truth. I almost didn't follow the lead because by then I
didn't want to know. I'd fallen in love with you and—"

"You thought you could have it all by marrying me," he
interrupted bitterly, "the Hartesite name, your daughter—"

"I want *you*, Rand! Yes, I want my daughter, but—"

He shoved her back, his hands clamped around her upper arms. A look of dawning horror crept across his stunned
features, as if he'd finally seen the whole truth. "You came
to take her away from us! All that stopped you was not
knowing which one to claim! God, when I think how moved
I was by your tale of losing a child, when I think . . . *He* was
the one who broke your heart, my damnable *brother*." He
squeezed his eyes shut against a thought too bitter to bear,
and when he opened them again, they were cold as gray

stone. The last faint spark of hope guttered and died in Gail's heart. He suddenly opened his hands and stepped back, as if touching her had soiled him, sickened him. "You won't get her," he promised coldly. "So help me God, you won't!"

"I know," she answered wearily. "I could never take her from you now, Rand. I admit that I meant to when I came here, but that was before I realized how much the girls mean to you, before I . . . came to love you all so much."

"I don't care what you mean to do," he told her coldly, "just stay away from me. Stay away from me *and* my family." He turned and strode around the desk to snatch up his hat.

"Rand, please!" Gail pleaded. "Whatever you think, I do love you."

He bowed his head, shaking it from side to side before fitting the hat into place. "I think you've got me mixed up with my brother."

"I hated your brother."

He pinned her with the most disbelieving look. "Then why did you have his baby?"

He might as well have slapped her. She reeled, literally, grasping the chair back for support. She had to catch her breath and swallow before she could speak. "You can't ask me to regret a child you've held and loved all these years."

For a moment, it seemed as if something changed behind his eyes, but then he turned away, his hand going to the doorknob. "I don't ever want to see you again," he said, his voice utterly devoid of emotion.

"You said you'd always love me," she reminded him softly.

He stepped back as he pulled the door open, then paused there on the threshold for a tense, immeasurable space of time. "I guess we both lied," he finally said, and then he stepped through the door and pulled it closed behind him.

Gail stared numbly at no one for a very long time before she gently pulled the diamond from her finger and slipped it into the pocket of her lab coat. Only then did the tears begin to fall.

Chapter Fifteen

Rand sat with his head in his hands, his body numb, his mind a whirl of pain and loss. He almost wished for the blazing anger that had sustained him through that horrible confrontation with Gail and the first few days without her. Anything would be better than the stupor of depression and raw emotional pain that seemed to have engulfed him since. Seventeen days. If he allowed himself a look at the clock, he would know how many hours and minutes since his dreams had gone up in smoke, thanks to a dead man. His brother, his own personal nightmare. Again. His brother, the child stealer.

One of my girls, he thought. *One of my girls is hers, Gail's and Carel's, together.*

God, how had he managed to do it again? How had he managed once more to follow on his brother's heels? It was almost laughable, considering that Carel had been dead over eleven years. Carel, the worm. And Gail. Carel and Gail. The very idea seemed to split his soul, not to mention his head. He held it and gritted his teeth in despair, but his mother was not one to give way to something as inconsequential as despair.

She sat down on the edge of his bed, not directly beside him, but near the bedpost so she could use it for leverage when rising again. "Look at me, Rand," she ordered sternly, and he complied from nothing more than habit. "Look at me and think. How would you feel if your infant daughter was stolen right out of the hospital?"

"You don't know if that really happened," he snapped, swallowing with bitter pride the fact that he was actually defending his lousy brother.

Belle made an impatient gesture with her hands, lifting them, then dropping them. "I wish to God I didn't," she said flatly, "but we both know all too well what your brother was like, what he was capable of. She explained it all to me, Rand, and I believe her."

He turned his face away. "It doesn't make any difference."

"Doesn't make any difference?" Belle echoed. "She's been deprived of her daughter for thirteen years, and you say it doesn't matter? Twice now, she's been deserted by a man who claimed to love her."

"That's not fair!"

"Each of them, in his own way, has taken her child from her."

"Stop it!" But one look at Belle's face told him quite plainly that she had no intention of stopping, and he knew with a sinking sense of powerlessness that he couldn't make her stop. She was his mother, and she always had her say— and she was usually right.

"She could have forced our hand long ago, Rand. A simple blood test would tell us which one of them is hers. All she had to do was hire a lawyer and lay her case before a judge, but she didn't. Have you ever wondered why?"

"I've given up trying to figure out that woman," he grumbled.

Belle gave him that mother's look that unilaterally declared him a very foolish boy. "It seems simple enough to me. She didn't demand her daughter—even though she has every moral and, I suspect, legal right to—because she didn't want to hurt you."

"Well, someone ought to tell her that she screwed that one up," he said bitterly, "because she sure as hell hurt me." He bounded up off the bed, throwing up his arms for emphasis. "For Pete's sake, she slept with my brother! She was *in love* with my brother! She had a child with my brother!"

"A child you have raised as your own, Rand. You've had all the benefits and joys of fatherhood because of your brother and, in part, *that woman.* You know what he was like. She wasn't the first woman he duped. She probably wasn't the last. God only knows how many others there are. But as far as I can tell, Rand, you've reaped all the rewards."

"You call Lynette—"

"No! Marrying that girl was a terrible mistake, and I let you make it, God help me, for my own selfish reasons. Thankfully she bailed out of the marriage before she completely ruined your life. But Gail Terry is not Lynette, and her child was not stillborn, she was stolen. Despite that, she's given me her word that she won't sue for custody."

"And you believe her?"

"Yes!" Belle looked down at her hands, composed herself, and lifted a steady gaze to her son. "I also believe that it is unfair of you to punish her by keeping her daughter from her simply because she knew your brother first."

"Oh, she knew him, all right," Rand quipped sarcastically, his hands at his waist. "She *knew* him in a very *Biblical* sense. Surely you don't expect me to just forget that!"

Belle sighed and rose laboriously to her feet, assisted by the bed post and a sleek cane with a gold head. "No, Son," she said resignedly, "I expect you to go right on letting a dead man cheat you out of everything you deserve." With that, she turned and made her way toward the bedroom door. She moved slowly, laboriously, as if she'd aged twenty years in the space of as many minutes.

Rand's heart suddenly spasmed, and an awful truth hit him like a ton of bricks. She couldn't live forever. Even this strong, stubborn woman was one day going to die, and then the girls would grow up and leave him, too, and he would be alone, so alone. As Gail was alone, had always been alone. Belle slipped out the door, and Rand put his hands to his head once more. Where, he wondered, was he going to find the strength to do what he had to do?

The new receptionist tapped at her office door. Gail laid aside the journal she was reading and faced the door. "Yes?"

Holly opened the door a few inches and slipped inside. "He's here," she said in a voice imbued with deep meaning.

Gail could only blink at her. Her mental powers were not what they should have been. For the first time in her entire career, she could not seem to make herself concentrate. She went through the motions of each day in blessed numbness, but she could not seem to think in any substantive way or climb up out of the heaviness that seemed to weigh her down.

"He has the girls with him," the receptionist went on. "All three of them are here."

Rand? Rand was here with the girls? The unlikelihood of that was so great that it seemed impossible, and yet, who else could it be? Gail got up from her desk without a word, but then she remembered the ring in the top drawer of her desk, and she paused to retrieve it, slipping it into her pocket. Perhaps he had come for that. She had hoped, senselessly, that he'd forgive her after a time, but she knew, after all these weeks that he couldn't possibly. And yet, it was the Christmas season, wasn't it? Might he possibly relent enough to let her see the girls? She couldn't think beyond the questions to form possible answers. Nervously, she left the office and walked briskly out into the hall.

They were following the receptionist into the examination room. The girls filed in ahead of Rand, who stopped suddenly at the door and turned his gaze on her, his hat in his hands. The anger that flashed in his eyes extinguished that stubborn flicker of hope, and the futility of it all suddenly overwhelmed her. It crashed down on her from above, swirled up from below, flew at her from every other direction, a thousand hot, sharp arrows of hopelessness. It doubled her over, sent her spinning away to the relative safety of the office once more. She leaned against the door and hauled air into her scorching lungs. Her eyes were so dry they felt as if they might crack, her tongue was like hot lead in her mouth, and the blood that pumped through her heart seemed to boil. She stood there until the worst of it passed, then jumped when the receptionist tapped on the door again.

"Coming," she croaked, knowing that she had to go. Her daughter was in that room, her only family, her only other link with the human race, but the thought brought her no solace, no pleasure, no hope. Still, it had to be done. There had to be some sort of closure. The ring. She put her hand in her pocket and closed it around the engagement ring he had given her. She had to give that back, and then it would truly, irrevocably be over between them. She could stop hoping then, and she could go away from here, away from the mingled hope and dread of seeing him again.

She pushed away from the door, took a deep breath, opened it, and stepped out. The hallway was empty. She put her head down and forced herself to walk toward the examination room. As she drew near, she heard the receptionist's voice prattling jarringly in the heavy silence.

"So she said she's putting the practice up for sale, and isn't that just my luck? I like this job. Dr. Gail doesn't make me feel guilty if I have to go take care of my boy. She's really big on family, you know, really understanding about a mother's responsibilities."

"That'll be all," Gail interrupted in a voice roughened by the fire burning her alive inside. "You can go on home now if you want."

The young woman abruptly shut her mouth and slipped out of the room. Gail flicked her gaze over Rand. He was staring at the floor, which was just as well. She wasn't certain that she wanted to look into those smoky-blue eyes again. Quickly, she turned her attention to the girls. They were sitting side by side on the examination table, avid expressions on each of their faces. Mary's seemed tempered by something else. Fear? Gail couldn't be sure in her state of emotional trauma. It took all her strength to put on a smile and mouth the requisite doctor-speak.

"Hello, girls. It's wonderful to see you. What can I do for you today?"

"We've come for the blood tests," Rand said flatly behind her.

"B-blood tests?"

It was Carel Belle who slipped from the examination table to stand close to Gail. "Are you really one of our mothers?"

A wave of intense love flowed over her, cooling the fires of pain somewhat. She clasped Carel Belle's hand in hers, but it was to Rand whom she turned. "You told them?"

"You expected something else?" he shot back.

She bit her lip, wondering what she had expected, then shook her head and lifted her chin. "Th-thank you."

"I didn't do it for you."

"I didn't think you did."

He turned his face away, nodding, his hands at his waist. "Get on with it."

She turned back to the girls. Mary Grace was looking at her lap. Gail wanted very much to reach out to her, but she was afraid of being rebuffed. Still, she told herself, how bad could it be? Certainly it could be no worse than what she'd already been through. She reached out to pat Mary's knee. The girl didn't so much as lift her head.

"Are you going to split us up?" she asked softly.

"No!" Gail shook her head. "I would never keep you apart o-or take you away from the people you love."

"Then why did you come?" she demanded, looking up suddenly to pin Gail with her eyes.

Why indeed? It seemed so long ago now that she had settled into Marfa, hoping to find her daughter and build a life with her. So much had happened. The steady pressure of Carel Belle's hand on hers gave her strength to find and voice the answer. "I've never had anyone to love," she said softly, "but my daughter. I couldn't let go of that. It's kept me looking all these years."

Mary frowned, but her gaze seemed to soften somewhat. She held out her arm. "I'll go first," she said to her lap.

Gail wanted to hug her. Instead, she managed a shaky smile. "I, um, have to get my lab kit from the other room."

"I'll get it," Rand said, the words rumbling up from somewhere deep in his chest. He was through the door before she could stop him.

Carel Belle's fingers threaded through hers. "What about Uncle Rand and you?" she asked softly. Tears flooded Gail's eyes and a lump swelled her throat shut. All she could do was shake her head. Carel squeezed her hand, whispering, "It'll be all right."

"No," Gail whispered. "No, it won't. I-It can't. You mustn't—"

But just then the door opened and Rand pushed the rolling metal stand with her lab kit on it inside the room. She broke away and hurriedly began preparing by drawing on protective gloves and picking out the needed materials. Her hands shook, and she began telling herself that this was strictly routine, but the retreat to professionalism didn't happen. She wrapped the rubber tourniquet around Mary's upper arm and swabbed the bend of her elbow with an alcohol prep, but when she picked up the lancet, her hands froze. For a long moment, all she could do was look down at the vials and tubing on the tray. Did she really want to do this? What difference would knowing make now? She loved them both, and she could have neither, because whatever happened she couldn't take either of them from Rand, not now, not ever. Even if she could have one of them, how could she bear to be separated from the other? It would be like giving up half her heart. Better a clean cut than this awful rending. Besides, wouldn't the best thing for all of them be just to let them alone?

She dropped the lancet on the tray and pushed it away. A feeling of great relief came over her, of rightness. What loving mother destroyed her daughter's home and family? She had loved from afar for a long time. She could go on doing so. Better that than this. Quickly, before she could change her mind, she snapped the tourniquet apart and dropped in on the table, then stripped the gloves from her hands.

"I want you to leave," she said, her voice strong, her shoulders once more squared, despite the tears that stood in her eyes.

A moment of stunned silence followed. Then Mary hopped down from the table and bolted for the door, running as if her very life depended on it. Carel grabbed Gail's arm. "Don't you want—"

"Listen to me," she said, folding the girl in her arms and holding her close. "The things I want can never be. I lost a baby, the most precious thing in my world, but I found two extraordinary girls to love in her place, and no one can ask for more than that." She dropped a kiss on top of Carel's head, then set her carefully at a distance. "I want you to go home," she said gently, "and I don't want you to even look back. Go on now, and tell your sister for me . . . tell her that she's half of wonderful and that you're the other half. Go on. Your unc—Father will be right behind you."

Carel shot a confused look at Rand, then slipped from the room. Gail took a deep breath. She could feel the tears uilding to the spilling point, and she wanted this done with efore they started. Once they began again, they would not e difficult to subdue, but that didn't matter. She had plenty f time, a whole lifetime, in which to dry her tears. She urned to Rand. He was standing with his legs spread, feet raced, his thumbs hooked into the rims of his hips pockts. His face was a careful, wary blank.

"I guess genetics doesn't have quite the importance scince would have us believe," she said wryly. "I have to now one thing, though. What did you tell them?"

"Nothing. That one of their mothers is dead and that ou're the other."

She swallowed twice, then cleared her throat. "That's robably best. I didn't want either of them thinking they veren't wanted."

"They *are* wanted."

"I know. If I didn't believe that, I couldn't... Well, that loesn't really matter anymore, does it? Here." She reached nto her pocket and took out the ring. "This is yours." Vhen he didn't reach out to take it from her, his eyes ooded, chin down, she stepped forward and slipped it ginerly into his shirt pocket, then quickly stepped back again. I'll be leaving here as soon as all the necessary arrangeents have been made," she told him. "I-I'll leave a forvarding address with your mother, so that if one of them hould ever need...something only a biological parent could ive them... That isn't very likely, but... doctors have to hink of things like that, you know, so..." She swallowed nd wrapped her arms around her middle. She couldn't look t him any longer, but there was one more thing she had to ay. "I never meant to hurt you. I never meant to fall in love vith you or... I'm not making excuses. I-I knew it was vrong, but I couldn't seem to stop..." She had said enough.)ne more deep breath, and then, "Goodbye, Rand." She urned her back and pretended a great and sudden interest n the lab kit she hadn't even opened. He stood there for a ong time, and then he simply walked away.

* * *

Mary Grace dropped her books and her jacket on the dinner table and glared at him, her hands on her hips in a gesture very reminiscent of one of his own. Rand sighed and stared into his coffee cup.

"What is it now?"

"I heard it in school today," she said accusingly. "She's just closing the office and she's going away."

He took a sip of coffee and set the cup down again. He didn't need to ask who *she* was. It seemed as though Gail was continually on everyone's mind, even after all this time. She might have been a ghost in his house, slinking around just on the edge of his vision, always there but not quite real. He tamped down the surge of panic that he felt at Mary's statement and disciplined his expression, keeping his face devoid of emotion. "She must have found a buyer for the practice," he said lightly. "We knew she was trying to."

"No," Mary insisted, "she didn't find a buyer. She's just closing the door and walking away. Don't you understand? She's giving up everything she's worked for because of us!"

Rand felt a flash of guilt, but he ruthlessly suppressed it. So what? So what if she did love them? What if she did love him? That didn't mean he was responsible. That didn't mean he could snap his fingers and all the deceptions and mistakes that lay between them would disappear. *But she's paid for her mistake in spades,* said his better self. *She's paid with everything that could possibly matter to her. She's paid for the lies and the schemes and...* No, he wouldn't tell himself that lie. There had been no scheme. He had pursued her. She had tried to discourage him, had even turned him down initially when he'd asked her to marry him.

Because I love you, she had said. *I can't marry you because I love you.*

He got up so suddenly that he bumped the table and sloshed coffee over the rim of the cup. It was, he reflected bitterly, just another mess he'd made. He turned away from the sight of it, desperate to escape his own feelings.

"It might be just a rumor," he said to Mary Grace. "You know how talk gets around—"

"She sent a letter, Uncle Rand! She sent the same letter to all her patients. I think she even sent one to Grandmother. I saw an envelope like the ones she uses with Grandmother's name on it in the mail today."

"I'll leave a forwarding address with your mother, in case one of them needs something only a biological parent can give... Doctors have to think of these things."

Dear God, she was going then. She was really going. And what the hell was he supposed to do about it? He closed his eyes. Oh, if only it had been any man but Carel.

His mother's voice reproved him. *"I expect you to go right on letting a dead man cheat you."*

Was he doing that? Was he letting Carel decide who he could love and who he could accept love from? Was he letting Carel steal his happiness and ruin Gail's life again? Why? Because of Lynette? Because of a woman he hadn't even loved?

Carel is dead, he told himself. *Carel is dead, and Gail is leaving forever if you don't stop her. You know she loves you. She loves the whole lot of you, if you haven't killed it, or punished it out of her.*

"God, what an idiot!" he said, neither realizing or caring that he'd said it aloud as he strode purposefully from the room, leaving a shocked but gleeful Mary Grace behind.

Gail smoothed the tape over the flaps of the box and set it aside. She pushed up the sleeves of her long knit gown and looked around at the books still waiting to be crated and the dishes stacked on the kitchen table. For a nickle, she'd walk off and leave the lot of it. What did it matter anyway? None of this stuff mattered. But it was too late to think of what mattered most. Too late. She pulled a chair out from the table and sat down, resting her head on her folded arms. She was so tired. Why was she always so tired? She slept and slept, and she woke up tired. It was the depression, she knew, but she didn't care. It was that simple really. She just didn't care anymore.

After a few minutes she began to feel chilled. Warmed earlier by the constant movement involved in packing, she had turned the flame down on the old space heater that rested against the bedroom wall. She supposed she might as well go back to work. She could always turn up the fire, but either way she was going to have to get up, so it might as well be work. She had just lifted her head when she heard the gentle screech of the screen door as it opened. She groaned. She couldn't bear one more parting. She just couldn't. She made up her mind before the first knock even came that she wasn't going to answer it. She had seen all the long-faced patients she cared to see, heard all the best wishes and goodbyes she ever wanted to hear. Whoever it was could just go on their way without inflicting their unintentional pain on poor Dr. Terry. She simply couldn't do it any more. And then she heard his voice.

"Gail? Are you there? I know you're there. Please, for God's sake, open the door."

She got up, leaning on the table for support. Rand? Here? Suddenly her mind was racing. Why would he be here? Did she even want to know? Her feet answered that for her, carrying her swiftly toward the door, but then she stopped, uncertain, even frightened. Before she could decide whether or not to let him in, the doorknob turned and the unlocked door swung slowly inward.

The first sight of him was like water to a parched throat, but suddenly it was too much, and she dropped her gaze, wrapping her arms about herself protectively. "Rand," she said, and then, in a masterful stroke of understatement, "I wasn't expecting you."

He looked around the room at the stacked boxes, the strewn newspaper and odd items awaiting packing. "You really mean to go then."

She turned away, walking back toward the little kitchen. "There's nothing for me here."

"There could be," he answered softly.

She stopped at the end of the coffee table, afraid to hope that he might mean himself. No, not that. But maybe… She turned back suddenly, her breath held as he moved slowly to the sofa and sank down onto it. He sighed, as if weary to the bone. She swallowed the lump in her throat and ventured a timid supposition. "You've changed your mind about the girls."

"Oh," he said, slumping forward with his forearms laid across his knees. "The girls." He bowed his head.

A bittersweet shimmer of joy wafted through her. She dropped down onto the end of the coffee table, desperate to claim even this consolation prize. "Just two or three times a year," she promised. "You won't even have to see me, I swear. You can pick the dates. Your mother and I will take care of all the arrangements. I know you won't want to send them to me, so I'll come here… or Fort Davis, maybe… Alpine. I don't care. I'll do anything you say. I'll crawl over broken glass if you want. I'll—"

"No," he said flatly, his bowed head slowly moving side to side. "You don't understand."

That "no" was reverberating in her ears. She was not to see the girls. There would be *no* trips back here, *no* joyous reunions to lighten the otherwise bleak weight of her existence, just "no." She closed her eyes, absorbing the disappointment as she'd absorbed all the other pain. "Then why?" she finally demanded, anger momentarily overshadowing all else. "Why are you here, Rand? Did you come to punish me some more for being nineteen and alone and stupid?" She leapt to her feet and took two stiff steps toward him. "What else do you think you can do to me? Maybe you just want to be certain that I'm getting the hell out of town? Well, I'm going, all right? Just as soon as I can, I'm leaving this place and you'll never have to—"

"God, no!" he said so softly that at first she thought she had misunderstood. It was when he wiped his hand across his face that she realized he was crying.

Stunned, her knees gave way and she sat down quickly on the coffee table directly in front of him. Mere inches separated their knees, three at most. For a long, charged moment, she could do nothing but stare at the top of his hat in astonishment. She didn't know what to do, what to think. Was he crying because of *her?* It occurred to her suddenly that she didn't have anything to lose by finding out. She reached out, peeled the hat from his head and tossed it aside. He sat back abruptly, turning his face away and sliding his fingers over it.

"Cowboys don't cry," she said gently.

He made an exasperated sound somewhere between a laugh and a sigh. "They do if they've ruined the best thing in their lonely, stupid lives."

She wondered if she was going to wake up or if wishful thinking had become insanity, but again, what did she have to lose by finding out? She eased over onto the sofa, turned slightly toward him. He laid his arm along the back of the couch, skimming her shoulders.

"Are you saying that you've forgiven me?" she asked hesitantly.

"No," he said, sighing. "I'm not here to dispense forgiveness. I'm here to ask for it."

If she could have spoken in that moment, she might well have demanded a refined explanation, she might have railed at the time lost, she might have cried out absolution, but she could only press her trembling fingers to her trembling lips and feel hope soar once more.

"Oh, honey," he said, gathering her to him. "I'm sorry. I'm so very sorry. Please, I'm begging you, don't go. Let me make it up to you. I'll find a way, I swear it! Just please don't...don't leave me!"

"Rand!" She was finally able to gasp his name, and doing so seemed to free her somehow. She threw her arms around him, curving them up and over his shoulders. "I should have told you! I should have told you in the very beginning!"

He shook his head, his hands pressing her against him. "You couldn't. I know that now. There wasn't a *good* time for telling me that. Everything I've done and said has proven it. I've reacted exactly as you feared I would. At least this way I had a chance to know and love you. If you'd told me in the beginning, I'd never have known that you were the most important person ever to touch my life."

She pulled away a little to gaze up into his face. The tears had dried in shiny tracks that crisscrossed his lean cheeks. "Rand, are you actually saying that..."

"That I love you," he whispered, "that I need you, that I'll do anything for another chance."

This time when she put her hand to her mouth, it was to stifle the laughter that bubbled up. "I love you, you big dope! I've loved you from the beginning. I'll always love you!"

"Thank God!" He crushed her hard against him. "I'm so sorry. Oh, baby, I'm so sorry! And I swear, never again. I don't ever again want to be without you, not for a day, not for a night, ever!"

"Never!" she promised, hugging him tight. It was over. The long dark night had passed into day at last. The sun had indeed risen again, and all the nights to follow would be soft and warm and incandescent. The proof was in her arms and holding her tight. It was not, she remembered suddenly, on her finger. She jerked away and shoved lightly at his shoulder. "I want my ring back!"

His mouth hitched up in a lopsided grin. "Oh, you do, do you?" He fished into his shirt pocket with thumb and index finger, quickly coming up with it. His hand shook as he slipped it onto her finger. "This time it stays there," he said, lifting her hand to his mouth.

"This time it stays," she echoed, her voice thick with promise.

"And so do I," he whispered. His eyes shimmered brightly, but it was the smile that lit his face as he shifted and lay back, pulling her down atop him—and flattening his hat.

"You squashed your hat," she told him needlessly. "Cowboys don't squash their hats. It's a definite faux pas, a very uncowboy thing to do."

"To hell with my hat," he told her. "I can get another hat, but there's only one woman in all this world for me, one love and only one."

He began to demonstrate, in classic Hartesite style, that she was that one woman, that only love. And she gave as good as she got. Her heart, you see, was very much in it.

*   *   *   *   *

COMING NEXT MONTH

MAN, WOMAN AND CHILD

Three provocative family tales…three wonderful writers…all come together in a series destined to win your heart! Beginning in June 1995 with

A FATHER'S WISH
by Christine Flynn
SE #962, June

Alexander Burke had never understood why Kelly Shaw had given up their child for adoption. Now she was back…but she didn't know she'd also found the son she thought she'd lost forever.

And don't miss one minute of this innovative series as it continues with these titles:

MOTHER AT HEART
by Robin Elliott
SE #968, July 1995

NOBODY'S CHILD
by Pat Warren
SE #974, August 1995

Only from Silhouette Special Edition!

MWC-1

He's Too Hot To Handle...but she can take a little heat.

SILHOUETTE

Summer Sizzlers

This summer don't be left in the cold, join Silhouette for the hottest Summer Sizzlers collection. The perfect summer read, on the beach or while vacationing, Summer Sizzlers features sexy heroes who are "Too Hot To Handle." This collection of three new stories is written by bestselling authors Mary Lynn Baxter, Ann Major and Laura Parker.

Available this July wherever Silhouette books are sold.

ANNOUNCING THE

PRIZE SURPRISE SWEEPSTAKES!

This month's prize:

L-A-R-G-E—SCREEN PANASONIC TV!

This month, as a special surprise, we're giving away a fabulous FREE TV!

Imagine how delighted you and your family will be to own this brand-new 31" Panasonic** television! It comes with all the latest high-tech features, like a SuperFlat picture tube for a clear, crisp picture...unified remote control...closed-caption decoder...clock and sleep timer, and much more!

The facing page contains two Entry Coupons (as does every book you received this shipment). Complete and return *all* the entry coupons; **the more times you enter, the better your chances of winning the TV!**

Then keep your fingers crossed, because you'll find out by July 15, 1995 if you're the winner!

Remember: The more times you enter, the better your chances of winning!*

*NO PURCHASE OR OBLIGATION TO CONTINUE BEING A SUBSCRIBER NECESSARY TO ENTER. SEE THE REVERSE SIDE OF ANY ENTRY COUPON FOR ALTERNATE MEANS OF ENTRY.

**THE PROPRIETORS OF THE TRADEMARK ARE NOT ASSOCIATED WITH THIS PROMOTION.

PTV KAL

PRIZE SURPRISE
SWEEPSTAKES

OFFICIAL ENTRY COUPON

This entry must be received by: JUNE 30, 1995
This month's winner will be notified by: JULY 15, 1995

YES, I want to win the Panasonic 31" TV! Please enter me in the drawing
and let me know if I've won!

Name_____

Address _____ Apt. _____

City   State/Prov.   Zip/Postal Code

Account #_____

Return entry with invoice in reply envelope.

© 1995 HARLEQUIN ENTERPRISES LTD.   CTV KAL

PRIZE SURPRISE
SWEEPSTAKES

OFFICIAL ENTRY COUPON

This entry must be received by: JUNE 30, 1995
This month's winner will be notified by: JULY 15, 1995

YES, I want to win the Panasonic 31" TV! Please enter me in the drawing
and let me know if I've won!

Name_____

Address _____ Apt. _____

City   State/Prov.   Zip/Postal Code

Account #_____

Return entry with invoice in reply envelope.

© 1995 HARLEQUIN ENTERPRISES LTD.   CTV KAL

OFFICIAL RULES

PRIZE SURPRISE SWEEPSTAKES 3448

NO PURCHASE OR OBLIGATION NECESSARY

Three Harlequin Reader Service 1995 shipments will contain respectively, coupons for entry into three different prize drawings, one for a Panasonic 31" wide-screen TV, another for a 5-piece Wedgwood china service for eight and the third for a Sharp ViewCam camcorder. To enter any drawing using an Entry Coupon, simply complete and mail according to directions.

There is no obligation to continue using the Reader Service to enter and be eligible for any prize drawing. You may also enter any drawing by hand printing the words "Prize Surprise," your name and address on a 3"x5" card and the name of the prize you wish that entry to be considered for (i.e., Panasonic wide-screen TV, Wedgwood china or Sharp ViewCam). Send your 3"x5" entries via first-class mail (limit: one per envelope) to: Prize Surprise Sweepstakes 3448, c/o the prize you wish that entry to be considered for, P.O. Box 1315, Buffalo, NY 14269-1315, USA or P.O. Box 610, Fort Erie, Ontario L2A 5X3, Canada.

To be eligible for the Panasonic wide-screen TV, entries must be received by 6/30/95; for the Wedgwood china, 8/30/95; and for the Sharp ViewCam, 10/30/95.

Winners will be determined in random drawings conducted under the supervision of D.L. Blair, Inc., an independent judging organization whose decisions are final, from among all eligible entries received for that drawing. Approximate prize values are as follows: Panasonic wide-screen TV ($1,800); Wedgwood china ($840) and Sharp ViewCam ($2,000). Sweepstakes open to residents of the U.S. (except Puerto Rico) and Canada, 18 years of age or older. Employees and immediate family members of Harlequin Enterprises, Ltd., D.L. Blair, Inc., their affiliates, subsidiaries and all other agencies, entities and persons connected with the use, marketing or conduct of this sweepstakes are not eligible. Odds of winning a prize are dependent upon the number of eligible entries received for that drawing. Prize drawing and winner notification for each drawing will occur no later than 15 days after deadline for entry eligibility for that drawing. Limit: one prize to an individual, family or organization. All applicable laws and regulations apply. Sweepstakes offer void wherever prohibited by law. Any litigation within the province of Quebec respecting the conduct and awarding of the prizes in this sweepstakes must be submitted to the Regies des loteries et Courses du Quebec. In order to win a prize, residents of Canada will be required to correctly answer a time-limited arithmetical skill-testing question. Value of prizes are in U.S. currency.

Winners will be obligated to sign and return an Affidavit of Eligibility within 30 days of notification. In the event of noncompliance within this time period, prize may not be awarded. If any prize or prize notification is returned as undeliverable, that prize will not be awarded. By acceptance of a prize, winner consents to use of his/her name, photograph or other likeness for purposes of advertising, trade and promotion on behalf of Harlequin Enterprises, Ltd., without further compensation, unless prohibited by law.

For the names of prizewinners (available after 12/31/95), send a self-addressed, stamped envelope to: Prize Surprise Sweepstakes 3448 Winners, P.O. Box 4200, Blair, NE 68009.

RPZ KAL